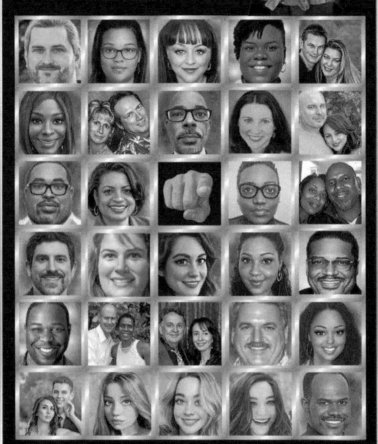

BELIEVE IT! SEE IT! TELL IT!
DAY AFTER DAY

Faith Faces

BISHOP LATERRA D. RUFFIN & FRIENDS

FAITH FACES

BELIEVE IT, SEE IT, TELL IT! DAY AFTER DAY

BISHOP LATERRA D. RUFFIN & FRIENDS

FAITH FACES

For additional information, please contact:
FaithFaces2023@gmail.com

For information about special discounts for bulk purchases please contact the Special Sales Department at FaithFaces2023@gmail.com Published by Executive Business Writing
Moreno Valley, CA 92552
(951)488-7634
https://www.executivebusinesswriting.com
executivebusinesswriting@gmail.com

Edited by Julie Boney
JB Editing Solutions

Graphics by Tracy Spencer
Legacy Media, LLC
Moreno Valley, CA 92552

TABLE OF CONTENTS

You are the modern-day Hebrews 11,

"By Faith Trailblazers."

Thank you for becoming living letters

read by others desiring to walk by faith,

beyond what is seen. Because of you,

great Faith Faces arise.

Let God be glorified in all things!

To All Faith Faces

AN OBSERVATION OF FAITH

When thinking about faith, it is impossible to dismiss the great pioneers of Hebrews Chapter 11. The same faith that Noah used to build an ark for impending rain, the faith Abraham demonstrated when he obeyed God to leave his home, to the faith Moses' parents showed when they hid him for three months, realizing he was a special child, and we cannot forget Sarah's faith that made it possible to have a child in her old age. In this "arsenal," you will find that same faith. Yes! The same level as those great pioneers is here. It stirs that great cloud of witnesses of Hebrews 12:1 to cheer us on today! You will find mountain moving faith, the kind that pushes us beyond the limits of our natural understanding.

This intentional work is constructed with stories of "Bishop LaTerra Ruffin & Friends" faith filled adventures that can be easily read and will benefit generations to come. These pages will serve as a reminder of what can be accomplished by faith.

Bishop LaTerra Ruffin has a remarkable faith journey that captivates the hearts and minds of the masses. Reared in a sound Christian environment, Bishop LaTerra was trained and postured to walk out her entire life by faith, no matter the circumstances. Her experiences as a young believer in the Lord paved an uncanny example of faith for all she encountered. Ironically, her formative Christian years were spent in a church, aptly named The Church of Faith, that produced a well-informed and thoroughly grounded young believer. She has developed into one of the most faith filled leaders and disciples of Jesus Christ of our time, hands down. If any modern human being was a true example of Hebrews 11, Bishop LaTerra is that one! From believing God for her now seventeen-year-old twins, experiencing the death of her only biological sister, overcoming breast cancer, and the passing of her mother, by faith she stood strong. These, among other life events more than qualify her to share, teach, and lead others in the realm of faith.

This woman of God's life and legacy defines "Faith Faces." Because Bishop LaTerra's walk in the Lord is not common, it has successfully commandeered what many would deem insurmountable odds. Through life's twists and turns, she never wavered. Whenever necessary, she can draw from bottomless wells of faith developed from her Christian training and time spent with the Lord.

As her brother and lifelong cheerleader, I have watched Bishop LaTerra's journey unfold wonderfully. She has always felt responsible to elevate the people she meets, even complete strangers. Whether speaking from a pulpit, walking her local park, or shopping at her favorite grocery store, her assignment remains to catapult you forward. An encounter with Bishop LaTerra will leave an indelible mark on your life, one that cannot be easily scrubbed away, forgotten, or misplaced. After reading this work, your faith will never be the same.

Thirty-one chapters demonstrate faith's aptitude. They expose the palpable nature of faith while drawing you closer to the Creator. These next chapters will work to recover your faith, provoking you to believe the Lord one more time. It capsulizes those testimonies, propelling you onward to a faith filled journey in the Lord.

As she often refers to them as "Thank you Jesus stories," they will leave you yearning for a deeper relationship with the giver of all faith. You will be taken on an expedition of faith beginning, faith renewed, and faith repositioned.

Throughout the pages of this great work will unfold stories of the impossible, tales of triumph, and victory snatched from the jaws of defeat.

If your faith needs a jolt, "Bishop LaTerra Ruffin & Friends" through Faith Faces have more than delivered! This is just for you! Enjoy the adventure!

Timothy Baldwin, MDiv.
Senior Pastor, Bethel Deliverance Church Northeast
Philadelphia, PA

An Observation of Faith

FOREWORD

It was one of those moments. I had heard so much about her and now I found myself diligently scanning the sparsely populated hotel lobby to greet my new colleague. My role on the pastoral team at Victory Christian Center in Rancho Mirage, California, was officially underway and core leaders were gathering for a strategic planning session. They included Congregational Care Pastor LaTerra D. Williams Ruffin. As introductions were made, she quickly stood from the well-upholstered chair, impeccably dressed from head to toe. However, that would quickly pale in comparison to her inner beauty that poured out during the exchange that followed. Charismatic to be sure, her warm smile and dancing eyes enveloped me like a cozy blanket. Her gracious welcome was followed by her diligent focus solely on the divinely appointed moment at hand. Words, beautiful words, encouraging and stirring faith-building words, which she shared with me that day eclipsed her natural beauty. They penetrated my heart and provoked me to love and good works. And so has every exchange with her that has followed over our nearly 20 years of ministry and friendship. Simply put, she is a God original, an iron-sharpening-iron living legend, a living epistle read of men whose words, whether written or spoken, refresh our souls.

So, it comes as no surprise that as she embarks on her 40th year of ministry, once again her consistent, intentional, laser-like focus is not to draw attention to herself, but instead is squarely fixed ON US to challenge and stir IN US the God kind of faith that literally moves the mountains we face. In this book, not only does she share her voice, reflecting on her personally walked out, one step at a time, intimate, God-led faith journey to date, but she has prayerfully invited and collected the voices of others to do the same.

As the chapters unfold, ordinary men and women like you and me who are geographically dispersed across this great country have put pen to paper at Bishop LaTerra's urging to encapsulate a bite-sized "look what the Lord has done" snapshot. It is one designed to steady and strengthen us in our own journey. Here you will find 31 deeply personal, individual stories of the tragedy and triumph, pain and purpose found in the real lives of believers who have set their faith faces like flint on the promises of God, and provoke us to do the same.

As Bishop LaTerra shared her vision for this book with me, I was reminded of the Great Faith Hall of Fame cadence and parallel found in the Bible's book of Hebrews, Chapter 11. Many times in my life, I have reached for, read, and rehearsed the examples of men and women outlined there who dared to believe God no matter how impossible the circumstance appeared.

Pick up reading where you will; the stories found in Faith Faces can be ordered and relished at your discretion and choosing. I encourage you to find yourself in the faces that grace its cover, to slowly savor each detail, allowing their stories to wash over you, and to listen intently to glean the "ah ha" impartation tailored to the present "opportunity" giant you face. No matter your approach, one thing is certain. The testimonies of the contemporary Faith Hall of Famers found here compel us to reexamine our own journey, recognize God's hand of protection and direction within it, and reach forward to the next rung of the faith ladder.

And so, the story continues, from Bible heroes and heroines to Bishop LaTerra and her contributors and ultimately to you and me. The invitation is clear! Catch the baton, dear reader, as you run your race so that you, too, may continue to grow as a God original, a living epistle read of men who confidently live faith out loud in a world desperate for the hope that only exists in relationship with God. This focused, daily walk with Him not only leads us but also provokes us to love and do good works. May our lives be consumed by literally living faith.

Rev. Deci Connelly, M. Min.

La Quinta, CA

Author, Educator, Prolific Defender of the Faith

Foreword

DEDICATION

"May God be forever glorified in all things!"

I decree the visible and eternal blessing of the Lord Most High upon the 30 plus transparent, generous, relevant, spiritually availed, FAITH FACES who understood the assignment! From all over the nation, you collectively delivered a full month of faith for today in beast mode!! Your innate drive withheld nothing as this anthology solidifies the God kind of faith in the earth!

The Lord and I dedicate the spiritual fruit of this work to your heart. Thank you for releasing fresh "by-faith" trajectories, possibilities, and productive hope for the world! Your "faith-i-monies" awaken nations to repeatedly BELIEVE IT, SEE IT, and TELL IT. Future FAITH FACES, having come this way are, undeniably, your spiritual heritage!

Well Done!!

Bishop LaTerra D. Ruffin

Dedication

Day 1: FAITH FACES

LaTerra Ruffin, MDiv., CPE, CPMLC, is unapologetically in love with Jesus. Believing Him for all things is first nature. She proudly leads Life Empowerment Church (Moreno Valley, California) as Bishop alongside Pastor Marcus Ruffin, her eternal husband (two decades plus). Together they parent their "by faith" miracle twins, King-Marcus Oral & Queen-Majesty Acacia (b. 2005).

LaTerra possesses grounded giftedness and is accessibly anointed to raise and marry mounting moving faith with destiny. The results reiterate, "With God all things are possible to those who believe." She is a prolific communicator who stirs faith in those attending church, conferences, and non-religious events each year. She wisely enlarges the Kingdom of God through ministry and church planting around the world (Africa, Trinidad, Antigua, Jamaica, Europe, Bahamas), and domestically wherever God grants breath. LaTerra is the encourager supreme, par-none. The words she speaks are birthed from the Spirit of the Lord and bring life on and off "the platform." LaTerra's best friend is the Trinity! When you see her, take the opportunity to just say hi. You will never be the same again.

No joke! Elder Robert McBay, my uncle, truly founded an amazing church in 1950. Under the instruction of the Lord, he named the church "Prayer Warriors for Christ, Church of Faith." Uncle McBay believed God on the inhale and exhale. Without reservation, this man of unrelenting and precise faith spoke and decreed God's heart, strategies, and plans with profound accuracy. Through the Church of Faith (Philadelphia, Pennsylvania), individuals and families were taught to walk and live by the word of faith. Close encounters of "the faith-kind" became common, expected, and contagiously normal. Under Elder McBay's demonstrative, faith-laden leadership, God's power remained tangible, and miracles were woven into life's tapestry. Uncle McBay raised up generations who unapologetically believed God.

In the early 70's, during a visit to Many, Louisiana, he dropped a clarion prophetic word over a three-month-young baby. The prophetic proclamation stirred the baby's 18-year-young mother, Anita Elayne Sibley Williams, to exercise faith in the direction of what she heard spoken over her child. Anita believed God.

Imagine such: A failing new marriage, a young life quickly shifted with a baby girl in tow. The future's certainty is confusing and thickly blurred. Heartache and depression become fast friends. They meet up in the journey. Suddenly, you're sitting at the anointed and proven spout from which accurate, faith fueled, prophetic words shower. This promising moment belongs to you. You immediately inhale the proclamation, "Sam is coming! Sam will bring about a change! Sam will do great and mighty kingdom works. Sam will be a blessing to many nations," poured out over your infant daughter (aka LaTerra DeKarla Williams) as sudden instructional manna. What do you do with that?

Philadelphia is a far cry from Many, Louisiana. Moving seemed doable, within reach, and the only viable option. You've been there and are maybe there even now. That valley of decision has one way out, by faith. Faith has a way of seeing the how. As the superior spiritual superfood, faith arrives power-packed for the battle, securing the God win! It snatches the wind from every contender. When allowed, faith aligns and unveils unprecedented strategies, wisdom, endurance, and favor required for every season forward. What a substance!

Each time Mommie shared this "faith-i-mony," intrigue filled the air. Through the years, she has repeatedly said, "I knew something better awaited me there. I felt everything said through Uncle McBay would come to reality. I believed God." Anita left. She went to the land, the "there" shown to her by the Lord, and continued living and reaping by faith.

At the tender age of nineteen, nearly one year to date of the prophetic proclamation, my mother, Anita (aka Eunice), left her mother, Ora (aka Lois), to ensure pronounced generational faith would grow and burn through me, LaTerra/Sam (aka Timothy). I was barely 13-months when we began our "Faith Faces" pilgrimage. We flew from Many, Louisiana to Philadelphia, Pennsylvania. Uncle McBay and Aunt Johnnie-Mae welcomed us into their heavily faith-driven home.

Within a few years after our arrival, Uncle McBay went to Heaven. His great faith mantle fell upon many, including his wide-eyed, committed, hungry-for-greater, spiritual son, Claude R. Barnes. "Brother Barnes" became the next and only pastor, now Bishop, of the Churches of Faith, Inc. Under his faith-powered ministry, miracles, signs, wonders, and extreme-faith soldiers mounted. The household of our Mommie, LeRondya DeMarla Williams (Ronnie), and yours truly became chief amongst those extreme-faith soldiers. (That's how I tell and live the story.)

Bishop (Dad), now over eighty, remains an iconic faith pillar. He nurtured the hunger for and cooperation with Elder McBay's proclamation over my life for over four decades and counting. The power, presence, and provisions of God, by faith, were carved and branded into my family of origin's soul through this spiritual giant. We grew to believe God!

It's been 50 years plus since those initial faith days. The decades brought copious opportunities to mold, shape, challenge, strengthen, and cement my "Faith Face" as flint! I believe God! The bulk of those stories are too numerous to account here. Oh but wait!! Blessed be His perfect name forever and throughout all of eternity.

Pastor Tim Baldwin (Bethel Deliverance Church, Northeast Philadelphia) says, "You can easily spot persons who come through the Church of Faith lineage. They believe God for any and everything!"

This chapter continues on the heels of asking "the Royals" (my anointed, beautiful children - King and Queen) the same question at different times, and while the other was not present. "What is your most memorable 'by faith' story?" I asked. Both responded immediately with tones dipped in expressions befitting one holding the "I believe God" baton.

Queen-Majesty quickly recalled sensing something was about to happen as we were suddenly standing five feet from Bishop Charles Blake, Sr. The Lord impressed upon me to have Bishop Blake pray for Queen. My part was to see the how, discern the timing and the space, along with execute wisdom with supreme grace that would bring Bishop Blake's security team on board this mission. I moved with purpose and precise timing as I presented Queen to him. I had never met Bishop Blake, yet this was a faith-driven carpe diem.

The words that fell from Bishop Blake's seasoned spirit to Queen's 10-year young spirit have been bumpers, guides, and gripping strength for her personal faith journey. Who knew just a few years later Queen would undergo two surgeries repairing a torn ACL and a torn meniscus? Her basketball stats were stacked amongst the best rising sophomores in the nation! Queen's game-IQ rendered breath-taking passes while dishing remarkable assists. Her reliable three-point shot widened the score, game after game. The tedious yearlong recovery more than knocked her off her feet. It directed her to Bishop Blake's prophetic words heralded over her life when she was just 10-years of age: "Lord make her name a household name for Your glory." God did it.

The fact that you're now reading a snippet of Queen's testimony speaks to the ongoing, resonating power of those words. Oh yeah, Queen bathed in those words on levels few will ever know. Her full recovery time was two weeks away. Medical clearance to resume playing the sport of her heart was near. Yet, it was somewhat awkwardly scheduled for after her final travel-ball tryouts. This is the moment where my seed's faith faces the evidence of things not seen but felt. Every prayer warrior who knew faith-rocking prayers, laced in the word of truth, was on patrol! Before she left for the final round of tryouts, she mentioned needing to demonstrate foot motion and competitive ability.

"Mom, I know I have not been medically released to play. I also know I will be cleared in two weeks. I am going to make this team, Mom. I'm going to play basketball today, Mom. I will fully tryout for this team today," she heralded with such conviction. My reply was simple, "I can't go this round. Your dad (a faith fireball with extended results) will take you. I will stay here and pray." Queen made the "A" level for an NBA-player sponsored travel team! Queen's generational faith was loud and clear.

"I have that feeling that I get when I am certain it's going to work in my favor. This is one of those times. I'm going to try out. I'm making that team, Mom," said the royal daughter.

Queen used that last round of travel-ball season as a strong senior year launching pad. Having been out of the high-school circuit for two crucial years presented uncertainties regarding college ball opportunities on the levels previously in pocket, prior to the injury.

This contributing, beast-mode, point guard started a new high school, fully confident and determined. She worked hard her faith, passion, leadership, and skills. The team made her the pre-game prayer connect after I declined their invitation with: "Thank you, girls, for asking me to pray before your games. What an honor. You do know Queen prays too. Don't be fooled. Ask her to pray. If you believe she needs back-up, I'll step in next time." They all agreed to the prayer plan. I checked in about three weeks later. The team captain said, "Queen's prayers are really good. She will not need back-up this season." Queen helped her team secure a 10-0 record, win regionals, and play in the Division (D-1) State Championship game.

Interviews, news articles, specialty teams, national and international college offers abound. We are currently in the thick of finalizing the flow of faith. Above all, "making her name a household name for His glory," while bending her knee in full allegiance, adoration, and honor to Him, remains the premiere pursuit and victory.

King-Marcus Oral Ruffin set his "by-faith" testimony recollection around a global and signature Ruffin "I believe God" moment, to describe it lightly! He is the tapped-in, discerning, inwardly cleaved-to-the-authentic-presence-of-God son of my right hand. King's answer to the original question, "What is your most memorable "by faith" story?" is remarkable. King knew his answer would show-up here and grip your heart now as this "faith-i-mony" has awakened him, many years beforehand and forward. His recall speaks to the combustible power of faith designed to inflame another's journey.

King believes God. His litany of personal "no faith to great faith" courses take second string this day. Well, not really. Let me quickly slip in a recent opportunity he seized to boldly display his "Faith Face." During the 11th to 12th grade matriculation, King made it adamantly clear returning to private school was not his desire. What he actually said was, "I am not going back to that school. I want to attend public school my senior year." Our response was surely going to dissuade said request. "Not."

"Research the public school the Lord has chosen for you. Let us know where He is leading you and we will follow," we said. This young man sought the Lord. When he learned the school was at full capacity (impacted), King was not moved. "Mom, this is the school decided by the Lord," he declared. What I heard was, "Partner with my faith!" The principal knew our family walked by faith. King was admitted after sharing with the principal God's leading of King to this public school. Within a month, King was standing before 1,000 plus superintendents, administrators, teachers, and parents as the student keynote speaker for the California Equity Conference. He received a standing ovation. Word has it the person over the conference was looking for another student when she came to recruit students from King's school for the conference panel. His principal suddenly gave King's name to the organizer. King was immediately interviewed and chosen!

The confidence that danced around in his eyes remains stellar as he adds, "I told you the Lord directed me to this school!" It's been six months since King's grand public speaking debut. The Lord keeps proving King's ear gates cleave to His voice. The California Teacher's Induction Conference (IGNITE) rendered another standing ovation as King confidently emceed the student panel segment with effective transitions and smooth segues from question to topic.

He is anointed in that "make room for you speaking gift." Over 600 attended the IGNITE conference. One, by faith decision, unleashes pronounced "nexts" often in the direction of exceedingly, abundantly above all you can ask or think.

King continues to abound in the "by faith" overflow. He accepted an invitation, through the same high school, to compete in his first speech competition, where he took first runner-up with a generous monetary award! King's new business, "King Speaks," will provide motivational inspiration for several graduations this year and a few conferences before "going on the road!" He's just 17 years young, and is learning to set his faith to face it all, through working in the direction he believes God has called and equipped.

Honestly, I'm amazed and honored as King discloses, "The story around our birth is my all-time favorite, Mom." "Yessss God!" I exclaimed! He has heard this faith buzz on a plethora of occasions. Sweety (my husband) and I have intentionally excised lesson after paradigm from its wells to King's God identity, character, and faith posture. King's knower knows what happens when faith faces a heart's desire. He is intimately acquainted with those whose faith faces intense opposition yet relenting has no penetrating portal. Read on. Allow these last few paragraphs to mold, embolden, and elevate how your faith faces the promises of God as final authority, regardless!

Five! Four! Three! Two! One!

While feasting on every premarital counseling session, we (Marcus Orlando Ruffin and I) learned each of us desired twins. Not only did we each desire twins but, get this: we desired girl/boy fraternal twins. Being cut from the same "I Believe God" cloth, we knew God placed the desire to have girl/boy twins within our heart. We were fully persuaded in His fulfilled promise prevailing. We said, "When we are ready, God will send the twins. That's our faith focus." We believed God for girl/boy twins.

Two years into our marital covenant we visited Christian Worship Center (Pastor Hansen Mettle) in Ghana, West Africa. While there, I was strongly attracted to the GYE—NYAME symbol affixed to the podium where we preached each day. I learned it represents the supremacy of God: EXCEPT GOD—ONLY GOD.

Our return trip had a one-day layover in New York. We came upon a material store selling GYE—NYAME fabric. The few yards purchased were taken to my Catholic seamstress. I looked her in the eyes saying, "Rosemary, we just returned from Ghana last month. My husband has informed me of his readiness to have children. We are believing God for girl/boy twins. Please use this fabric to make this two-piece maternity outfit I have designed." I then explained to Rosemary the meaning of GYE—NYAME. Rosemary looked at me. The presence of God was visible in her visage as she held my hand saying, "It will happen, LaTerra." Shock and glory overwhelmed my heart. ("She's clearly a spirit-filled woman," I thought.) We immediately acknowledged the Holy Spirit's presence. He was in the room confirming, assuring, and overseeing our way. One month later, I conceived!

Natural conception confirmation came in the form of two home-based tests. I handed the results to my husband while interpreting them at the same time. This man of vision and great faith was more than elated. We decreed, "The twins are here!!"

We cheered. We praised God. We BELIEVED GOD!

Our language was totally in sync with our faith. Sweety's announcement, "Pastor LaTerra is pregnant. We are having girl/boy twins," sent the congregation in a jubilant uproar. Over 1500 persons were present that day. Eventually thousands more joined this by-faith campaign.

You see...hmmmm...how do I say this but to say it? DIY pregnancy tests are just that. They do not determine how many "little people" are growing inside. When your faith is sealed, set, and signed, the complementary language along with continued mindsets and actions must follow in like manner. Sweety's public declaration of girl/boy twins, spawned from his strong faith background. His bold faith power and faith persuasion were consistently modeled by his mother, Sandra Uzzle Ruffin. As a matter of fact, she released a resonating, unique to her faith persuasion, "Hallelujah" followed by "You will have girl/boy twins LaTerra," upon hearing of our by-faith desire and proclamation. These children were set-up, on both sides, to walk by faith. (It matters how and whom you marry. That's extra wisdom for buying this faith arsenal!)

When Sweety spoke those by faith words to the congregation (three services and over fifteen hundred persons), all who heard were charged forward, even more, after learning WE DID NOT HAVE ULTRASOUND PROOF NOR HAD WE SEEN OUR DOCTOR. Pregnancy, for Team Ruffin, was synonymous with having girl/boy twins. No questions considered. We believe God completes what He begins. These children are His desire. We are conduits of the promise!

Dr. Blessing (truly her name) did not know of our faith declaration. She conducted a rather lengthy external ultrasound. As I watched her face, I sensed she heard two heartbeats. She moved the doppler to the left then to the right and said, "Hmm, okay." My sensing was confirmed when she said, "Mrs. Ruffin, I want to send you for a special ultrasound. You're a little bigger than what I expect for this gestation." When Sweety and I left the appointment, I could barely speak. This was our first physical confirmation of the by-faith twins' arrival!

It's here! The day for the special ultra-sound has arrived. Everyone, and I do mean everyone, is awaiting this report! We decided a long time ago, our faith faces God's promise. He will not be denied! By this time a significant number of persons who clearly have their faith facing doubt, jealousy and ridicule, decide to take turns asking (nearly every Sunday before the specialty ultrasound), "Do twins run in your family? Do you have a family history of twins?"

Oh my word, you have to know how to love people to life and stay in your faith lane as you respond from that "well able to quench the fiery darts of the enemy." "Oh yes, by faith, girl/boy twins run in your family and in mine. We are the family of God, you and I. Thank you for believing what God has done," was dropped in love, on repeat…UNTIL the same question was asked by the medical provider during the specialty ultrasound! "Do twins run in your family?" she prodded! My head whipped around quickly, disengaging my chat with Sweety. The two round sacs on the screen brought instant tears along with a forever praise to THE FAITHFUL GOD!! "Look Sweety!! There they are!! The twins are here!! Glory be to God!! You are the keeper of Your desires. God, You reign! We bless Your name forevermore!!" I exclaimed.

The medical provider identifies our son, King and then states not being able to determine the sex of the second. Both Sweety and I smile saying, "It's a girl!" Then suddenly, closer examination, with my own eyes, turns my attention from the children. I see "other details" in my uterus. "Are those fibroids?" I ask. Sheepishly, the medical provider confirms my observation. Fibroids can cause intrauterine growth retardation. They can impede development, smother the fetus and so on. I learned such during my Bachelor of Science in Nursing (BSN) studies.

When your faith faces potential and sudden worry, fear, and shock, guard your heart with all diligence. Remember the Lord your God. Override every thought sent to undermine His purpose and process. Gnaw, chew on, and digest His Word. The steadfast Word brings assurance of His presence in the journey from His desire birthed in your spirit to His promise revealed and fulfilled.

JESUS TODAY. I refused to give place to facts when the truth of His work was already at hand. Never did I share such facts with Sweety. Continuing to rejoice in the Lord was my decision. The Lord can be trusted. He is the keeper of His own Word. His Word has never returned to Him empty, weak, or void. We believe God!!

"Ouch! That hurts. What is happening?" Those were feelings and inquiries with which I tussled, March 8, 2005. The pressure was strange and the generous blood running down my legs, punched my faith in the heart. The Lord immediately brought to remembrance the doctor's appointment scheduled for later that day. "Do not worry. They will admit you during this visit. Pack your bag," the Lord so sweetly directed as I wiped my tears. I was alone. Bedrest had been prescribed due to previous spotting. This was more than spotting!

Linda Young called within seconds of this whole scene. "I have a surprise for you. I'll be there in a moment. Wait for me outside," she said with such glee." "I'm resting, precious. The door will be unlocked. Please come in," I offered. She agreed. Upon her arrival, Linda asked me to close my eyes and not open them until she said so. I followed her instruction as I lay on the couch privately nursing my soul. She went back outside, returned and when instructed to open my eyes, my heart exploded. Surely all is well as the Lord has said!! Mommie was kneeling down beside me. I kept blinking in shock, holding her hands, hugging her neck, kissing her face while crying over the Lord's timing.

God sent Mommie for such a time as then. The very next day, after I was admitted (as the Lord had said), my sister (LeRondya DeMarla/Ronnie) whom I love as myself, walks in the hospital room. She was singing our signature song, "Always sisters, Always friends." God prepared and sent my "by-faith" roots (all the way from Philadelphia - the Church of Faith and our faith alive home to Palm Springs), as "surprises for me." More importantly, He sent them to sure-up my focus in the flow of His undefeated, "by-faith" victory!! Mommie, Sam, and Ronnie believed God with unfailing generational faith.

The next 10 days turned into 30, then 58, and ultimately 72 days in the hospital, protecting the promises. Desert Regional Medical Center (DRMC) became the "Church of Faith."

I had contractions every single day and mostly throughout the night. Every week, the reports did not favor the report of the Lord. That was just fine because THE REPORT OF THE LORD DID NOT FAVOR THE TESTS!!

The hospital room became a season of pure isolation and determination to see what God has said. Guarding all portals was critical and crucial. Having no visitors became a necessary decision, as ordered by the medical team. Regardless of the tests' results concluding the children are at risk; they will arrive premature and will not survive, we believed God!

We repeatedly declared beyond and over every test, each untimely contraction and even naysayers, "The children will arrive full-term (beyond 37 weeks). They will weigh over five pounds each. They will not require time in the Neo-Natal Intensive Care Unit (NICU), and they will leave this hospital when we leave!"

I sang the songs of Zion to the children. While reading Psalm 91 as daily manna, verse 14 became personally ascribed to the children. I heard the Lord declare He would surely deliver them!

I told the children every day how much they were loved and what a miracle God was performing through their journey. They heard a wealth of "Thank You Jesus" stories reiterating God's certain power at work. I prayed for their lives, friends, love for the Lord, spouses, callings, gifts, talents, professions, character, and their voice to echo God. I prayed beyond what appeared to be at hand, yet in sync with God's plan for the up-and-coming stages of their lives.

When your faith faces the valley of the shadow of death, how do you fear no evil when literally everything is visibly in opposition of what you believe? Try closing your natural eyes. Never open them again. Spiritual sight silences, tramples upon and then commands everything in the natural to demonstrate the unequivocal, glorious splendor of God! This is true 20/20!! It's the breeding ground where miracles populate.

May 20, 2005, bedrest ended under the unforgettable care and love of Dr. Ralph Steiger, my top OB specialist in the nation. We grew together as he would take time to chat, share his life, and understand how my faith worked with his training. Several times, I was offered the opportunity to continue bedrest at home. We contended, respectfully and kept true to the weekly "agreement sessions." The medical team cared well for us. We were 34 weeks strong when I was discharged from DRMC. Bedrest restrictions were lifted.

The next three weeks were filled with nesting and preparing for the children's soon arrival. I was free to roam the land. Whew!! The 37-week marker (full-term for twins) was in sight. We believe God.

Mommie and Ronnie wanted to return for the children's birth. I asked the Lord to keep me in that loop so I could tell them when to arrive. He did. Sweety and I believed the Royals would arrive after the full-term decree. When the sensing from the Lord was precise, Mommie and Ronnie returned. Five days later, the "by-faith" girl/boy twins were delivered by c-section. GLORY BE TO GOD!! The Royals arrived June 11, 2005. Queen-Majesty Acacia weighed in at six pounds thirteen ounces. King-Marcus Oral was suited in six pounds fifteen ounces of faithfulness. They were born thirty-seven weeks and one day!! NICU intervention was not needed, and we all left the hospital together!

Pastors Marcus and LaTerra believe God from desire, through process to promises fulfilled!! The Royals' intentional names reflect the presence and authority of God.

King (after his KING OF KINGS).

Marcus (after his faith-filled, faithful and praying warrior Father: Pastor Marcus Orlando Ruffin).

Oral (after Granville Oral Roberts, a general in our lives. We met at his university. The legacy of faith is taught and caught there. It's alive in us).

Queen (after her living in and "by faith" Queen-Mother).

Majesty (after her Lord).

Acacia (the durable wood of the desert used to construct the Ark of the Covenant, which housed the presence of God).

As previously inferred, the Royals nursed on this testimony (many others too) for almost two decades. This June welcomes their 18th birthday. Academic and athletic offers abound as do several entrepreneurial and internship options. King and Queen's "by-faith" future is yet being molded by their own God-life. Their generational "by-faith" posture is evident and growing with much to fill in as and when their own faith faces God. All that was spoken over and regarding them from the Lord, will be fulfilled.

King wanted you to have this piece of "our faith faces, and believe God's legacy." He holds the many "by-faith" lessons drenched in those 72 bedrest days, not shared here but stay close. Those testimonies will pop-up in the "encore/sequel." In the interim, hold on to this:

My prayer for you:

Thank You, Father for aligning Your beloved's steps to this sacred and holy ground. As their faith faces real life, deals with extensive, sudden types of situations that are not exactly how and what they planned, thank You for the divine assignment of this space. Even now, it enlarges their hope and the scope of their measure of faith. Your beloved, oh Lord, will not be consumed or derailed. In truth, the very opposite is their lot and assurance. Yes! This is also the portion for all who come to know Your name because of Your beloved's faith decree.

Amen.

I hear the Lord saying even now:

"While you ingest these life delivering words, I am multiplying the fruit of your efforts and establishing immediate results upon your expectations. You are one who dares to believe Me. When all appeared bleak, you believed. Through dense fog, you fixed your eyes on Me and allowed My voice to compass your way. Now, you are one who sees and hears Me, before your faith faces sudden grief, an uncomely diagnosis linked to a dreary prognosis, defiant offspring, family disputes, professional disparities, betrayal, adultery, addiction, recovery, forgiveness, restoration, healing, promotion, new beginnings, favor, success, and sustained victory. Remain unwaveringly reminded of My inability to fail. I am drawing the harvest to believe it, see it, and tell it, pursuant to your clarion example. I have sealed this Word to you in My Son's perfect, trusted, all powerful, supernatural, enduring, and true name."

You BELIEVE God!

Day 2: THE LIFE AND NEAR DEATH OF A MISSIONARY

 Lloyd Hanebury holds a Bachelor of Science Degree in Business Administration and Marketing from California State University East Bay, and a Master of Divinity and Master of Arts in Missions from Oral Roberts University. Lloyd and his wife, Nataliya, are proud parents of two boys, Liam and Fáelán. Lloyd and Nataliya served in missions from 2002 to 2009 in the nation of Ukraine. In addition to being Global Infusion's Ukraine contact, Lloyd served as the National Director for Global University in Ukraine and taught mission courses at the Kyiv Bible Institute. Lloyd and Nataliya were members of the elder board at the International Christian Assembly in Kyiv for 6 years. Lloyd trained both short-term mission teams from the USA as well as Ukraine and hosted countless teams. Lloyd currently serves as the Long-term Mission coordinator at Global Infusion.

"And they overcame him by the blood of the Lamb and by the word of their testimony" (Revelation 12:11, New King James Version).
"But it was a beginning" - Robert Jordan

I was born on April 5th, 1973, in Oakland, California. Despite this, often when people ask me to share my testimony, I start with "It all began in 1954." Why? Because it was in 1954, in a tent in Alameda, California, that my grandfather and namesake, Lloyd Coley, answered an altar call at an Oral Roberts crusade. On a subsequent night, Lloyd Coley, a cripple and alcoholic, was healed and set free from his addiction. This miracle transpired as the power and grace of the Lord Jesus Christ flowed through Oral Roberts into my grandfather's life and body as Brother Roberts laid hands on him. So, this was not the beginning of my testimony. However, it was a beginning as was the conversion of Oral Roberts himself and the person who led him to Christ. These beginnings continue to go back through time, carving my spiritual ancestry, not only from the birth of Jesus but beyond to the time in which Jesus was the Lamb slain before the foundation of the world. This is pedigree.

What is a pedigree? It is an ancestral line, line of descent, lineage, or ancestry. It is distinguished, excellent, or pure ancestry.

This is my pedigree, which is not exclusive to Lloyd Maxwell Hanebury. This caliber of ancestry is attributed to all who bow their will to that of Jesus. Their stories have many beginnings, but they all trace back to the same beginning, Jesus. *"We love Him because He first loved us"* (1 John 4:19). Jesus. *"And He is before all things, and in Him all things consist"* (Colossians 1:17). Jesus. It all starts with Him (John 1:1-3). Jesus.

The reality of these statements is quintessential to the story I am about to share. This is not a tale that I weave. This is not a fable that has been constructed to convey moral truth. Although there are truths to be gleaned from this narrative, it is not fiction. This is my history. My His Story. This is the story of His and mine. This is my testimony. This is His testimony.

A Beginning...not the beginning.

I was born to a family of mixed faith. My father was raised as a holiday church attender in the Episcopal church. His faith ultimately turned to atheism at worst and agnosticism at best.

In contrast, there was a strong Christian faith on my mother's side. Yet, it was the legacy of my grandfather and grandmother, who had very powerful and miraculous experiences with God as revealed in the Bible. It was they who had given their lives to Jesus at the Oral Roberts' Crusade in 1954.

From an early age, I believed the Biblical account of God and Jesus were real as I saw and experienced the supernatural and miraculous move of God in response to my prayers and the prayers of others. I remember the first answered prayer when I was five years old. My great-uncle was a nicotine addict who smoked like a brisket. All day. I don't even know how many packs he would go through each day. Even the news from the doctor that he would die imminently if he didn't stop immediately did not sway him in the least. His wife, my great aunt by blood (my grandmother Lee Coley's sister), was distraught. I was only a child, but children have ears, so I was aware of the situation.

I was spending the night with my grandparents. My grandma and I were praying as I was getting ready for bed. I asked the Lord for something, and my petition was not well planned nor well laid. It was simple and seemingly impossible for any adult. However, it seemed a simple matter to a child who believes that God is whom He says He is. My supplication was thus, "Jesus take cigarettes and coffee out of Uncle Dean's life." The doctors had also said Dean needed to stop drinking coffee as well as give up smoking. So, I asked, not sheepishly but largely. *Let us, therefore, come boldly to the throne of grace, that we may obtain mercy and find grace to help in time of need*" (Hebrews 4:16). I didn't come with mature faith...but that of a child. "*Assuredly, I say to you, whoever does not receive the kingdom of God as a little child will by no means enter it*" (Luke 18:17).

The next morning, my aunt called my grandmother. She was astounded as she relayed what had happened that morning. As she packed my uncle's lunch, she felt the urge to ask him if he wanted, to put his coffee and cigarettes in his lunch box as per her standing orders. He responded, "No." He quit smoking and drinking coffee that very morning. I testify to you that he never touched them again from that moment forward. Yet this was not the biggest miracle. When my grandmother heard this testimony from my aunt, my grandmother relayed to her how "Little Lloyd" (that's what the family called me) had prayed for the Lord to do this very thing just the night before. You see, my Uncle Dean wanted nothing to do with God. However, he was best friends with my grandfather. He had heard the testimony of my grandpa, of his healing and conversion, yet he was completely unswayed. However, Jesus!!!! Jesus was unrelenting. When Dean heard later that day that his little nephew had prayed for his deliverance from his addiction and when he realized that he had tasted and seen the goodness and mercy of God, he gave himself over to the saving grace of Jesus! After this foundational experience, I could never doubt that there is a merciful God, that He hears our prayers, that He has the power to move on our behalf, and that He honors faith in His Son where He finds it.

Who was shown mercy when I prayed? Clearly, my Uncle Dean who needed to be saved and freed from self-destructive addictions. But wait, clearly the one who received mercy was my aunt who desperately wanted her husband to live and be saved. But wait, the target of mercy was obviously my grandmother who got to see her sister and brother-in-law touched by God in a miraculous way and the seeds she had sown in her grandson bear fruit. But what about me, wasn't I the recipient of grace? A grace that has not left me but rather has branded my soul forever, showing I am not my own but owned by my Lord. What about you? Was this moment not for you? Is not your heart burning with the realization that God is not swayed by words no matter their grandiose scale nor depth of elucidation but rather by the simple boldness of faith that asks for what only He can do? What is it that only He can do for you? Are you ready to ask?

There was a man. He was a paralytic. Mark Chapter 2 conveys his condition and the quality of his friends. But this story does not begin, nor does it end in the pages of scripture. I believe in eternity we will get to hear all the beginnings of his story. His story, like mine and yours, has many beginnings. Let me share a few as my spirit and heart imagine them. One starts with a child, a boy his age but not him. He is a young, Jewish boy from a poor family but rich in faithfulness to the mandate given to them through Moses. Every Sabbath, that boy listened, quietly enthralled by the stories shared by the rabbis in the synagogue. How he marveled and his heart leaped as he heard the story of the dead man, carelessly thrown onto the bones of Elisha, who was resurrected by the power of God that was still residing with Elisha, even after death. He pondered in his heart, how if only he knew where those bones lay, there would be more miracles to be seen. Years later, that boy hears about Jesus doing miracles. Is this Elijah returned? Can he heal my friend like he has healed so many others? The testimony in scripture planted in his heart brought forth a harvest of faith that carried a friend onto a roof. Another friend of the paralytic, who had heard of David, undaunted by a giant and won the hand of a princess, was not put off by a mere rooftop standing between his friend and the one who could heal him. He began to use his hands, when no other tool could be found, to tear apart that rooftop. He didn't stop until the hole in the roof was large enough to lower his friend through it. Every man on that rooftop, the paralytic and his four friends, all had expectations, and they all had reason to believe. Each had heard the testimonies of who this man Jesus was. They all expected one thing — the healing and restoration of this paralytic.

Imagine the room in which Jesus was teaching and preaching. It was just an ordinary home. Someone had opened their home to host Jesus. Imagine the audience. People were enthralled by this teacher. His followers, His critics, and everyone in between flooded the home to overflowing. As they sit transfixed by every word that left Jesus' mouth, there is a hushed silence over the crowded room. Everyone wants to hear everything He says, but as He speaks, noise from above grows ever louder as at first small dust begins to fall from the ceiling. The noise and the descent of debris continue as the noise grows louder and the larger pieces of the ceiling begin to fall to the ground in front of Jesus. Jesus ceases speaking and like everyone else present, He turns his gaze upon the light now peering through the shadows of the room from the rooftop. As the circle of light grows bigger, everyone can see that there are men, desperately working to make the hole bigger. The owner of the house isn't happy and is confused as to why someone would be trying to destroy his roof. The crowd begins to murmur as the men stop working and an elongated shadow eclipses the light shining from above. "What is going on?" the crowd wonders as the witnesses question each other. But soon everyone can see there is a man on a mat being lowered through the hole in the ceiling. They recognize this man. They know this man. He has palsy, and he can't walk. They know why he is there; it is because of Jesus, the healer. He will work a miracle. He will do something wondrous. They know it, yet what they will witness is beyond the pale. They think they will witness something supernatural but what they will witness is something beyond imagining. What they will see and hear is something at the pinnacle of audacity.

As the man lies before the Master, their eyes meet. This crippled man knows why his friends brought him there. He knows why they paid such a price and dared so greatly to bring him face-to-face with Jesus. He had expectations of what this moment would be. He hoped beyond hope that the God who had brought the walls of Jericho to the ground would in His infinite mercy lift him off the ground to which he was bound. However, this man could not fathom the depths of mercy into which he was about to be delivered. Not until he looked into the eyes of God, Emmanuel, did his expectations implode, and he was left with only one thought. "I am undone, a sinner far from God, a wretched soul worthy of judgment." But then, JESUS!

Jesus looked at this man and saw the condition of his heart, and the greatest need that this man could not meet for himself. He saw his sin and his contrite heart. Jesus peered into his soul and saw what this man wanted more than anything. Forgiveness. Jesus gave this man exactly what he wanted. "Your sins are forgiven." No one expected this. It was outrageous! It was apostasy! Heresy! But that man lying in front of Jesus wasn't disappointed that he was still paralyzed. He didn't feel cheated or grifted or incredulous. He felt, for the first time in his entire life, whole. He was healed, not in the body, nor by some temporal experience. He was free. He was saved. He was rescued, redeemed, restored, and reconciled. Jesus gave this man the deepest desire of his heart. He forgave him.

The crowd didn't believe it. The friends probably didn't believe it. Many were confused and some were even offended and angry. But JESUS!

His mercy was not just shown to that man. Consider what happened next. Jesus told the people, "But that you may know that the Son of Man has power on earth to forgive sins" -- He said to the paralytic, "I say to you, arise, take up your bed, and go to your house." Immediately he arose, took up the bed, and went out in the presence of them all, so that all were amazed and glorified God, saying, "We never saw anything like this!" (See Mark 2:10-12.)

Understand this...Jesus didn't heal the man because the man was crippled and needed to be healed. He healed him because he wanted to show the same mercy that he had already shown to this man, to everyone else. He wanted to forgive their sins like he had forgiven this man's sin.

The miracle was mercy shown towards this man, but even more so and even more importantly, it was mercy shown to those who bore witness and to those of us who would eventually hear of it. Why? Because we could trust and believe that He could do the same for us. He could forgive us. He can forgive you.

In the same way, my story is not for me, at least not alone. It is for you, too, so I can't keep the story hidden. It must be shared.

So, at the age of five, I knew there was a God and that He answered prayers, but it wasn't until I reached the age of 13 (Presidents Day Weekend, 1987), that I realized that my need for God stretched well beyond my need for a genie who could answer my temporary wishes.

It was that weekend that I was awakened to the reality of my spiritual need. It was that weekend that the Spirit of God convicted me through His Word being preached. It was such a simple thing! Hearing a young man preach God's truth from God's Written Word with humor and boldness, changed my life. God used that moment to illuminate the truth — that I was not a good boy; that I wasn't holy, or blameless, or righteous. I was instead a criminal who had violated God's laws, and the statutory punishment for that was death and suffering for eternity. I was a liar, a thief, sexually immoral, and a murderer all before I reached high school. How is that even possible? Because I was deceitful, I had coveted, I had lusted, and I had hated! Furthermore, I couldn't save myself or even change myself. I was guilty with no way of escaping the consequences. I was diseased without a cure or the ability to heal myself. I was doomed and without hope. Just like the paralytic, I was hopelessly lost, damned, and in need of forgiveness. But...JESUS! But Jesus saw fit not to leave me in that condition. He sent someone to help me to develop a saving relationship with God.

He was just a man, a young teacher, a youth pastor, and a newlywed. He took the time to invite a group of 8th graders to go to a Christian Snow Camp at Old Oak Ranch in Sonora, California. That invitation brought me into a close encounter with a personal God. He was not just the idea of a creator or some intelligent designer, but a personal God! I am talking about a God that speaks to individuals and has a plan for them.

It was at that snow camp, sitting in an audience with about 200 other 7th and 8th graders, that eternity was altered. There was a young preacher teaching, very humorously, about David and Goliath. He was so funny, so irreverent in comparison to how I had heard preachers in the past, that he captured our attention. The message was clear, God had called David as a youth, and He was calling us too!

However, it was in the middle of all the laughing, the jokes, and the descriptive storytelling, that I heard someone talking to me. This voice cut through all the ambient noise, not audibly, but in my heart and mind, as clearly as if someone was speaking out loud. It was God. He told me that I was His. He showed me that I needed Him. He asked me to surrender, and I did. I wept so hard and for so long, I thought I might never stop. Somewhere in the middle of that experience, the reasons for my crying shifted from guilt, confession, and repentance to praise, thankfulness, and joy.

What has my life been like and whom have I become since that day? There was no static. I didn't reach a destination when I called Jesus Lord. I didn't become perfect. Not everything in my life went perfectly from then on. I didn't attain any sort of perfection in any way, shape, or form. My journey didn't end there but it was from that moment onward, that I was never again lonely nor journeyed alone. I had a companion, a friend (who is closer than a brother, a blood brother), who was with me through every part of this life journey, and He is perfect. He is a guide, a teacher, a defender, and a confidante. He sometimes steers me around a storm, and at other times walks me through it. He keeps me from falling when I listen to Him and graciously picks me up when I don't take heed of His advice. He has both sheltered me and challenged me. He has saved my life and made it worthwhile. He is my Master, and He is my friend.

I made my third trip to Ukraine in 1998, leading a team from Oral Roberts University. It was a small team of eight people. We arrived at a village called Teplik. We ministered in the church, we evangelized in the streets, and we demonstrated our love to the local pastor through acts of service.

During one of our endeavors of physical labor, I was severely injured internally. I didn't quite notice at first. It took several minutes for it to affect me. I was walking and standing one minute and the next, was on the ground, barely keeping my breath and feeling as though I was being stabbed in both clavicles as well as my solar plexus. Two team members who were local ministers picked me up and carried me into the small nearby cottage around which we had been working. My abdomen had swollen and was as hard as a rock by the time they had gotten me into the single large room in the house. I was sweating from every pour in my body. Spoiler alert: my digestive system had completely shut down and my body was desperately trying to find alternate ways to eliminate all the deadly toxins our body normally excretes through the digestive process. Weeks later, an ER nurse told me if I had been stateside in her hospital at that time presenting those symptoms, they would have operated immediately. However, I was four or more hours away from anything near western quality medical services.

They laid me on a bed in the room and began to pray. The Holy Spirit whispered to me, "Hezekiah." I knew in a moment the Spirit of God was telling me that I was dying. Like Hezekiah, upon receiving this grave news, I turned my face both literally and figuratively to the wall and cried out to God. I said, "Lord, forgive me of my sins. I am Yours and Yours alone, to live and to die for Your glory." I knew I was dying, but peace came over me. It was a peace that surpasses all understanding. *"And the peace of God, which surpasses all understanding, will guard your hearts and your minds through Christ Jesus"* (Philippians 4:7).

Something else began to happen at that same time, around the world. Daniel Olorunda, a friend, was leading a team from Oral Roberts University (ORU) to China. The team was praying before an outreach they were about to do. The same Holy Spirit that whispered "Hezekiah" to me, told Daniel that I was in trouble, and they needed to pray for me. He immediately redirected the teams' prayers to intercede for me.

At that same time, my friend and team leader from the previous summer's trip to Ukraine, Dr. Jeremy Wallace, was leading a new team from ORU to Israel. As the team was resting from the summer heat of midday, the assistant team leader, Angie Teater, was asleep. The Holy Spirit of God gave her a dream, and in her dream, I was sitting in a chair. Leaning forward, I put my hand on my face and said to Angie, "You need to pray for us. We're not doing so good." She immediately woke up, gathered the team, and had them start interceding for me and my team.

At that same time, another ORU seminarian was hanging out with a couple more. They were having a time of fellowship and prayer. The Holy Spirit spoke to all of them and told them they needed to intercede for me. They knew I had planned to go to Ukraine, but they didn't know where I was at that time. The compulsion to pray was so strong that they called my home number (this was before I had a mobile phone) and left a message on my answering machine. They told me that the Lord had told them to pray and although they didn't know what was going on, they wanted me to know that they were interceding on my behalf.

At the same time in Oakland, California, Grandpa Lloyd Coley, my namesake, was fast asleep but not for long. He was awakened by my voice, my childhood voice, crying out, "PAPA!" Just like I used to when I was sick as a child and desperately needed prayer. The Holy Spirit had moved another one to prayer on my behalf.

At the same time in Pittsburg, California, my mother was already awake. She was reading in scripture an account of someone's only son dying. The Holy Spirit spoke to her and said, "Your only son is dying." Immediately, my mother began to travail and weep, as she prayed for the Lord to save me.

Back in Ukraine, in the village, the pastor in whose bed I lay dying, felt compelled to go to a neighboring village and bring back an old woman in her 70s to see if she might be able to help me. This old woman, his grandmother, had only been a Christian for about six months. She entered that room, saw me laying on the bed, and began to weep and pray on my behalf. She paced back and forth for a while on the other side of the room, and she cried out to God. Eventually, she approached and examined me. She took her hand, hard, rough, strong, weathered by a lifetime of sun and work, and extended a single finger. That finger was more of a raptor's talon. She stuck that talon into my navel and pressed her ear to my stomach. It felt as if she was trying to locate my spine with her probing finger and she pressed so hard that I couldn't keep my breath in my current state. The look of care and concern was ever apparent upon her face. After she had listened for a short while, she declared in Ukrainian, "It isn't speaking" referring to my stomach. She understood that my digestive system was no longer functioning. She explored other sections of my abdominal cavity and determined that things had been shifted internally, precipitating the shutdown of my system. She took her weary hands of sandpaper and began to massage my stomach, moving my organs back into their proper alignment. My stomach had marks scoring it from top to bottom from her efforts. It hurt more than you could imagine. Eventually, she started using soapy water to help lubricate this process which she continued relentlessly for hours. Eventually, she stopped and said she could do no more that day without "breaking something." Following her instructions, the two pastors in the room, Roma and Vasya (her grandson), bound my torso with a large shawl, tightly to the point I could barely breathe. She said I would need to wear that the rest of the day and the following day, and that she would work on me again the next day as well.

The next day I preached at the local church. Vasya's uncle repented and went on to become a pastor in a neighboring village. I shared the experience with a policeman that pulled us over the following day. He was looking for something when he pulled us over that was very different from what he received. He was looking for silver and gold but found something infinitely more valuable. However, after we presented him with the Gospel, he said he would repent when he was older. I responded by sharing my near-death experience as well as the death of a 19-year-old friend that had just passed away that year. The fragility of life became apparent to him as I told him no one including us, was promised tomorrow. His repentance was the fruit of suffering and the faithfulness of the Holy Spirit.

My life was saved by a little old woman, who had almost died in World War , which was a miracle. What was the beginning of that miracle? Was it the prayers of my grandfather? My mother? My fellow students and missionaries around the world? Was it my cry out to God from that bed, while I faced the wall? Was it the commitment I made at the altar? The answered prayer of a five-year-old boy at his grandmother's house? Was it a man lying on his hands so that God would heal a broken, crippled alcoholic? Was it that crippled man who made his way to the front of the tent amongst 10,000 people to be prayed for? Was it that man's parents who had named him after a Welsh itinerant evangelist? Was it that evangelist, who traveled and lived by faith so that he could share the Good News? I could go on, but the answer is yes to every one of those and no. They were all the beginnings and yet none of them were. If all those events, and an infinite number more going back to Adam, were the bones of the miracle, then it was the Holy Spirit who breathed life in their midst and caused flesh and sinew to wrap around them. It was the Holy Spirit who breathed life into the body they formed (read Ezekiel 37), until that moment when what was nothing gave birth to a miracle. All good things start with Him. He is the author, the perfecter, and the instigator of our faith (read Hebrews 12:2).

And the miracle? Who was it for? Me? What about Pastor Vasya, his grandmother, my teammates, classmates, fellow missionaries, family, friends, that policeman on the road looking for a bribe...and what about you? Were not my trials and my miraculous experience not for your sake as well? (Read Philippians 1:14.)

Today is not the beginning, but it is "a beginning" in the next part of your testimony. You are surrounded by the testimonies of the Saints for your benefit. Who will benefit from yours?

My prayer for you:

Gracious Heavenly Father, You are worthy of all praise. Your mercies and grace are so often left uncelebrated. I remember, as do You, how only one leper came back to thank Your Son for the miraculous mercies He had shown to them. I pray that this will not be the case with those who have read this testimony of Your unfailing mercies today. Fill their mouths with praise. May their thankfulness compel them to share

Your goodness, reality, and light with the multitude of people in this world who have not known good, who don't know the truth, and who are living in darkness. You have given this reader all that they need to be Paladins of Christ. For He has given them His blood, shed upon that cross, and You have given them their testimony as You have worked in their lives before the universe was formed. Your Word declares in Revelation that it is by these two weapons, the Blood of the Lamb and the Word of our testimony, that the enemy of our souls will be defeated. So, fill them, O Lord, like a vessel of oil, overflowing, running down, and saturating everything that encounters it.

Father, if Your children reading this are unwilling to share that which You have so freely and with such a high price given to them, with what authority You have given me, I release Your Holy Spirit to break these vessels over the nations, that Your anointing oil may flow out of them, willing or not. But I also pray, Lord, that they will be willing, for a willing and generous sacrifice is always better, for it demonstrates not only thankfulness but love. Thank You, Lord, for Your children, and thank You for the story that You are authoring in their lives. I don't pray for their story to be safe, or pleasant and comfortable, but rather that it be glorifying and honoring to You, Your Son, and Your Spirit.

Amen.

Day 3: PROMISE KEEPER

Kimberly Carter Lassiter is a native of Philadelphia, who currently resides in a small rural town in North Carolina with her husband of 31-years. She has a Master of Business Administration Degree and works in Human Resources. Her Bishop would lovingly say that she had a Ph.D. because she could Pray Heaven Down. She has a love for serving the people of God. However, her biggest blessings call her mom and grandmom. God has gifted her with three children and four beautiful grandchildren (two girls and two boys).

HOUSEHOLD SALVATION

My salvation story is so "me," a quiet person who likes to work in the background, not the spotlight. It doesn't include a trip to the altar of a church on Sunday, a pastor, or even a saved individual inviting me to recite the Sinners' Prayer. It involves me sitting in my bedroom with a Bible in my hand reading the unadulterated truth and knowing that I needed something different in my life. I needed to be different and live differently. So, at eighteen years old in the back bedroom of a row home in southwest Philadelphia, I asked God to come into my heart and live in me. He has never failed me from that day in May of 1990, to this one.

Early in my salvation walk, God made me a promise that my whole household would be saved. In my infancy, I thought that meant me, my spouse, and the children. However, GOD is so much bigger than that! HE meant my family and as I have worked out my salvation for the past 31-years, I have been blown away by the unfolding of His promise to me. It was a promise to not leave any one of my relatives to the devourer.

I would get to see the unfolding of His promise just one year and nine months after accepting Him into my life with the passing of my grandfather. He was my everything (my grandparents raised me). He was not a church-going man. He drank, smoked cigarettes, was one of the highest-ranking members of the Masons, and was notably not what Christians would call a shoo-in for Heaven. When he went into the hospital in 1990 for a colon resection, we were all summoned to the hospital to say our goodbyes. I was not saved yet and the one person that I knew without a shadow of a doubt loved me was dying. The person who drove seven hours to Pennsylvania and turned around and drove seven hours back to North Carolina every holiday and summer, the person who taught me how to ride a horse, the person who taught me how to drive a car...MY Pop-Pop was coming to the end of his time on earth and something in me ached.

The family split duties. Someone stayed at the store and kept it running (my paternal grandparents were entrepreneurs) and someone stayed by his bedside 24-hours a day. As the youngest of the bunch (freshman in college) who was under 21-years of age, I couldn't help in the store, which sold liquor, so I spent most days at the hospital keeping watch. I spent many days in the green chair in his hospital room hoping...dare I say praying that tonight would not be the night that he took his last breath. God would move in this situation even prior to me knowing Him. The man whom doctors had given up for dead recovered and was released from the hospital.

I would have a year of salvation under my belt and be attending a Pentecostal, Holy Ghost-filled church with a bishop who took me under his wing and fathered me by the time I would have to face my grandfather's mortality again. My grandfather was able to see my middle son be born but would not live long after seeing "Tattoo," (his nickname for him because he said he looked like the actor from *The Love Boat*). He would only be four-months old when he died.

When he was at the end, my husband and I went to visit him at home where he was lying on the couch in the living room, a shell of the man I once knew due to cancer and chemo. My husband asked if he wanted to be saved and to my surprise, he said, "Yes." There in the living room of the house I loved to visit, with just the three of us in the room, MY Pop-Pop repeated the Sinners' Prayer and invited God into his heart. The prayer would be the last words he would ever speak. A week later, he was gone. February 29, 1992, MY Pop-Pop closed his eyes here on this side and opened them in Heaven.

I had so many questions and I took them to the source. I asked God how He could take him now that he was saved. Why now? I would get my answer in the sweetest way possible. I had a dream where MY Pop-Pop looked like himself again and he told me he was okay. God told me that he wouldn't have made it in if He had let him stay. My faith increased and I knew that God would keep His promises to me. Household salvation was happening right before my eyes!

However, time would not be my friend, as in just four short years I would be facing yet another cancer diagnosis. This time my beloved grandmother, who never smoked or drank a day in her life, who ate healthily and always watched her weight, would battle stomach cancer. When she went in to have surgery, we were hopeful that they could remove the orange size mass from her stomach, and she would live. Maybe she would have to have chemo and radiation, but she would get to stay with us a little while longer. When the doctor came to the waiting room and invited us to the consultation room, it was as if everything was moving in slow motion, and I was watching it on a black-and-white TV screen. Is he really saying they could not remove the mass? Is he saying it is inoperable and wrapped around her organs and they just closed her up and are sending her home to die? I never saw my grandmother express emotion growing up and that is the way she approached cancer. There were no tears, just an emptiness in her eyes. I wish I could have heard her thoughts over the next few months, but those thoughts would go with her to the grave and remain completely hers.

Yet, God is a promise keeper, and He would show up once again and allow me to see household salvation with my own two eyes. A group of church members came to visit my grandmother in that same living room that my grandfather got saved in and offered salvation to her. My humble, reserved grandmother praised God and accepted salvation as the tears rolled down my face.

I was at work in the bank when I got the call. My aunt was on the phone saying the dreaded words, that she was gone. At this point, I had been saved for six years and I knew to be absent from the body was to be present with the Lord. I knew she was no longer in pain and once again with MY Pop-Pop, but it still hurt.

God was continually proving Himself to me and my faith was growing in Him. When my next grandparent was in the hospital facing death (10 years later) it was not even a thought that he wouldn't get saved before he took his last breath. Even so, God allowed my husband to be the one to repeat the Sinners' Prayer with him in his hospital bed. Once again, God proved to me that He is a promise keeper and household salvation was mine.

Out of all four of my grandparents, the only one that I never worried about was Roberta. She took my sister and me to church every Sunday when we were little girls. She seemed to have a relationship with the Lord growing up. She is the reason I had a foundation on which to draw when I wanted to change my life in that bedroom. Calvary Baptist Church was where I was baptized and learned to recite the 66 books of the Bible in Sunday school. When she died in March of 2008, I was at peace with God's decision to take her home. She had dementia and was living in a nursing home. God had not failed to keep His promise to me in the 18 years that I had been saved. He had even on numerous occasions allowed me to witness my loved ones get saved with my own eyes.

I did not know then that He was building my faith, strengthening my muscles, and teaching me to adjust my armor for my biggest test that would come in 2015. I did not think that it could get any worse than losing the people who raised me. I serve an amazing God who, even though He knows when and where, is still concerned with my heart. This was so much so that He would slowly walk me through what would happen over the next two years. I had visions and dreams that showed me what was to come, and I would awaken in a cold sweat, and sometimes in tears. My secret closet is not a closet at all; it's my shower, and God and I had several conversations in there about me not being ready. I pleaded with Him many days to not let it happen yet and many times He obliged me.

The week of Thanksgiving in November 2014, I received a call alerting me that my oldest son was in the ICU. We immediately drove to Philadelphia to see him on a ventilator with tubes running everywhere. They asked me if I wanted to see the chaplain and I was numb. I stood by his bed, and cried out to God to not take my son, to grant him another chance. Once again, I was bombarding Heaven pleading to not take him now, letting God know my heart was not ready. Once again, God obliged my request. He recovered and was released from the hospital but was still daily battling the demons of his addiction.

My son was back in the hospital in January 2015 from an apparent overdose. Once again, we drove to Philadelphia to see him in the hospital. This time would be different though. He told us he was tired of fighting his demons, and that he wanted to change. On January 30, 2015, Dorian got saved in a hospital bed at Jefferson Hospital. God had allowed me to see with my own eyes and hear with my own ears so there would be no doubt in my mind that he was saved, and Heaven bound. He proved to me yet again that He is a promise keeper and household salvation is mine.

In March 2015, he came home to North Carolina to celebrate his nephew and uncle's birthdays. I did not know that March 8, 2015, would be the last time I would see my son alive. If I would have known, I would have held him a little longer when we hugged and said goodbye. The week of April 10th we talked on the phone for over two hours. He went on and on about one thing or another, he laughed with that infectious laugh (that sounds like it is coming from the pit of his stomach) that I miss so much, and he was making plans for a future that would never be. On April 6, 2015, at 3:08 PM, he sent me a photo and text that read:

"...I had to go to the pharmacy to pick up Valium. They're helping to wean me off. I just can't stop completely because I've been on for seven years and I will have a seizure, so we're taking less each month until I'm off completely. I'm trying, Mommy; I'm already taking half of what I was..."

This would be the last text that I would ever get from him, the last communication ever. On Friday, April 10, 2015, we received the phone call that no parent ever wants to get. My precious little boy was gone. There would be no Narcan, no hospital visit, no intervention...he was gone.

On April 17, 2015, I buried my firstborn child, and something inside me was broken. As I am writing this almost seven years later, I can see that God cradled me in His loving arms, slowly walking me to what He knew would happen on April 10, 2015. I can see His love for me and my son.

God took the time to show me He could be trusted. He helped to build my faith in Him. Over 24 years and many tests and trials, He proved to me that He is a promise keeper. Have I experienced more deaths...yes. Have I ever doubted if they made it into Heaven...No! God said it and I believe it!

PROMISE KEEPER: If you build My house, I will build yours.

Our bishop (a man who was like a father to my husband and me) had been in ministry for over 30 years when he expressed the desire to build a fellowship hall on the existing land that the church owned. My husband jumped on board and set out to raise the money to build the fellowship hall debt free. As the church members got a hold of the vision, they began to give toward the project. Before we knew it the metal frame had been ordered, the foundation poured, and the men of the church were working on the project days, nights, and weekends. A visiting preacher prophesized over my husband that God was going to build his house because he was building God's house.

My husband came home one day and told me that he had found some land for sale. We got in the car and drove to see it. I could not believe that no one had already purchased this perfect piece of land right outside of the city limits. We were not looking to build anytime soon so we made a ridiculous offer thinking that there was no way they would accept such a low offer...But God!! We got right under 12 acres for the going price of one acre of land. When we had the grass cut and began cleaning off the land, we got more offers to buy it than I care to mention. The real estate agent said she had not gotten any inquiries into it until it was sold. It was as if they had not seen the 'For Sale' signs prior to us buying it. They did not know how they could have missed it but of course, we do. God had it hidden in plain sight just for us!

In 2006, the fellowship hall was dedicated (debt free) and my husband put a FOR SALE BY OWNER sign in our front yard and told me we were going to build a house. This was a BIG deal for my husband because he is a very black-and-white person who wouldn't normally move on faith. What I need to mention here is that we had just moved into our brand-new house in 2001. Within one week we had an offer and a move-out date. The buyers wanted to do a quick sale because they wanted to be in the home and their children settled by the opening of school that year.

So, here we were, no boxes to put anything in, nothing packed, and nowhere to go. We literally could not find anything to rent to stay in during the construction of our house. We had land but it would take a good year to build a house from the ground up. We finally found an old house to rent with just a few days to spare. This house had a front porch where you could see the ground through some of the floorboards and when you stepped on it you were scared you might fall through it. The bathroom was straight out of the sixties, and I am sure the tile, toilet, and tub had been there at least that long. The kitchen was like a little box that my side-by-side refrigerator swallowed whole. There were old curtains hung in the living room reminiscent of the movie, Gone with the Wind. The front door had a gap at the bottom where you could easily slide mail under it without having to open the door, which also let in the cold air and heat from outside. We had gone from our less than five-year-old home where everything was new to this.

The rumor mill was busy in our small town but so was God. My husband had begun studying for his contractor's exam. He would not only see the fulfillment of prophecy, but he would get to build his house with his own hands. In 2007, my husband became a licensed general contractor and we moved into our home, for which we paid ½ fair market value. God had proven to us yet again that if He says it, it's a done deal. If you build His house, He will build yours. He is a promise keeper.

PROMISE KEEPER: I will bless your children

When my middle child was six months old my Bishop prophesied to me that I was going to have a baby and God was going to bless it. We did not plan to have any more children and didn't want to hear that with an infant in diapers and a four-year-old. God truly has a sense of humor because when the boys were 11 and 15 years old, we found out we were pregnant with my daughter.

It was a very eventful pregnancy. The devil tried everything to keep her from being born. I was diagnosed with placenta previa at my first ultrasound. The church mothers prayed, and that was corrected. I was diagnosed with gestational diabetes in the sixth month and had to take insulin daily until delivery. I was told she was transverse at my second ultrasound, and they wanted to do an external cephalic version, or we could wait and see if she would turn into the proper birthing position on her own. I opted to give her time to turn on her own. However, at my last doctor's visit on 8/12/2003, the ultrasound revealed that she was still transverse. I was given the option to go to the hospital and allow them to try and turn her or have a C-section. I opted for the C-section and was told to be at the hospital the next morning at 6:00 AM.

On August 13, 2003, when they cut me open to get her out, it was discovered that the umbilical cord was wrapped around her neck three times. Therefore, if she would have turned, or if I would have let them turn her, she would have been strangled. We named our miracle baby Moriah, God is my teacher, Danielle, God is my judge.

She has been one of the biggest blessings that God has given to me. She is destined to do remarkable things for the Kingdom. God kept a promise that we didn't even think we wanted. He is faithful!

If you are dealing with a prodigal child, God is with you. If you are gripped by the pain of grief and loss, I want you to know that God is with you. If your loved one is fighting for their life in a hospital, God is with you. Everything (every child, family member, mortgage...etc.) that concerns you concerns Him. He is not absent in your suffering. Know that most of the time when you are taking a test, the teacher is silent. Just because you don't feel His presence or can't hear His voice doesn't mean that He is not there. Some of my greatest testimonies (the three that I shared with you) came from my hardest tests. I pray that these pages give you confidence that God is faithful, and He keeps His promises.

My prayer for you:

Father, I pray that the person reading this will freely bring their concerns, doubts, disappointments, and triumphs to You. Give them beauty for ashes, joy for their mourning, and put a praise in them that drives out the heaviness of what they are facing. Give them an assurance that You are a God who keeps Your covenant with Your people who obey Your commands and that You see farther than we can see and know more than we will ever know, and You have everything under control. Let them know that Your grace is sufficient for them, that Your strength is made perfect in weakness, and You will never leave them nor forsake them. In Jesus's name.

Amen.

Day 4: FAITH THAT GOES THE DISTANCE

 Pastor Vonoka Dingle is an exciting speaker and teacher of the Gospel nationally and internationally. She desires to impart wisdom and occasions of laughter to all with whom she connects. She and her husband, Dennis, are the pastors of Covenant of Love Christian Church located in North Carolina. They have been married for more than 40 years and have two children.

There may be those who view the title and wonder what is meant by faith that goes the distance. I assure you that as you continue reading, you will fully grasp and understand its meaning. First, before I go any further, let's look at three important words in the title. They are faith, goes, and distance.

To help you understand, "faith" is simply to trust, have confidence in, and have an unshakeable belief. I have learned and you will too, that having faith to trust God, to have confidence in God, and an unshakeable belief in God is what will get you through life's journey. Have you said or maybe heard someone say, "If it had not been for God, I don't know what I would have done or even where I would be?" As you read further, you will understand the magnitude of God's power and His Word.

Let's now look at the word "goes." Goes means to move, to proceed, and to advance. It is imperative that you and I always allow our faith to move forward, not backward. That's what proceeding and advancing is all about. Goes is not going backward nor is it becoming stagnant. What happens to anything that becomes stagnant? It begins to release an unpleasant odor.

I was determined to have my faith move forward not backward, even though sometimes it appeared I was not even taking baby steps, but instead crawling. Guess what? A crawl was still moving. No matter how small the movement, I'm still advancing. I made up my mind that I was not going to allow the pitfalls of someone else's words, actions, or nonverbal expressions to cause me to waiver in what I firmly believed. I will continue to declare and decree my declaration of faith in all situations by the authority and power of Almighty God. It does not matter how ridiculous it may appear.

Lastly, when you think about the word distance, you think about how long. Please understand that there will be times when things you pray for will happen quickly, while at other times, you wait, and wait, and maybe are still waiting.

I love the verses of scripture in Isaiah 40: 30, 31 (The verses I will be referencing will be from the King James Version): *"Even the youths shall faint and be weary, and the young men shall utterly fall: But they that wait upon the LORD shall renew their strength; they shall mount up with wings as eagles: they shall run, and not be weary, and they shall walk, and not faint."* You may have said "Oh, how I wish I was young again" while the young say, "Oh how I wish I was older." I say to you don't despise or regret where you are at this moment. IT IS NOT OVER!! We must learn how to wait, and in our waiting, wait patiently. I must admit, patience is not always easy, but you and I must trust God in the process.

Job said it like this in Job 8:7: *"Though thy beginning was small, yet thy latter end should greatly increase."* These are words you can decree over your life, family, health, finances, and all that is connected and pertaining to you both near and far. I urge you to never, and I do mean never, allow doubt and unbelief to interfere with your visions, dreams, and plans no matter who or what is the source. You will see, as you continue to read, the faithfulness of God. Always remember God is working behind the scenes, even when we don't realize it.

Faith came on the scene while I was a child. I remember my mom saying I was a "strange child." Strange to the degree that I loved to go and get that great big Bible and read the stories in it. I called them stories because that's exactly what they were to me, stories with some colorful pictures. I loved reading about Daniel in the lion's den. Little did I know I would be facing a lion's den of sickness not too long from then.

I loved getting up every Saturday morning and watching cartoons. There was one Saturday morning when I woke up and tried to get up but couldn't. I was literally paralyzed, stiff as a board, from my neck down. I screamed out for my mom and dad. They came running to my room. I remember my dad grabbing me. My mom and dad were doing everything they could to help my limbs move by moving them up and down. Finally, I began to move but was in excruciating pain. Now that I'm older, I had a physician say to me that my pain tolerance level is very high. I can see that when I reflect on all the physical pain I experienced. My parents wanted me to go and see a physician, but I would say to them "I don't want to go. I'll be all right." Little did they know I had a fear of doctors, but as you continue reading you will see my mind changed.

I would go into my parents' room, lay across the bed, and read in that great big Bible the story of Daniel in the lion's den. It came to the point where I could no longer sleep in my bed but had to sleep sitting up. One day the pain was no longer sporadic, but consistent, as if somebody was jabbing a knife in my shoulder. No matter how I would try to position myself, I felt nothing but PAIN!! I knew at that point I needed help. Fear of the doctor left. I just wanted to stop hurting. That's when I told my parents I want to go to the doctor. After I made that statement, they realized, even the more, that something was going terribly wrong with me. I had pretended that all was well but couldn't pretend anymore.

They took me to the hospital. They gave me different tests but could not find what was wrong with me. They also gave me an injection of penicillin in case there was an infection present that they couldn't detect. Then I was sent home. The next day the physician called and wanted me to come back to get another injection of penicillin. Guess what? Those injections didn't work.

One day I decided I was going to lie in my bed. I grabbed the great big Bible and began reading about Daniel. While reading, I fell asleep and had a dream. My dream was so vivid and clear. In this dream, I was walking with Jesus. Jesus took me by the hand and as we talked, He led me to what looked like a beautiful blue partition. Jesus had me stand behind the partition and told me to wait right there. The next thing I hear is Jesus and it sounds like He is arguing with someone. I said to myself, "Whom is He arguing with?" As a child, that's what it sounded like to me. I distinctly heard this male voice say, "I will have her." Jesus said, "No you won't." The male voice said, "Yes I will." Then Jesus said, "You wait right there." Jesus came around the partition with this beautiful bottle. This bottle reminded me of the bottle Jeannie lives in, from the television series *I Dream of Jeannie*. That's exactly what it looked like to me. It was a beautiful purple and gold bottle. This explains why I love purple so much. Jesus handed me the bottle, and after taking off the lid, said, "Put this on. Rub it all over your body." I looked inside the bottle and saw a red liquid. I said, "This looks like ketchup!" He said, "It does, doesn't it?" Then Jesus said, "See, I have it all over me."

When I received Christ into my life and began to reflect on this dream, there is no way Jesus would tell a child His blood is in the bottle. So, all He did was agree with me that it does look like ketchup. I put that "ketchup" all over me like a bird washing in a bath. Then once applied, Jesus grabbed my hand, and we walked around the partition. As I came around the partition, I saw a dark figure some distance away. Jesus and I lit up like a light bulb. I remember us being so bright that the dark figure ran away. Jesus turned to me and said, "Whenever you need me, call me, and I'll be right there." Then I woke up.

When I awoke, I felt very hot. I got out of my bed and walked towards the den of our home. There I saw my mom crying because of my condition and my dad trying to console her. They didn't see me, but I saw and heard them.

I could still hear Jesus' words ringing in my ears, "Whenever you need me, call me, and I'll be right there." I didn't want to see my mom cry. I walked in and said, "Look ma! I can move my arm!" I began to literally force the raising of my arm. My mom and dad began to smile and hug me. Little did they know, when I got back to my bedroom, I grabbed my shoulder because the pain was so great from the force of raising my arm, and the hugs they had given me intensified the pain.

That night I went to bed. I thought I had been sleeping for a while and looked at the clock. It was literally midnight. I sat on the side of my bed and was in so much pain. I said, "Jesus!" Suddenly, I heard a very loud pop in my shoulder. I have not had any more pain from that day to this. Glory be to God!

There were other instances in my childhood that were not pleasant, but God has always been there. Sure, you wonder and say to yourself, "Why is this happening to me? What is going on? Where is God?" Believe me when I say to you, He is right there!

You have read thus far about me as a child. Why you may ask, am I speaking of my childhood? I am reminded of the scripture in Mark 10:15, 16, "*Assuredly, I say to you, whoever does not receive the kingdom of God as a little child will by no means enter it. And He took them up in His arms, laid His hands on them, and blessed them."* Just think for a moment. When you say to a child you are going to do something, they take you at your word. They believe you. They have faith that you're going to do what you say. They trust you. They have confidence. Does this sound familiar? People will try to determine in their mind's view the dimension of your faith and if it meets up to "their standards."

Understand this. In Matthew 17:20, it says, *"So Jesus said to them, Because of your unbelief: for assuredly, I say unto you, if ye have faith as a mustard seed, ye will say to this mountain, 'Move from here to there' and it will move; and nothing will be impossible for you."* Even in your adult life, have faith like a child. You must believe and remain focused on the Word of God. Allow the Word of God to have the final say and be the final authority in your life.

I was a child when Jesus spoke to me. I believed what He said and that all I had to do was call Him. I said his name, Jesus. That pain no longer exists in my body. Glory to God!

Let's fast forward. I married a wonderful man and have two children, a son, and a daughter. Approximately 14 years ago, I was in a car accident that severely damaged my back. At the time our son was only three months old. From then until he was between the ages of 14 and 15, I had suffered from pain in my back. The pain would at times radiate down my legs. It was not a constant pain, and I was very thankful for that.

All my household loved God, during that time. My husband and I were ministers of the Gospel in our local church, yet I was still in pain. I was praying for others and seeing the manifestation of God, but I was still in pain. I didn't grow bitter, but guess what? You will find yourself becoming acquainted, accustomed, and adjusting. That's what I did. I loved God and believed His word, but then I found myself just going on with daily living. It's not that I didn't believe God. The fight within me somehow grew less. It's amazing how the prayer fight of faith for others is intense. You'll encourage other individuals, but when it comes to yourself the fight is not as intense when you have been going through it for an extended period. You still fight; however, it becomes a little different. I got out of that slump and began to not only fight the good fight of faith through prayer and intercession for others but for myself too!

I want you to remember the time span. The accident happened when our son was three months old. He was now 14 almost 15 years of age. That's a long time to be in pain. isn't it? As I was getting ready for work one morning, I was listening to the telecast, *This Is Your Day* with Benny Hinn. The children were getting ready for school and my husband was getting ready for work. I was sitting on the side of our bed, getting ready to put on my pantyhose when I heard Benny Hinn say, "There is a person that is being healed of back problems right now." I heard it but proceeded to get ready. Suddenly Benny Hinn said, "Hey lady!" I looked up and he said, "Yes, you. God is healing you now." Suddenly I felt a push to the back of my head, and I bowed completely to the floor. I was unable to do that before! I could not bend over at all! I began to cry uncontrollably and scream with joy. My husband and children came running wanting to know what happened. I began to tell them, and they were overjoyed. I did not know how bound I was until the healing power of the Lord Jesus set me free. I exclaimed to my husband, "I'm a new woman-lookout! HALLELUJAH!!!

I want you to not give up. No matter how long it takes, keep loving God. Keep being faithful to God and His Word. Have the trust, confidence, and unshakeable belief to know that Jehovah-Rapha is your healer, and He is the One who will make bitter experiences sweet. Begin to roar the

Word of God and prophesy. Speak into existence those things that be not as though they were. I'm a witness!

Let's move forward a few more years. Our son, DJ, was now between the ages of 21 and 22. He was helping my husband and me move his sister into her dorm. As he reflected on his life, he said, "I should have been out of college a year before my sister started her college career." He decided to change his attitude and get serious regarding his studies and graduating college. He only needed 21 hours to graduate. He had to get approval to take a 21-hour course load and the approval was granted. You know what? He made the Dean's list. I thought to myself, "You could have been doing this all along."

Things didn't get better with our son, but grew worse. We raised our children in a Christian home, they went to church and attended youth services, but there are times when our children will make decisions that can cause heartache in their lives as well as that of others. I would talk to our children and inform them that they must remember the decisions they make not only affect them but us as your parents, as well as those outside of our home.

Please never stop praying. Always keep your children and others covered in prayer. It doesn't matter their age or what they have done. Never stop praying. Plead the blood of Jesus over their lives. Speak forth great things for their future. Reference the latter part of Romans 4 verse 17 *"and calleth those things which be not as though they were."* I declared and decreed the magnificent things for our children's lives and not the problem.

One morning as I was praying, I heard a gunshot. I immediately stood up. I heard the Lord say to me, "This must be, but he will not die." I knew this was regarding our son. I began to tell my family what God had said to prepare them. I continued to pray as I normally did and thanked God for our son having long life.

A few months later, DJ decided to go out one night with a friend and drive my car. He was supposed to be in one place but decided to go to another. During that time, our phone was constantly ringing with young ladies wanting to speak to our son. On the night DJ decided to go elsewhere, the phone rang. There was a young lady who called to speak to Dennis. Note that our son is a Junior, so I proceeded to ask, "Which one would you like to speak with?' I knew which one she wanted, but I asked anyway. She responded, "There are two of them?" I thought to myself, "You've got to be kidding." I said, "Yes, there are two of them. Then there was silence. I broke the silence by saying, "Once you figure out which one you would like to speak with, call back." I proceeded to block her number. I'm the queen of a block (smile) and taking the phone off the receiver. This was going to be one night I was going to sleep undisturbed.

I had gotten up early and put the phone back on the receiver. As my husband and I were preparing for church, the phone rang. It was a young man, the friend our son had gone out with. He stated he had been trying to contact us. DJ had been shot. He'd had surgery and was doing okay.

We got to the hospital quickly, fast, and in a hurry. When we arrived, we spoke to the surgeon. She said our son was a very lucky young man. I knew luck had absolutely nothing to do with it. She said that when our son arrived at the ER, he was alert and asked who in here is a Christian. A couple of people said, "I am." Our son said, "Pray!"

The doctor said DJ was not bleeding externally, so they had to perform surgery to see if he was bleeding internally. I want you now to look at your little finger on either hand. The bullet she removed was the length of your little finger and the bullet did not hit any internal organs. WOW! PRAISE GOD!

She said the bullet hit him on his right side and it was like something stopped it. I said, "Not something, someone, God."

She said this type of bullet is made to fit the gun and seeks to kill and destroy. Those were her words. When the bullet hit his side, it went down, turned, and went under the skin like a splinter. You could see the bullet by his navel. Look at God!! The surgeon and all the staff had never seen anything like this.

When we went into DJ's hospital room, he assured us that if he hadn't made it, he was going to Heaven. He said he repented and rededicated his life to Christ and had even asked the ambulance personnel if they were Christians. They all said, "We are." DJ told them to pray, and the ambulance staff prayed.

While in the hospital room, DJ dosed off to sleep. I proceeded to pick up the slacks that he had been wearing. I looked and only saw three small drops of blood around the waistband. I said, "Lord, where is the blood?" Immediately I heard, "He's covered with it." I cried and rejoiced in the faithfulness of God.

Prior to our son leaving the hospital, I was shown how to apply sterile gauze and pack his wound. The hole in our son's side was about the size of a golf ball and remember, there were only three small drops of blood on the waistband of his slacks and none in my car. This is undeniably God moving in our son's life. I want you to know He wants to move in your life as well. No matter what's going on, He will never leave you or forsake you. You may get in your feelings and emotions, but know, He's right there.

A home care nurse came by a couple of times to check on DJ. She stated I was doing an excellent job. She would let her superiors know she was no longer needed. I saw the healing of that wound from the inside out. Some would say to me, "How can you pack that wound? I wouldn't be able to do it." I gladly let them know I don't mind. I have my son and I will do whatever is necessary to make sure my son thrives.

Was everything great after this incident with DJ? No, it wasn't. I say unto you, "Keep praying and stay committed to God." The word of God tells us to fight the good fight of faith. You and I must fight in faith, in confidence, in unshakeable belief, even when it's hard. I did it and you can too! I know you can!

Today, my husband and I are pastors, and our children are assisting us in ministry. Let me tell you about DJ! He is over the audio/visual department in our church. He celebrated two years of marriage in September 2021 and is expecting his first child in May 2022. God, I thank you!! *Behold, I am the LORD, the God of all flesh. Is there anything too hard for me?*" (Jeremiah 32:27).

On a beautiful summer day, I decided to go to an evening church service of a friend. At that time our daughter, Starr was two years old and had fallen asleep in my arms during the service. As the man of God was ministering the word of God, he came to me and said that when my daughter gets older, let her hear these words of the Lord for her life. I listened to what he said and was and still am excited for our daughter. As he walked away, he turned back around and said the Lord wants me to say this and you will understand. The Lord said tell your daughter that whenever she needs me, call me, I'll be right there. These are the exact same words the Lord said to me!! For a moment I was speechless. Then I began to cry, and I still cry to this day when I think about God and His love for us. God does care about every aspect of our lives.

For years Starr has been going through physical problems which consisted of pain, lightheadedness, anemia, and fatigue, just to name a few. She exercises, takes supplements, and eats well, but still, nothing was working. On one of her visits to a physician, he stated her iron was so low he could not understand how she was even functioning. This undoubtedly is the grace and mercy of God operating in our daughter's life. The physician gave her an injection, but she had to have someone come and take her home. He was not going to allow her to drive in the medical condition she was in.

Things that were happening in Starr's body grew worse at the end of 2020 into 2021. She could not figure out what was going on. In the middle of 2021, she finally got answers as to what was going on in her body. At first, they were talking about blood infusions. That changed to another procedure because they found four tumors in her uterus. This procedure will annihilate the four tumors over a course of time. They also wanted her to have an iron infusion. These tumors were thriving off the blood supply and making her menstrual cycle almost nonexistent. The largest tumor was the size of a woman being five months pregnant and was also pressing against her spine. These tumors were holding the blood and literally trying to take over her body.

The procedure to destroy the tumors has been scheduled for July and Starr has now had her first iron infusion. July's procedure was canceled due to Covid-19. August, September, and October's procedures were canceled, due to Covid-19.

The procedure was rescheduled for November. Starr was thinking, well maybe this is a sign that I shouldn't have the procedure. She got a notification stating everything was on point for November's procedure.

We never stopped praying. We continued to give thanks to Almighty God that all would be successful. After the procedure, the surgeon came and stated that it went perfectly. It couldn't have been any better.

Now Starr was home and the pain, oh the pain. She was second-guessing herself, wondering why she did this. She could barely walk. There was a time in the wee hours of the morning when the pain was so intense nothing was working. In the darkness, as tears streamed down my face, I said "Lord I don't know what to do. Jesus, we need you!" Immediately I heard, "What did Paul and Silas do?" They were beaten and in tremendous pain. I remembered they prayed and praised God. I told Starr we're going to worship God. As I began to sing and worship God, Starr literally fell asleep, and her sleep was sweet. God, I thank you!

Fast forward. Starr went to the doctor who performed the iron infusion. The doctor began telling her she would have to come back more often than planned originally. She was feeling defeated. Always remember, the feeling of defeat, despair, or whatever it may be doesn't have to remain when you proclaim the word of God. Starr continued to confess her healing.

On January 21, 2022, Starr went to the infusion doctor. The entire team was asking how she felt. She proceeded to exclaim she felt great and prayed that all the labs come back great today. The nurse said, "Amen," but the doctor just kind of shook his head like yeah, right. Starr didn't care what the doctor said; it was her confession of faith and healing. The doctor stated, "Ms. Starr, your labs look excellent, and you don't have to come back next month. We'll see you in three months for blood work. But honestly, I don't think we will have to have you come back in six months; maybe a year, if at all." He stated, "It's obvious those tumors are shrinking." GLORY TO GOD!

Starr is now telling everyone she knows about the goodness of God. In her words, when you are going through difficulties in life, "Do thoughts come? Yes! Sometimes you will cry BUT know you are a child of the Most High God, and you walk in healing, prosperity, and abundance."

I pray that you all understand you have faith that can go the distance because of who God is and who you are in Him through Christ Jesus.

My prayer for you:

Father, in the name of Jesus, Your word says in 2 Chronicles 7:14, *"If my people, who are called by my name, will humble themselves, and pray and seek my face, and turn from their wicked ways; then will I hear from Heaven, and will forgive their sin, and heal their land."* I pray that Your healing power will engulf our land, families, and ministries in Jesus' name. I cry out to you, Jehovah Rapha (The Lord that Heals). You sent Your Word and healed them, and delivered them from their destructions. Oh that men would praise the Lord for His goodness, and for Your wonderful works to the children of men! Hallelujah!! Thank You, Father, for divine health, for healing of families, ministries, and all who are in authority over their wounds. I speak crop failure to every tactic, strategy, and deception from the demonic realm in Jesus' name. I release divine wisdom and clear understanding from the Lord God Almighty. May this wisdom and understanding flow into and through the hearts and minds of the people in Jesus' name. I pray that the body of Christ and all who will receive you as their personal Lord and Savior live in and forever walk in love and forgiveness. I declare and decree that our homes overflow in the fruit of the Spirit, love, joy, peace, patience, kindness, goodness, faithfulness, humility, and self-control. We are fully armored and ready for spiritual warfare in Jesus' name. Give us eyes to see, Father, and ears to hear that there is more with us than against us in Jesus' name. Absolutely no weapon will ever be formed against us; it will not prosper in Jesus' name. May the body of Christ forever roar into the atmosphere of the word of God and testify of His goodness, grace, power, love, and favor that surrounds us as a shield.

I thank you, Father, that we can say like Jesus said, "I know You hear me always." We are more than conquerors through Christ Jesus our Lord. Therefore, WE WIN, THEY LOSE.

In Jesus' name, Amen!!!

Day 5: FAITH BEARS FRUIT

Naomi Kiah Handsome was born and raised in Philadelphia, Pennsylvania. She hails from a beautiful, faith-filled, large family raised by her loving parents with many siblings. She has attended Bible Union Fellowship Church since birth and serves in various ministries. She attended private and public schools throughout the city and participated in the Gifted Program. In 2007, she married the love of her life, Esdene, and they are raising 5 children. Naomi is gifted with many talents, most notably, styling hair. After years of providing amazing hair services, she attended cosmetology school for her license and later received a license to teach cosmetology as well. Naomi is the founder, owner, and operator of a successful business, Naturally Handsome Hair. Naomi has trusted the Lord and seen how He has opened doors for her and her family. She is simply grateful.

Today and every day to come, I am grateful to the Lord for His promises kept and His miracle-working power in my life. Something I've experienced many times on life's journey is how the Lord doesn't need the world's approval to elevate or bless us. He is so faithful and kind, and His mercy endures forever. It warms my whole heart how God has chosen to bless me. Every day He shows me that He is still working all things together for my good. My faith story today is about my barrenness.

Circling down the proverbial drain by choice is sadly a place I've been before. I made lots of decisions that did not honor God. It was a time in my life when I felt unworthy of love from God or anyone else for that matter. However, God showed Himself faithful, mighty, and strong. God snatched me back from Satan's clutch.

My mother led me to a counselor who was able to help me break free from the disaster I called my life. Every shattered piece I left in God's hands. I gave Him everything I had, no matter how broken. I watched Romans 8:28 unfold in my life.

Some of the consequences I deserved, which made me pray for death, God has used to shine His glory on my life. It doesn't matter what you bring to Him. He can use it all. He used all the "stuff" to send the one who would love me despite my past.

God showed His great favor in allowing my husband and me to find love, joy, and friendship from our first date, August 31, 2006, to our wedding day, April 7, 2007. During this time, I had the honor and privilege of meeting our first daughter Sydney. I'd also gained 60 lbs. in the six months we dated that I'd kept off for five years prior.

We desired children together as a couple. After one year of marriage, and zero pregnancies, we sought the help of a medical professional. Medications were prescribed, instructions were given, and instructions were followed, to no avail.

After two years of marriage and zero pregnancies, we sought a specialist to help further the process. Medications were prescribed, instructions were given, instructions were followed, and further instructions were given. There were insults about my weight followed by hurt feelings. We left this doctor after several weeks of appointments and no real help, heartbroken.

We weren't sure how to proceed. We left the doctors alone for our sanity. My husband and I started attending parenting classes just to check things out. We hesitated to choose the reason. When we filled out our forms every week, we didn't choose whether we were looking to be respite care, foster parents, or adoptive parents. We attended class until it was over and before our certificates were delivered, we received a call asking if we could take in two children. From the moment they walked through the door, they were home.

Then I met my next two children, Marianna and Amos. Isaiah 43, my life scripture, was coming alive before my eyes, specifically verses 5 and 6. My children were being gathered from every direction to which they had been scattered, and I knew in my heart what some others couldn't understand. Some would try to disqualify our love for them because it wasn't biological. That couldn't be further from the truth.

Throughout the years, life went on as we served our church and family. We built businesses and worked hard. We were grateful to God for His faithfulness to us. However, in the back of my mind, I would sometimes hope to become pregnant. Some would encourage me, although there were others who would say very hurtful things under the guise of curiosity among other intentions.

Ten years of marriage, zero pregnancies, and then one of my routine appointments alarmed my doctor. She wasn't calm and it showed. She told me my test results were concerning and they sent my lab results to Johns Hopkins. She also said, "It looks like cancer." She went on, "I could keep you in my network or send you to my friend who is really good." I chose her friend. She hung up and called back very quickly to tell me I had an appointment in two days. That was the only time in my life an appointment had ever been made for me. She didn't even ask if I was free. I felt her urgency, but I had peace.

Oh, peace! What peace! Jesus didn't lie about the Comforter. I had lots of experience taking the low road after spending so many years of my life lost, in turmoil, or depressed. My way used to be not getting out of bed, sad songs on repeat, and two ears full of tears. Yet, that's not where I was anymore. This time, I got to see my life differently than before. I could stand in the eye of the storm, not being swept away by it.

I met the doctor who would make sure I didn't have cancer. The conclusion seemed to be a diagnosis of cancer-like behavior for which she would have recommended a hysterectomy if I were just a few years older. Then she asked the question I'd been asked so many times I'd lost count. "Do you want to have children?" The answer was, "Yes." Then she said, "We will make sure you are clear and then I will send you across the hall to the specialist."

I was cleared in May. In early June, I met the only fertility doctor who didn't bring up my weight as a barrier to pregnancy. As all the testing commenced, God sent several vessels to encourage us, pray with us, and pray for us. The results came in. The good news was there were no blockages, but the not-so-good news was, my egg count was low.

Medication was prescribed, instructions were given, instructions were followed, and on the very first try, for the first time in my life, I was pregnant! Just four weeks along and we told everyone. We were so happy and ready to share what God had done. It was a miracle, but at our next appointment at about seven weeks, our miracle no longer had a heartbeat.

This part was hard for a few hours. It was Sunday morning, and we left the office hurting. We went to church and while there, my sorrow was literally traded for joy. My perspective shifted. I wasn't hurting the same way I was when we left the office. I was encouraged because it happened. My womb, which gave me trouble for 20 years in my 34 years of life, carried life for a short time. It was therefore possible, and I knew God could do it again.

Pastor LaTerra was such an encouragement to me during these times. I thank God for her life, her faith, and her willingness to help. Amazingly, I was able to console so many loved ones and encourage them when they heard the news.

Several months and several tries to repeat our former success failed. There was also a growing and paralyzing pain that accompanied each round.

Our oldest daughter, Ashayah, came to live with us after the new year. She is the older, biological sibling to the two children we'd adopted eight years prior, so they were finally reunited. Several attempts we had made to prevent her from being bounced from home to home were blocked. One social worker looked me straight in the eye and said, "Stop trying! They will never be placed together."

It was Super Bowl Sunday, 2018. The Eagles had just won it all and I could barely move. The pain. The growing pain that had reached a point I couldn't handle anymore was back, and I was done. I'd had enough. "Lord if it's your will, it will be, but I'm not doing this anymore."

I was perfectly fine and at peace. At this point, we had four children, and they were all a handful. I decided we will be just fine. I had been putting undue pressure on myself because I had a real desire to give my husband children. As he came from a strong legacy himself, I felt like I was letting the village down. Mr. Handsome had enough grace and peace in this area for both of us. He never pressured me nor made me feel unloved.

The very next month I ovulated without medical intervention and even though I hadn't taken the pills, that terrible pain still came. I had determined that it didn't work and continued my way.

While attending a women's retreat, my sister who gets sympathetic symptoms around pregnant people yelled at two of us, "Y'all better get a test, cuz somebody's pregnant!" I did and I was. God had done it again! The next thing I saw was a small figure that looked like a superhero on the ultrasound screen from which I heard a strong heartbeat. I am still amazed at what God has done.

Later that year, after so much prayer and praise, fighting every worrying thought, catching each one captive, and keeping a song in my heart, our son was born despite every concern the doctors had. They made promises about me getting gestational diabetes. I did not.

Yet, after everything was said and done, the doctor still wanted to give me the hysterectomy. Following multiple tests, the abnormalities are gone and there is now no need for that. My pre-diabetes is also gone, and my thyroid is normal. God healed me in so many ways. I'm just grateful for the opportunity to write, speak, and sing His praises.

My prayer for you:

Heavenly Father, I am grateful and thankful for everything You have done. I thank You for bringing your son or daughter to my testimony. Please bless their barren places. Open up, clean up, plant, and cultivate a new life in places they thought were dead; in places where they need Your life to light the way.

Thank You for being a way-maker, miracle worker, and promise keeper. Remind them over and over of Your faithfulness. Walk closely with them in these dark times. Heal, encourage, and strengthen them.

We thank You for Your forgiveness and love. We bless Your holy name. We love You and thank You so much for loving us. Help us to be a blessing and a light to Your people everywhere, even if we are facing challenges. Do what only You can and lead us into Your faithful truth, Lord.

In Jesus' name, Amen.

Day 6: BUT GOD

Scott and Kristin Gilbert have been married for over 24 years and have 3 children: Allison, Kenzingtin, and Aydon. They were both raised in a Catholic household. However, Kristin gave her life to the Lord at the tender age of 15. Scott did the same in his early 20's. Daily they do their best to live life according to God's will. Their struggles, failures, and successes have brought them to this faith point. They believe, "God did not promise an easy faith walk but He promised us a blessed one. We are for sure, without a doubt, very blessed."

"Now faith is the substance of things hoped for, the evidence of things not seen" (Hebrews 11:1). Goodness, FAITH!! It is an amazing and frustrating word and journey all at the same time. Though there have been many faith journeys we have traveled, there are a few which stand out vividly.

The early to mid-twenties can be a very lonely and sad time for single people. Don't get me wrong, it is fun and exciting as well. However, when you are waiting for the Lord to bring your perfect soulmate, the waiting process can be both exciting and devastating. Waiting stinks. Walking out one's faith is not always fun. There is great emotion, both good and bad. Sometimes, you just want off the rollercoaster as it is not fun anymore, or too scary, or maybe it is the same old ride and you're over it. Though all the emotions are normal and part of the journey, there are times in the midst of it all when you just cry out, "HELLO GOD!! DO YOU SEE ME? DO YOU HEAR ME? HAVE YOU FORGOTTEN ME? HELLO, HELLO, HELLO" …. silence!

But God

My journey to the long-awaited husband I was praying for truly started when I was about 20. Well, the trials and tribulations of it all started then. I started dating a young man when I was 17. I just knew I was going to marry him. It was ok, he was not as handsome as my friend's boyfriends. It was ok, he struggled a little with pornography. I mean it was just a little, and he confessed it and he was sorry he struggled with it, so it was ok. It was ok he was a more difficult personality to handle. Meaning, people didn't really care for him. He was too "weird," too "nerdy," too "different," and not "friendly" enough. Still, it was OK, because I could make up for what he lacked, and I just knew we were going to get married young. We were going to have a family and "I" was going to live happily ever after. It was all OK! But it wasn't. OK is not what God wanted for me. God did not want me to be satisfied with just "ok." God did not want me to compare Him to others. It was not fair to Him. It was not fair to me, and it was NOT God's best. I however, did not want to be obedient at this time because to break up would mean I don't have a boyfriend, I don't have false affection, I don't have the fake future I dreamed of and knew deep down I deserved and wanted with all of my heart.

Don't get me wrong. He was not mean, abusive, or ugly to me. He was just not God's best for me. Well, as God does, if we don't listen, He takes care of it for us. So, after almost three years of dating, we broke up. It was devastating, to say the least. All my future plans were shattered, and I was lost. I wasn't really lost; God had me just where He wanted me, but I did not know this at the time.

As I am a teacher, one of my students drew me a picture during this turbulent time. It was a man and me under an arched gazebo arbor. We were getting married. This picture, I knew, was God-given and prophetic from the moment little Sara gave it to me. First, Sara had met my boyfriend and she knew he had blond hair. The husband in the picture did NOT have blonde hair; he had dark hair.

Second, call me superficial but a blue-eyed man was on the "List" and this was non-negotiable. The man in Sara's picture had blue eyes. I knew this picture was a crayoned snapshot of my future. Yet, it made no sense at the same time, because I was still praying that I would get back together with the old, blonde-haired boyfriend. But I still could not dispose of this drawing, and I knew the Holy Spirit was instructing me to keep this picture and to keep it visible. I did. I didn't give it much thought other than, it was such a great picture; too bad he was dark-haired and not blonde.

Well, blonde haired ex-boyfriend got a new girlfriend. It was still OK; he would see the error of his ways and he would come back to me. Precious reader...let me save you time...Ok is not OK and you DON'T want them back!

The summer I was 23 I was in four weddings. May, June, July, and September. Four! This was an exciting time. I was proud of myself because though I was sad that I did not have anyone, I was not jealous of these brides. I was genuinely happy for all of them.

I was skeptical about one, however, as it was the ex-boyfriend's brother's wedding. I hadn't seen the ex-boyfriend for about a year, and he was still with his new girlfriend, which meant I would see her. All I knew was she, too, was blonde, and she sang opera. She was Christy Brinkley in my head.

However, all that anxiety aside, I learned so much from watching these brides travel through the process of planning and dealing with life during this exciting time. The "maybe we shouldn't get married" to the "I can't believe he lied to me." The stories are endless.

There is one story, however, which to this day, was the loudest I have ever heard the Holy Spirit YELL at me. This encounter changed my perspective and strengthened my faith in an oral and visual capacity I recognized. My dearest friend, the June bride of the four, was struggling with her fiancé's past. She was struggling with the physical experiences he had and was grasping so hard to find a "first" they could have together. Her last-ditch effort at a "first" had just been blown out of the water and she was feeling betrayed and defeated. We regularly took walks in the hills surrounding the neighborhood we lived in. We were out on one of our walks on this night, and she just needed to vent. So, we walked.

I listened and she vented, yelled, cried, screamed, you name it. I was there for moral support and didn't do much talking. I just took it in and listened. I prayed for words to comfort her but had none.

Our normal three-mile walk was almost seven miles that night. By the last mile, after six miles of listening to her struggle, listening to her try and find peace and finding none, and listening to her talk about this man whom she was going to marry but was having very, very serious red flags and doubts about, my spirit could not handle it anymore. I heard the Holy Spirit tell me to tell her to "Give the ring back!" No, I could not tell her this. She was living the "I am engaged" dream. She had the love story we all wanted. I surely was not hearing the Spirit properly.

Again, I heard the same words, so loudly, so clearly, almost audibly, "Tell her to give the ring back." I won't lie, after three hours of listening to how she was feeling, I agreed with the Holy Spirit's prompting, but was this too honest? Would I be acting as a good friend to suggest such drastic action? Was I being obedient? I knew it was the Holy Spirit, not me, and I 100% agreed. But this was a level of honesty for which I was not sure neither she nor I was ready. This was deep. She started in on the "He is such a bleepity, bleep, bleep, liar." I then blurted out, "Give the ring back."

She stopped dead in her tracks and said "WHAT?!" I repeated, "Give the ring back." It was at this point she called me a B****. Never in my life had I been called this to my face, and with such disdain, from one of my best friends!

I knew she was hurt. I knew she was scared. I knew she was disappointed with her "happily ever after." I was not at all offended by her comment. I went on to explain, if she was this worked up over everything prior to even being married and questioning it all, then how would a lifetime as his wife change things? Her trust in him was gone. She needed to get over the things he did in his life prior to knowing her. She should forgive him for sins he committed not even against her. She needed peace with accepting he is not a virgin by any stretch of the imagination, or she needed to give the ring back.

Silence. The last 20 minutes of our walk was utter silence. I knew I had been obedient, but did I just lose one of my best friends? I was not going to apologize for saying what she needed to hear. But I had no words. I just prayed for her for the rest of our walk. As we approached her door, she said, "You are right. If I can't deal with things he did before knowing me, I can't marry him."

This night and other conversations over the next six to nine months would lead me to a revelation. I was a virgin. I knew I was going to remain a virgin until I was married but what if my future husband was not? Could I handle this? Prior to watching friends on their relational journeys and being called a B****, the answer was NO. I could not handle it, but God grew me. I wrestled with myself over my "List" during these months as well. Was I selling God short or was I selling me short? Funny enough, the shower held all the answers and is where I found my peace.

I was in the shower one day, crying out to God. "Lord, I do not know whom You have for me in this world. But I also know, he has had a life before me. He may have not always been a Christian. He may have fallen away from You and come back. He may not be a virgin but if he is Your best for me, and will love me, ALL OF ME, all my insecurities, all my doubts, and all of my what-ifs, do I really want to throw all of Your perfect love away because he is not a virgin? NO! I cannot hold his past life, struggles, burdens, and sins against him. You don't."

I even took it further. "Lord, if he is a divorced man with a child, but is Your perfect love for me, then let him be a divorced man with a child. Lord, if he is a divorced man with two or three kids, but he is Your best for me, then who am I to judge? He is Your best for me.... Lord, please don't let him be divorced with two or three kids ... lol!! I am pretty sure this is too much for me, but if he is Your best, then I guess You will make it all as it should be."

I left that shower with 100% confidence my "List" was of God and not of me. My "List" was not unreasonable, and I had perfect peace knowing all these years of praying, all my maturing, and all of the faith I was holding onto while seeking for this man would not be in vain. It was not a long wait either.

Just after my 24th birthday, I walked into the Vons Pavilions where my mother worked to show off my new car. As I walked in, I saw a produce clerk. He was tall. He had dark hair, and he was beyond handsome. I literally pointed to him and said to myself, "Oh look, the guy from Sara's picture," as if it was just another day, and there he was. As I checked out, he was called to come bag groceries. Goodness, he was handsome and as I got a closer look, he had blue eyes! A non-negotiable on the "List" (God and I talked about this in the shower...lol...blue eyes was staying).

However, he did look to be about 18 years old, and "older" was also on the list so, it was nice to look at you, you sure are handsome, but you are far too young for me is what I said to myself. The total was given to me, and I realized I did not have my savings card so I asked my mom for hers. She was the checker in the next lane, as a family could not check out family.

Scott grabbed the card from my mom, as he, 1. Put together I was her daughter and, 2. Did not take his eyes off me once. He swiped the card and while still looking at me handed the card back to my mom.

I was thinking, little boy, do you realize I am 24? You are so handsome but that was bold. The checker must have recognized something as well because she said, "Is this your girlfriend?"

Again, I thought, um Karen (that was her real name), he is like 18! My mom answers for him, "Scott? No, he is too old for her." TOO OLD!!! TOO OLD!! HOW OLD IS HE???? Again, Karen must have been reading my mind because she asked him, "How old are you?" "... 25." 25!! 25!! He is 25!! He is older than me. He IS the guy from Sara's picture. HE HAS BLUE EYES!!

I was dancing in my head. My mom came home, and I said, you have never told me about him! Why? You always tell me about the cute ones. She said, "Scott? I have known him forever; I was his trainer for checker school. You were too busy for him. Remember when you were dating your ex-boyfriend?"

She had known him for seven years! My mother has known this beautiful man for seven years and here I am just seeing him this day! Of course, my mother cannot keep a secret to save her life and tells him the next day about how I thought he was just the most handsome man I had ever seen.

He said, "Here, give her my pager number and have her call me." When my mom handed me the number I was like, "A pager?" A pager!! The guy from Sara's picture has a pager.

Ok, not playing the pager game. I don't have time for that. So, thinking this was short-lived and I would not waste time on the pager boy,

I took the number and paged it. Twenty minutes later, he called back. I answered. "Hi, this is Scott. Sorry I was playing basketball and didn't get your page until just now." "Well, hi Scott. This is Kristin," I replied. (Again, I am in the mindset of I am not playing, and I am just going to cut to the chase, take me or leave me, I don't have time to play.)

So, I said, "Well Scott, tell me about yourself." Clearly, Scott wasn't playing either because he said, "Well, I am 25. I am divorced and I have a two-year-old." Ok, I thought, we are not playing. So, I responded with, "Well, I am 24. I am a virgin, and I am staying that way until I get married."

We both laid out all our cards. No games. Here is a list of things you may have an issue with concerning me. If they aren't issues for you then let's move forward, we shared. They were not issues for either of us. I saw him at the grocery store on October 4th, 1997. I talked with him on the phone on October 7th, 1997. I came home from my vacation in Colorado four days early so we could go on our first date on October 11th, 1997. He asked me to marry him on November 17, 1997. I got my ring on December 17, 1997. We planned the wedding for June 7, 1998. We eloped January 1, 1998, and have added a daughter and a son to this family of ours over the past 24 years. He is to this day beyond "OK." He is exceedingly and abundantly above and beyond because God is the God of exceedingly and abundantly above and beyond.

Fast forward 15 years and our daughter is getting ready to finish up middle school and transition to high school. Well, this child and her best friend have planned out their high school journey. They are NOT going to go to public school; they are going to go to the local private school. Dear sweet girl, I love how you are planted in faith, and you want to be educated with like-minded students in a smaller setting and with our bonus daughter (her best friend since 5th grade to this day. They are now 22 and 23).

However, your father currently does not have a job. Our car has just been repossessed and your sister is headed off to college. Please explain how we are going to pay for your private school. I tried to explain in kid's terms that this may not be her reality. She vehemently stated, "Gabby and I ARE going to this school. God will bring the money, Mom." It was a no-brainer for her. There was not a shadow of a doubt so much so, she filled out the application for herself. She gave me the link to fill out the scholarship papers and just knew we would qualify for a scholarship because she was going to go there. "I am going to the school, Mom," she chimed.

As middle schoolers, they take a tour of the neighboring high school and fill out the paperwork to get a jumpstart on the following year's enrollment. This girl did NOT fill out the paperwork. She did not even mention there was paperwork to fill out. She explained to the enrollment woman she was going to a private school for high school and returned the unfilled paperwork back to her. Lo and behold, this child is accepted into the private school. She is given a scholarship. Her father, who up to this point was unemployed as he was working on finishing up college to become a teacher, passed all his tests and was hired as a teacher. The tuition payment portion we were responsible for did not make a dent in our family budget. There was a blow, however. Gabby's father was transferred shortly after she was accepted to the private school. Gabby and her family would be moving to the state of Washington.

The high school journey plans, with her best friend forever, were shattered. She would be attending high school on her own. She would be making new friends without her constant sidekick. Of course, you know God worked this all out for her as well. Turns out a young girl who lived literally on the street behind us was new to the school as well; her mom could take them to school, and I could pick them up.

God set this girl up as she never doubted that He would. Even when I doubted, God remained faithful! Like, hello God! How are we going to pay for this? We were one income at the time and our oldest had just left for college! Kenzingtin, however, never doubted it would all work out. Her teen faith was very adult!

God also worked out and made up for the missed high school opportunity with the BFF as well. Kenzingtin was dually enrolled in high school and Grand Canyon University (GCU) for college. Gabby was going to attend Arizona State University. They are 20 minutes away from each other! After taking a tour of both schools, however, Gabby felt at home at GCU and GCU transferred more of her college credits from her high school program as well. Again, God made a way where there did not seem to be a way, and for 1.5 years of Kenzingtin's college journey, she was able to live the college campus life with her best friend. God has protected, hidden, encouraged, and without a doubt, directed the comings and goings of this girl.

On Halloween morning, 2016, as she was on her way to work, she was in a single vehicle crash on the freeway. She was not hurt, as God's protecting angels guarded her car. Her driver's door flung open before she knew what was happening, and a concerned woman asked her how she was doing and if she was ok.

Kenzi jumped out and hugged this woman, having no idea where she had come from but 100% needing a hug at that moment. The woman and her husband had been on the opposite side of the freeway. She saw the accident, pulled over, and jumped the median to make sure Kenzi was ok. Once she knew Kenzi was good, the police were there, and we were on our way, the woman left because she needed to get to her brother's house.

Later that evening as we were gathered in the neighborhood, passing out candy, Kenzi and my sister decided they were going to take a walk around the neighborhood. As they set off, my sister noticed a gorilla-masked person was analyzing Kenzi. As my sister's comfort level was reaching the point of "back off please," the gorilla took off its mask, walked up to Kenzi, and asked, "Were you in an accident this morning?" Kenzi immediately hugged the gorilla. It was the same woman who had jumped the median earlier that morning to make sure she was all right. Kenzi and my sister brought her back to the house; they were about three houses down. I gave her a hug and thanked her for being there as well. Only God sets up divine appointments such as these.

As parents, you can have all the faith in the world for your children, but many times, the child must walk out their path as you look on. As my kids get older, Scott and I do a great deal of sideline watching as they navigate through life.

There seemed to be a few more bumps in the road for Kenzi than she would have liked regarding her college experience. They were all God's leading, obviously, but nonetheless, even at times, I found myself saying, "Girl, get it together! It is not this difficult!"

As she was approaching the final semester with only her student teaching left, she had not heard from the school about her student teaching placement. I continued to encourage her to make phone calls and get updates and see if there were any hang-ups. She continued to forget with days left for her to be assigned to a student teacher or be forced to wait until September, which she made clear ... "God I am not waiting until September to do my student teaching." Still, she received the "I am so sorry, but we are having a really hard time finding a host teacher for you to do your student teaching. We will have to place you on the list for September" call. Of course, this does not fall in line with "her" plan and we know it is not the plan we were believing for either.

Well, meltdown mode ensued, and this girl was feeling she needed an intervention of the highest sort, so she called all the reinforcements she could. I also knew the district I worked for was taking student teachers. So, Kenzi asked if she found someone to be her host teacher, would this work? She was told yes. Her dad and I sent out our calls and phoned a friend or two or three, and within 30 minutes we had a host teacher, a school site, authorization from GCU, and a start date. Kenzi would be student teaching in the Spring of 2021, not the Fall. Yet, God took it to another level for her. As she was tossing around the thought, "I'll just sub in the Fall for a year and get classroom experience," this mama was saying, "Lord, the girl needs a permanent contract. She needs her own classroom. Subbing can be Plan C, D, or E, but not Plan A."

Kenzi finished student teaching at the beginning of May. I knew this time she was believing for a full-time job by Fall. All her applications were in at the end of July. At the beginning of August, she had an interview, and one hour after her interview she was hired as a permanent kindergarten teacher. Funny enough, but just like God.

She had said two days before she got the call for her interview, "I think I either want a kindergarten position or a junior high school position." God was just waiting for her to say it out loud. God was just waiting for her faith declaration. Once she backed up her declaration with her unwavering faith, God moved.

The favor which surrounded her and all the behind-the-scenes action which has not been expressed in this "quick" version is remarkable. She had three people tell her now current principal she needed to hire Kenzi before Kenzi even knew there was a position available. Three! As I have said, God has provided for, protected, and poured out His favor, love, and blessings repeatedly on our family.

My husband, Scott, used to be the night crew supervisor many years ago for VONS. One night/day, early in the morning about 3:30 am, right around the time Scott should have been getting off to come home, I was awakened and just felt the urgent need in my spirit to pray for Scott's safety. I began to pray, "God protect Scott, keep him safe, bring him home safely."

We are talking about the early 2000's, so cell phones were not something everyone had and were not the primary source of communication. I could not track him with 'find my friends,' or 'find my iPhone.'

I called the grocery store. He should have been home by 4:00 a.m. at the latest. I was urgently prompted to pray for him again! Oh, and I, at this time of my life, was far more anxious than I am now. Philippians 4:6-8 kept saying, "Be anxious for nothing, he is fine."

The grocery store said he left about 45 minutes ago. It takes 20 minutes to get home, so where is he? My anxiety radar and panic were in full force. All I could do was pray. All I knew was Scott was not home yet! My gut was telling me bad things, and I had been awakened to pray urgently for him. Scott got home about 15 minutes later, and I met him at the door with all the "why are you so late" inquiries. "I called the store. They said you had left. Where have you been?" I asked. He initially replied with a question, "First, why are you up? Second, the strangest thing happened on my way home. I left at about 3:30 a.m. On my way out, I saw a co-worker coming into work and had to talk to him about an order. Then we chatted for a little more before I headed to the car. I felt like I needed to go home on a different route, but I didn't listen, and as I continued my regular route there was a terrible accident. Two cars had crashed, and one had flipped over. It was bad. I honestly could have been a part of that accident if I had not stopped to talk to him," to which I chimed in, "Well about 3:30 am, I was urgently awakened to pray for you. Thank goodness I listened!" He said, "Good thing you listened because I am sure your prayers helped to keep me out of that accident. I got stuck in the traffic because I did not listen and take a different route home!"

God has been faithful to our family. I won't say it has been an easy faith journey. I have protested, boycotted, moaned, groaned, cried, pleaded, and ignored. Thankfully, God is above all our temper tantrums and continues to be faithful to us even when we are faithless and pitiful.

My prayer for you:

Lord, thank You for always knowing what we need before we do. Thank You for Your promises and for Your faithful and faith filled "Yes and Amens." Your provision and blessings are far more than we deserve.

I pray for the individuals reading and sharing this prayer. May You give them the assurance to know You have worked all things out. May You give them the peace to journey through and the comfort of Your wonder and Your power in going before them and making a way where there may seem to be no way. Your constant is an anchor to our souls, Lord. Your promises are true, and Your love is endless.

Thank You for Your perfect will; may it be done in our lives. You are faithful and true. Thank You for guiding and showing us how to be faithful and true for Your glory.

In Jesus' name. Amen.

Day 7: NOBODY BUT JESUS

Lisa Douglas was born in Philadelphia, Pennsylvania. At age 12, she moved to Willingboro, New Jersey. Upon graduation from high school in 1981, she joined the U.S. Navy. Ultimately, she was sent to Japan, where she met and married her husband in October 1986.

After separation from the military, the couple moved to California and raised three children. She earned a Bachelor of Arts Degree in Japanese and Spanish 19 years after graduating from high school. Among many occupations, she worked as a substitute teacher. Later, she decided to pursue a teaching credential in public education.

Due to the economic crash of 2008, which resulted in massive teacher layoffs in music, art, and foreign languages, she was motivated to switch disciplines from World Languages to Mathematics. However, without a Mathematics degree, she spent many nights at the library studying for the Math CSET exam. After three failed attempts, she finally passed it and became a high school Math and Spanish teacher. She retired from teaching in 2021 and the couple then relocated to Middletown, Delaware.

Bishop Louder declared from the pulpit one bible study evening, "Sister Douglas is a genius. She could go to Harvard." He didn't know I tried to go to college several times, but my SAT scores were too low. My scores were an embarrassing 320 in English and Math. Paired with my C's, D's, and Fs in Latin, Algebra II, and Chemistry in the 11th grade, my only escape from my current situation was to graduate high school, join the military, and snuff out the loud thunder in my head of how unintelligent and worthless I was. I had confirmations all around me to support my private theories.

I was 12 when my mom sent me to live with my dad and his second wife. Shortly after a year, I ended up moving in with neighbors who lived on the same suburban street because my stepmom kicked me out.

When I arrived at my neighbor's home and told them I had been put out of my dad's house, I asked if I could stay with them. I was so relieved when they said yes. They both worked in Northeast Philadelphia and lived in Willingboro, New Jersey. I became a babysitter for their two elementary school-age children.

They received no financial support from my dad, who was an engineer for the Philadelphia Bell Telephone Company. Still, they let me share their daughter's bed, and I made sure to be home from school before their two kids arrived. I took care of them until their parents returned home. They brought an emotion into my life I had not experienced very often, laughter.

My mom, who for a long time did not know I lived with them, was very grateful for their kindness towards me. However, she had no extra money to send them as she struggled to support her drinking habit and to put food in the fridge for my other siblings.

As I walked down what seemed like a mile-long street, I thought about my life and the threat of returning to live with my mom in Philadelphia. I knew it meant being very hungry year-round and very cold in the winter. It also meant being around my alcoholic cousin, Nadine, who would be so drunk she needed me to tell her what she did while inebriated on Thunderbird. I always left out the part where her equally drunk father touched my private parts when he was drunk.

So, I didn't want to leave the suburban neighborhood and wealthy Black classmates that I admired and enjoyed watching. By my 13-year-old standards, wealthy kids lived in single-family homes with their own bedrooms, dressed in nice clothing, and had well-groomed hair.

So, even though I showed up at school with the same clothes and shoes year after year, it was better than going back to the roach-infested Philadelphia house where I slept fully clothed with my coat during the winter. It was also where my drunken relatives would visit on weekends.

In the 1970s, it was legal to turn off the gas during the winter months for non-payment. So, by the time I was 10, I had learned to make friends with people who had food in the fridge. I developed the fine art of listening intently and observing other people. I learned how to survive many nights without food, heat, and adult supervision in Philadelphia, but I still had no training in how to fit in around kids and their parents who lived in the suburbs.

I remember how unwelcome I felt around my classmates' parents, who took one look at my worn clothes and badly groomed hair and concluded I was unfit to befriend their kids. Naturally, I was not invited back to their houses. Who could blame them?

In the early '70s, when Blacks struggled to be treated with respect as hard-working educated members of society, why would middle-class Black parents allow their kids to be associated with me, the very image of the poverty that they were endeavoring to escape? When I asked if I could visit on weekends and was quickly told they could not have company, it became easy to convince myself that I was not good enough to socialize with them. They did not know that all I wanted was to be in something beautiful and clean.

When attending middle and high school in the suburbs of New Jersey, I watched my classmates closely because I wanted to be them. I watched them enjoying life as cheerleaders and members of academic and athletic clubs. Inside their single-family homes, they had what my 13-year-old mind longed for — their own bedroom with a canopy bed, desk and dresser painted and cascading in a sea of white and pink.

Growing up in a city row house where several houses were missing and replaced with broken glass and graffiti and houses struggling to remain erect after fires destroyed their roofs and second floor, I thought the bedroom I daydreamed about was for rich white people. It was a culture shock when I saw the homes of African American classmates in the suburbs of New Jersey who lived like rich people. I asked myself what I could do to make my neighbors want to keep me so I could be around kids like them. I would clean their house profusely. I ate whatever they gave me and never asked them to buy me clothing or shoes because I did not want them to see me as a financial burden and send me back to Philadelphia.

My classmates seemed to have so much more self-worth than me because of their nice clothes, their long well-groomed hair, their nice houses, and both parents. Besides all those things I admired, there was one thing they had that was more valuable to me than everything else I observed about them. I wanted to be smart like them.

One afternoon, shortly after moving into my neighbor's house, I tore into my homework assignment. I couldn't wait to write sentences for my spelling words so I could read them to my teacher and hear her say, "Wow what a great job, Lisa! You wrote really good sentences." If she told me that, I would start to feel smart like my classmates. I would want to try harder. I would start to feel like I was worth something. Instead, she responded with words that crushed my fragile self-portrait of a skinny, short-haired, raggedy-clothes-wearing girl longing to be smart like her classmates.

"Well," she sneered with a tone of disdain, "I don't know where you copied that sentence." I was crushed and scared all at the same time. "Did I copy my sentences?" I asked myself.

My own real experience of tearing into that homework assignment and giving it all I had was snuffed out by her authoritative, disapproving response. I wanted so much to run home and tell someone how much her words hurt, but whom was I going to tell? My neighbors with whom I was living? Absolutely not! I had a long, serious conversation with myself, declaring that if I did everything I could around their house, ate whatever they gave me, and never asked for anything, they would let me stay. I was not going to threaten the roof over my head by burdening them with my problems.

Do I tell my father, from whose house I was put out? No way. I was relieved to be gone from there. No more watching my father drink himself into oblivion and blow his cigarette smoke into my face. No more hiding in my bedroom to escape his mean drunken disposition. He had not allowed me to visit other kids, so my textbooks became my friends. Reading my textbooks was like having someone to talk to.

Would I tell my mother in Philadelphia who, for quite a while, did not even know I had moved in with the neighbors? No, it was safer to believe my teacher's words that I did not write the sentences but copied them. Her words influenced my already low self-efficacy that there was no way I was smart.

But that would not be the only experience that confirmed my evolving low perception of who I was. There were images and perspectives developed over many years. That reached a boiling point when I heard Bishop Louder declare, "Sister Douglas is a genius. She could go to Harvard." I was so angry with him. He was embarrassing me, and I had to stop him from uttering such foolishness in front of the whole church.

He really didn't know about my life. He wasn't present the night I watched my high school classmates graduate and get accepted to schools including Harvard, Cornell, and MIT. He wasn't there when I watched a classmate challenge a girl, Sheri Nixon, to an SAT battle. Yes, an African American girl actually did that, and it blew my mind. After the results of the PSAT scores were released, Sheri scored 600 in both Math and English and the other girl challenged her that she would score higher on the actual SAT when we all took it.

As I listened to them talking, I wondered how they learned to talk with confidence and courage and how they became so confident. I consistently scored under 350 on both the Math and Verbal section of the PSAT and SAT and concluded in the 12th grade that a person had to be so smart to pass those tests.

I did not know about cross-cultural knowledge, exposure to a world outside of the influence of poverty, nor about the hidden biased questions that Carl Brigham, the writer of the exam in 1923, crafted along with the skewed scale used to score minorities test results to defend his rationale that wealthy whites were superior in intellect to everyone else. It would be 60 years before scientists would prove that the exam did not measure accurately one's intellect. In the interim, my plan to escape poverty and my depressing existence was via the military.

In 1983, after several years in the Navy, I applied to the Navy's BOOST program. It was designed as a pathway to help minorities prepare for college while in the Navy. Approximately 150 African Americans were selected. It was 18 months of intensive, rigorous academic training in Science, Math, and English. At the end of the program, each student would be honorably discharged from the Navy, sent to a four-year college of their choice with all expenses paid by the military, and upon graduation from said college, they would re-pay the military by serving as commissioned officers for six years. I was thrilled about the prospect of one day being seen as smart. Shucks, if I pulled this off and became a Naval officer, no one would be able to tell me nothin' about what smart looks like. There was only one pre-requisite that we all had to meet to take advantage of the program. We had to score 600 on both the Verbal and Math sections of the SAT. Any score below 600 on either section would result in a return to active duty for the remainder of our contract.

Out of 150 African Americans, eight of us did not fulfill the requirement. I sat in class on the last day listening to students joyfully describing their upcoming trips home to celebrate with their families before going off to college. There was so much excitement in the air, but for me, there was only the voice yelling in my head how stupid I was to ever think I was smart like them.

I was sent to Japan to finish my contract and while there, I got married. I told myself that I was not smart enough to pass the SAT and get accepted to college, but maybe I would be good at marriage and never get divorced like my parents. When I finished my Naval contract, I returned to the United States, but my husband still had 18 months of military service to complete.

During those 18 months, I was introduced to God in a way I had not heard before. I was taught that if I had faith, it pleased God more than anything else. The only relationship I ever knew about God was through my Catholic elementary school in Philadelphia where I listened to sermons in Latin on Sundays and went to confession once a week.

Now, my Christian Bishop was teaching me about a Jesus who was pleased by my faith above anything. I had such a need to be liked and to be good at something. I wanted Jesus to like me so I decided I was going to become good at faith so I could feel like I was worth something. I got my chance to show God how good I wanted to be at it so that He would like me, and so that everybody would say I was good at faith.

I was seven months pregnant with my first child on the night I learned my husband was hooked on crack cocaine. Earlier the same day, I showed my friend my filthy bathroom sink that was covered with a charcoal-colored powdery residue that also housed one unidentifiable metal thing, and afterward, I went to church.

That night our Bishop was having an outside revival. I went up for prayer and told the elder what I had learned about my husband. He told me if I wanted him delivered, I could not tell anyone who would condemn him because it would drive him further into the addiction. I never told anyone in his family. Only God knew and the friend who told me what was wrong with him since she had already been delivered from a cocaine addiction in the same church where I was a new member and new at exercising faith. That revival service was the beginning of my faith journey.

For seven years I remained silent while my husband depleted our bank account several times to support his habit. Back then, my Bishop referred to him as Deacon Douglas even though he knew what condition he was in. "How is Deacon Douglas?" he would ask.

When I cried out to Bishop about the evictions among other things like being disrespected by his family and how my husband would not protect me, he gave me a sober smile and said, "You have to be long-suffering with your husband, Lisa." He repeatedly taught from the pulpit these words, "Do good to them that hate you," and "you will get the victory if you just don't quit on God."

The greatest challenge I faced early in our marriage, though, pertained to obedience, particularly in paying tithes and giving offerings. My husband would often bellow, "I'm not giving my money to no church, and let the pastor buy fancy cars and houses 'wit' MY money while I'm struggling. Lisa, you must think I'm stupid." I prayed all the time back then. "Lord, he won't tithe. How can I ask You for good credit and to let me buy a house without being a tither?"

I wanted to experience that verse about the windows of Heaven opening and not having room to receive it all. My prayer continued, "Lord,

You said if I had the courage to tithe, that it showed my obedience and how much faith I have in You." I went from wanting to be smart, confident, and valued like my classmates to wanting to be like those saved women at church whose husbands came to church with them, opened their Bibles with them, actually prayed for people, and testified about how God did wonderful things for them. But my husband wanted nothing to do with the church. That did not stop me from praying, reading, and learning all about God.

I was starving for some success in life, and I chose faith because it looked and felt impossible. What would people think of me if I pulled it off, if I bought a house with little money, F credit, and a spouse who repeatedly rejected the concept of putting God first in his finances?

"God is greater than your credit report; He just needs you to be upright. Answer the phone when creditors call and ask God to help you with payment arrangements. The Bible says, God will rebuke the devourer for your sakes, but you must put Him first in your finances." Bishop taught us that and I kept begging my husband to tithe and told him that God would give us favor with our creditors and we could buy a house. Finally, he let me. Tithing was a wonderful feeling because I knew I was doing something that was hard on our pocketbook at first. I was so full of glee. I was a tither. God promised to help me, and I believed Him.

We started paying our rent on time. The money was there. We went from paying late at our previous addresses to never being late with our rent on Canteberry Road. But I wanted more from God. I wanted the abundance that I heard came from giving after tithing.

I wasn't yet crazy enough to ask my hubby to do more because I knew it was still a struggle to tithe since sometimes, we had to eat less. One time, our money was so tight that he even ordered me to go back to church and get his money back! After that, Bishop told the whole congregation that if they tithed, they could not ask for their money back. Tithing was hard at first, but that didn't discourage me. In fact, it made me get excited about some big testimony I was hoping to have just like the ones I heard from other people.

Around the time we started tithing, a guest speaker visited our church named John Avanzini. He taught us how to go from F credit to A+ credit. "Pay your creditors what you owe them. The Bible says that a man is worthy of his hire. Be upright and God will give you favor with your creditors because He knows your heart. When you pay your judgments or charge-offs completely, ask the creditors to remove those negative entries from your report and get that in writing."

When I left that meeting, I couldn't wait to get home and tell my husband how I was going to clear our credit report so we could buy a house. I didn't care that we didn't make a lot of money. I read Mark 11:24 and believed: *"Whatever things you ask when you pray, believe that you receive them, and you will have them."* That was faith!

I was determined to show everybody that I was good at faith. I was going to prove it by buying a house. I called Zales Jewelry store and told them I was buying a house. I spoke by faith since I didn't even have a realtor. However, Bishop taught me to speak those things that be not as though they were, so I did. I asked if they could delete the charge-off entry from my credit report if I paid them and the representative answered with a hard no. John had already warned us that if we got someone on the phone who was not favorable, thank them, hang up, and call right back. That is exactly what I did. The second time, I got a person who sent me a letter promising to delete the entry upon receipt of my full payment.

God's favor was on us, and I could feel it. Our credit score was getting higher, and we reached out to a realtor named Dave Geary of Remax Realty. Every time he found a house in our low-price range, below

$125K, we got outbid. Finally, one day it happened, he found a house that was new on the market, in our range, that no one had bid-on. The sellers accepted our offer, and we met Dave's lender. Things were about to take an interesting turn.

Our church was planning to expand by tearing it down and rebuilding something larger. Bishop told the congregation they could sow a seed into the vision that would be a financial gift above our tithes. He wanted us to write down what we needed, place it in a capsule to be buried in the dirt, and after some years, we were to dig up our capsules to see what God had done. I knew I could talk my husband into giving something using a gentle reminder of how God was fixing our credit report so we could buy a house. I was hurt by the small amount he wanted to give, but God knew me and that, if I could get my husband to agree, I would give God so much more.

I was beginning to change the reason why giving and tithing were important to me. I read that God loved a cheerful giver. The Bible said in 2 Corinthians 9:7, "*So let each one give as he purposes in his heart, not grudgingly or of necessity; for God loves a cheerful giver.*"

I began to understand that God wanted me to give to demonstrate my love for Him. He wanted me to love Him more than proving I had faith, more than I wanted to be smart. He wanted me to give from that place. At the time that I began my faith journey, He never held my selfish motives against me. It was as though God knew that I would fall in love with Him just because of who He is.

I wrote down my desires, placed them in my capsule, and turned in our offering. At that moment, I didn't care if God answered my prayers. I just wanted Him to know that I appreciated everything He did.

My husband reached his lowest low with drugs and walked up to Bishop one Sunday and said he was sick with his life and wanted to be delivered. He never touched drugs again after that Sunday. Several years later, he became a deacon, just as my Bishop referred to him. What I did not see coming was that God would answer everything in my capsule and more because there were times when it looked like buying a house was not going to happen.

I thought I had fixed everything in my credit report, but one judgment for a car down payment of $3000 was still visible and the creditor was furious with me. He accepted my payment arrangement because the judge ordered him to, and I was allowed to pay $20 a month. The attorney stormed out of that courtroom furious. Even when I paid him in full, he was still angry.

There was nothing I could do. Our lender told us that VA loans must have squeaky clean credit and a judgment, even a paid one, would get us denied for sure. His only solution was to remove me from the application. Submitting the loan in my husband's name meant he had to qualify by himself without my income. That was financially challenging for us, but not as devastating as the news he got from his boss. He was being re-assigned to work in Blythe at the Chuckawalla State Prison and we lived in Riverside, 162 miles apart. Our car needed a tune-up, tires, and more, but he had to report to Blythe immediately.

He was furious, but then he called me from Blythe, and I could hear the excitement in his voice. "I am on mandatory overtime, Lisa. The prison can't fill the positions because people keep failing the background checks. I will be working six days a week, 16-hour days until further notice."

His boss wrote a letter to his lender informing him of the pay increase and said it would continue for a minimum of one year. His income qualified for the house, he got the loan, and we moved in. The first day he drove home to his new house from Blythe, he had more news. "Overtime is over," he said worriedly. I said joyfully, "NOBODY BUT JESUS did that in the first place!"

Dear Reader,

I want you to know that I learned no matter how lonely and dismal my life has been many times, God turned my mourning into dancing. Stay close to Him. Don't let your hunger for Him fade away. God is like the faithful watchman who stands guard at the tomb of the unknown soldiers. We are His soldiers, and He is standing guard, hoping we will not run from our post during the hard times, but instead courageously launch a grenade of faith as our powerful weapon. When we do that, it pleases Him.

During your most difficult hour, make a declaration to yourself that you just want to please God and through doing that, everything else will fall peacefully into its proper place.

My prayer for you:

Dear Faithful Father, I thank You for everything you have done in my life throughout this faith journey. There are so many people who may be feeling worthless, unappreciated, unimportant, unwanted, and unintelligent, but Your love is greater than it all. Wrap each reader, Lord, inside your blanket of hope like you wrap a newborn baby to give it a feeling of security, warmth, and provision. In Jesus' name, Amen!

Day 8: FAITH'S ADVENTURE: A LOVE STORY

Mike and Patti Storie have been married for over two decades. While in recovery in the early 90s, as friends of Bill W., they answered a stirring to carry the message of recovery to the Body of Christ. Together, they created and implemented Recovery Curricula which had glowing success in the church before recovery groups started in the desert.

They stood upon James 5:16; bearing one another's burdens and obtained their Substance Abuse Counseling certificates, (CCDC). The Stories interned at the ABC Club in Indio, California. Patti went on to work at Village Counseling Center in Palm Desert. There she worked with at-risk children in families with addiction and intervened with those families.

Mike has a heart for men's ministry and was very active in Promise Keepers, locally and nationally. They ran men's groups, utilizing John Eldridge's "Wild at Heart" curriculum. Together they continue to be committed to their local church in numerous capacities. They also enjoy ministering at the Coachella Valley Rescue Mission.

The Lord has provided numerous opportunities to pray and minister to customers through their air conditioning company (Amen Air Inc.). They have also raised two miracle children by faith, Praise God! One graduated with honors from Oral Roberts University (ORU) with a business degree. The other is a nurse at the Mayo Clinic in Phoenix, Arizona, pursuing her Bachelor of Science in Nursing.

Mike & Patti continue to live a life of faith. Their mission statement is: To encourage, educate, and escort people into the Kingdom of God.

Romans 4:17-18 says: "*Call those things which do not exist as though they did, who, contrary to hope, in hope, believed.*"

Remember to *"Call those things which do not exist as though they did"* (Romans 4:17). That is faith in action. It serves as the foundation of this love story. Through Mike's eyes, this is how our FAITH FACE unfolds:

I was in my garage working on an electrical panel. I looked up and saw a gorgeous woman with beautiful brown eyes. I was staying away from church at that time. I was in the wilderness, and God was there with me. I had been in a church and God's Word was alive and powerful there. God had never left me nor forsaken me. I believed that, but my heart was wounded and broken. So, I did what most of us do. I fed the flesh.

I had a house with two other guys and the party was on. Sin was fun for a season, but the Holy Spirit was still there with me. Greater is He who is in me than he that is in the world, remained true. I knew this to the core, yet I still lived for me.

When I met that brown-eyed beauty, I was not looking for anyone. She just joined the party, and she fit right in. That's what we did — "party," and according to the world, we were having fun. However, Patti had a big enemy. It was one of the first things in the world that we had to apply faith to overcome. I did not know the depth of the heartache behind it. Therefore, as I got to know her and the depths of her IV drug addiction, I wasn't sure I could trust her. Yet, I couldn't let go either.

I didn't know it then, but God had a great big plan. Amazingly, Patti was kind and full of love, despite all she had been through. She believed in the Hallmark Movie kind of storybook ending, love with a sense of innocence. She wanted a family and children, but I didn't want that at all. We had to deal with the demon of addiction if we were going to be in any kind of relationship. I talked about Jesus all the time. The Bible says out of the abundance of the heart the mouth speaks. So true.

Interestingly, she ate it up. She was Catholic and had a measure of faith, but it was based on works. One day we prayed, and I wrote on a red piece of construction paper, "Thank You, Jesus, for delivering me and healing Patti." Romans 4:17 in action. We confessed that every time we walked by the fridge. Everyone who got a beer out, including my two roommates, read that note on the fridge. We spoke the truth about believing God to anyone who would ask.

Some of those people, like my roommates, didn't care about God. Some did and were running like me, but the one who heard and believed the most was Patti. She only knew works from her Catholic faith. She tried to follow it, but she didn't have a personal relationship with Jesus as I did. I knew to go straight to the Father through Him. Patti's faith was growing. She hoped against hope that Jesus was real, and she was not disappointed. Her born-again experience was not 'churchie;' it was the polar opposite.

She was all alone in a very dire place when she read the Sinner's prayer in the back of a book and believed she was born again. No heads bowed, no singing choir. It was Holy Spirit breathing new life into a broken human, and it took. As you know, transformation is a lifelong process. We are still in the process.

Through a series of events, Patti got arrested for selling drugs. God "bailed" her out of jail in two days and she was able to go to rehab, where she defeated the demon of IV drug abuse. To God be the glory! Statistics say only 3% of IV drug users ever get free. But God! She has not stuck a needle in her arm for over 30 years.

Remember I said we were broken humans? The needle was gone but we still drank and partied. God was nowhere near done. Patti and I had an on-and-off relationship for a year or so and one day we had a big fight. I was tired of the up and down and she was too. She was already depressed when I said something mean to her. She then said she was done, downed a bottle of Xanax, followed by some vodka, and took off in her car.

My friend and I went looking for her but couldn't find her. I went back home, lay on my bed, and had a vision. I had never had a vision before, but I could clearly see where she was. It was like I was looking down from above. I wrestled with God and God won, after which I jumped in my car and drove to the place He had shown me. There she was, just like I saw in my vision. I rushed her to the hospital where they pumped her stomach. Patti survived, as God had a plan. Just as God used a donkey in the Bible to save the ones He loved, He used me to save Patti that night.

I didn't want to do this lifestyle anymore, so I asked Patti to marry me. But like the donkey I am, I called it off and that tore her heart out.

I wrestled with God again. God spoke to my heart and asked me why I wouldn't let this woman love me. That truth of being afraid pierced my heart. God spoke to my heart again in Romans 5:5, "*The love of God has been poured out in our hearts by the Holy Spirit who was given to us.*" I will ask her again. I cannot deny the power of God and His truth. I'll let Patti take over from here.

Patti's FAITH FACE:

Only through faith in God and the power of the Holy Spirit was I able to survive our breakup and the fact that God had a great big plan for our lives. I went to my Bible that night and flipped through the pages. I cried out to God to please speak to me! He led me to Isaiah 54. I was flipping pages, and this is where I landed, "*I will be your husband and you will no longer live in shame!*" I cannot express with words how that encounter changed me. God was so real to me now. I mean the God of the universe spoke right to my heart! He heard me and comforted me!

I then knew I would be OK, whether I was married or not. I believe I fully surrendered my life to Him that night. But God had a plan and Mike asked me once more to marry him, after his own encounter with God. We got married. We were totally in love! We spent just $500.00 on our wedding and $250.00 was for the church. We were in love and that's all that mattered.

We threw ourselves into church and the Word of God. We were in church every time the doors were opened. Some people say beans, rice, and Jesus Christ. We lived and ate Jesus.

We wanted a family and amazingly, God changed Mike's heart in this area. He had never wanted kids before, but God was in the process of changing our hearts. I wanted to be the mother I never had but I kept having miscarriages. I believed and prayed all the way to the hospital and was so discouraged when I lost that baby. I was so distaught!

What about my faith? Was this a punishment for all the bad things I had done in my drug-using days? I knew where to turn. I searched the scriptures and God led me to Proverbs 3:5-6: *"Trust in the Lord with all your heart. Lean not on your own understanding, but in all your ways acknowledge him and He will direct your path."* That gave me such comfort, again! God is faithful. God's timing is perfect. I believed in God, and I believed in prayer. I started praying. I found Mark 11:24 which says, *"Whatever things you ask when you pray, believe that you receive them, and you will have them."* I stood on Romans 4:17 again, *"Call those things which do not exist as though they did."* I prayed every day for a year! During that time, I confessed, "Thank you, Father, for my happy and healthy child!" I believe that time in prayer helped guide me into the bold, steadfast, and unwavering prayer intercessor I am today. Prayer changes things!

It just so happened that a woman at my church was starting a life group called "Woman Fully Persuaded" from Romans 4. I knew this was for me. This woman was told that she would never have children because she only had one tube, but God. She was the proud mother of three boys.

She wanted to give back what God had done for her. That group of women encouraged one another and prayed fervently for each other. There were many miracles out of that group.

I had a total of three miscarriages. Then I was pregnant again and started spotting, just like all the other rounds. This time someone suggested that I see a new doctor, so I did. I kept praying and believing. They got me right in and did something no other doctor had done. They put me on special suppositories. I stopped spotting and I stayed pregnant. God had answered my prayers. I was a mother! My precious Faith was born, literally! We named her Faith because it took so much faith in God to conceive her!

Writing about this gets me just as excited as I was then! This was a miracle. God was true to His Word, after all the pain, and despair over each miscarriage. As I delighted myself in Him, He gave me the desires of my heart. He will do it for you, too, as He is no respecter of persons.

Whatever you're believing God for, if it's in His will and being fruitful and multiplying is His will, it can be yours. Only believe.

I had another miscarriage after my daughter, Faith, was born, but honestly, the pain was not as bad. I had a child and was content with that. However, God's Word says He will give you the desires of your heart, and we desired two children.

At the age of 35, I became pregnant again. The doctor said, "You are at high risk for Down's Syndrome and other genetic abnormalities because of your age. You should have an amniocentesis." Mike and I prayed about this. It just so happened that I was sitting in a conference, the Norvel Hayes Convention. The speaker said he had a word for someone, someone who had problems with pregnancies, and he described my situation exactly. I went up and he prayed and prophesied over me. It all resonated in my heart and my spirit. Basically, he said this child will come forth.

Needless to say, we did not get the amnio and we had supernatural peace throughout the whole pregnancy. My precious Shelby (SHALL BE) was born! We were a family of four.

Please don't think for a minute that we used God's Word to get things willy-nilly. You would miss the whole point. No, we sought the Lord. He heard me and delivered me from all my fears! We sought Him. We stood on His Word that says, *"Call those things that do not exist as though they did."* At the end of that chapter in Romans 4, it actually says this was not for Abraham only but for all future believers! That's you and me! That makes me shout and Praise God! That is faith, *"Faith is the substance of things hoped for* (a child)*, the evidence of things not seen"* (looking at miscarriages). Another translation says, *"It's the confident hope that something we want is going to happen."* It did. If God said it, we believed it, and that settled it.

I didn't want to make God's Word sound like He is a genie, but if you know Him and you know His Word, you know better. If you don't, then I suggest you get to know Him. Have a relationship with Him and then you will know exactly what I mean.

We brought those girls up "in the nurture and admonition of the Lord." We taught them everything we could about God, and we had them in the same church we had been in. We prayed every day pretty much, and still do. We tried to show our gratitude to God in every way. Those girls are walking out God's plan for their lives, and I'm so grateful for that.

We wanted these stories to inspire you as we share what God has done for us. He will do it for you too. There are so many more "by faith" stories we could tell. This has been a 33-year journey between God and us. We are still going strong in faith today. We have had multiple trials as we all do. Life is in session, but we know where to turn when trials come.

We hope your faith has grown a little from reading a snippet of our faith journey. Just a little faith, that of the size of a mustard seed, which is super tiny, is all you need. We plant this story in your life and your faith journey.

My prayer for you:

Oh Father, when we look over all You have done, and we remember with great joy, we give You all the praise, glory, and honor.

Father, we ask that You bless anyone reading this. No matter where they are in their journey, touch them, strengthen them in their inner person, that Christ would dwell in their hearts by FAITH. We believe they will be rooted and grounded in love, that they know the love of Christ and by faith, would know that God is able to do exceedingly abundantly above all that we could ask or think, according to the power that works in us.

Open their eyes to see You, Father, perfecting every detail that concerns them. Be so real to them Father, IN JESUS' MIGHTY NAME, AMEN!

Day 9: WHAT MEAN THESE STONES?

Thurston Canada Harris was born in January 1961. He accepted Jesus as Lord and Savior in July 1975. Thurston has been an active member of White Rock Baptist Church, Philadelphia, Pennsylvania, since 1990. He is a father to one daughter and retired from a career in Compliance Management.

Thurston is taking time to enjoy each moment of life, at a slower pace. He is currently pursuing sculpting and lives appreciative of God's patience and direction while learning to seek Him in every aspect of life. He is currently active in His Ministry as a New Member Instructor.

What do these stones mean and why is it important to place them? It is vitally important to recall, review, and mark moments in life that we know, without doubt, that whatever just happened only happened because of God's direction, leading, and handiwork. True growth in Christ will begin when we recognize that God put a lot of work into assuring us that we would be standing at this very moment. A multitude of our ancestors were created and positioned, and persevered in a daisy chain of life events that allowed our birth and existence. All these occurrences were designed by God from the beginning of time. The love of God extended towards us through the generations. We offer Him a grateful heart because we are His unique creations. We give thanks to God because He has awesomely and wonderfully made us. He has approached even the smallest details with great excellence. His works are a wonder, and our souls know it very well (see Psalm 139).

What Mean These Stones?

This is written to testify about the excellence of God within our everyday lives. The story of God's everlasting love is extended past the scriptures and now gushes forward through testimony and witness of His greatness. *"One generation shall praise Your works to another, and shall declare Your mighty acts. I will meditate on the glorious splendor of Your Majesty, and on Your wondrous works. Men shall speak of the might of Your awesome acts, and I will declare Your greatness"* (Psalm 145:4-6).

We must learn to trust God for His infinite wisdom to have hope for today and tomorrow. This is not easy in a world filled with the static noise that resonates inside of our heads and that is always present in our immediate surroundings. A believer must learn to hear God's voice and then do as He says. Do not consume your mind and time trying to position God to fulfill your personal dreams. He's very good at ordering life and our steps for His glory. We should use prayer to align ourselves and others with God's will — NOT align His will with our own human desires.

This is my story and my song...

At the beginning of my new relationship with God through Jesus Christ, I saw everything afresh. The reds were redder, the water was wetter, the sun was warmer, and life seemed more at peace. Looking back, at the beginning of my journey I was very obsequious in serving Him in spirit and in truth. (Obsequious means "marked by or showing a fawning attentiveness"—in other words, too eager to help or obey someone important.)

Studying the Word of God was at first an exercise in understanding how to get Him to do my will — seldom to allow His Word to either change the focus of my life or to do His will. I didn't desire challenges and opportunities in my life intended to transform me into His image, but instead, I manipulated some parts of His Word to suit my thoughts and perceived needs.

Finally, I made the choice to deny myself, pick up my cross daily, and follow Him. I no longer asked Him to come where I found myself, but instead desired to go where He was, as I was placed there to do His will. It was not an overnight success, as I still must regularly refocus my wandering mind. Philippians 4:4-8 helps me center my soul when I feel unsettled, as well as when I feel collected.

He caused me to change how I viewed my battle scars – no longer as remembrances of how others betrayed and hurt me, but instead as a testimony and witness of how He healed and delivered me (mostly from myself). How great Thou art!

We cannot be selfish in our faith. The crucifixion and resurrection of Jesus are for everyone in the world – not just a select few. We must abandon seeing His world as we see it and learn to see this world as He sees it; to have our eyes opened to see His glory. God so loved the world that He gave His begotten Son. To live a life of faith with no regrets, it is necessary to put on God's whole armor and trust Him in the seen and the unseen. We must walk by faith and not by sight. If we trust and obey, we will find that He has little interest in changing the world around us, for us, but He is constantly changing us for the world around us, for His glory.

There would not be a need for Psalm 23 if we never saw it as a template for our life. Our prayer would be to avoid it. Instead, our prayers should embrace it and His will and proclaim His greatness in and through it all. I refuse to worry about anything that God already knows about. Whatever we imagine Heaven to be, there are two signs that we will never see displayed. One is "No Vacancies" – there is always room for one more. The second is "Help Wanted" – God doesn't need our help in getting His creation right, He desires that we obey Him and do as we are told. (Here I am Lord, use me.)

What Mean These Stones?

It took me 13 years to honestly desire to fully surrender myself and my life to His will. I was saved but not submitted and therefore found myself in an unimaginable place. I was on the verge of divorce and had lost every worldly possession I had stored up. My slate of friends had been erased and I'd lost my connection with my wife and nearly with my daughter. Even worse, I had to move out of my house and move to what I thought was a horrible neighborhood. I went kicking and screaming.

Thinking my world was falling apart, I could not imagine anything good coming from being in this place. I felt alone and embarrassed. Even worse for me, I felt it was due to no fault of my own. However, during this pruning and time of realignment, I met a wonderful member of the household of faith who became a friend. It was so refreshing to see someone who loved God and had the desire to learn more about Jesus. In my moment of despair, they caused me to see the wonder of God in a new way. Many years later, we are still great friends and God continues to use our relationship to refresh our souls.

Trust God in ordering the steps for your life. You will see a bigger, more loving God than you could imagine. I would never have seen His ability to reveal His glory while walking through the valley without the turmoil. Through it, I was able to focus on who God was and who I was in Him.

Tired of relying on others to tell me about God through Jesus Christ, I decided to read about Him for myself. I committed to open my heart and personally read the Gospels of Jesus Christ. While reading it, His Word revealed the extreme love He has towards me (us). Also, reading it for myself literally changed my perspective and my life.

Nothing changed humanly – I found myself dealing with the same stuff, and got divorced. However, it was I who changed spiritually. God was pruning me and my life by allowing me to be able to see more of His glory, power, strength, and love. More importantly, I was in the Refiner's fire and was being convicted and transformed into His image, as the dross rose to the surface. Most importantly, I knew that I was not alone in my personal desert and that He was with me (even when I felt alone) and that He loved me (even when I didn't love myself)!

The biggest breakthrough occurred when I accepted that I was the culprit and that I was guilty of turning away from Him. I was to blame for how I responded to His constant prompting and knocking on my spirit. I was purposely ignoring the Lordship of God in, for, and throughout my life.

Previously, I would blame most of my life's ill effects on others without taking responsibility for my own actions, which pushed me away from God. We must own our stuff and then accept His faithful forgiveness after we confess them. He already knows – so we should start with being honest with God. All have sinned and fallen short of the glory of God. I had to accept that the "all" included me.

Once I realized that the log in my eye was much larger than the speck I saw in the eyes of others, I was able to humbly receive His healing. It was me standing in the need of prayer.

We must get it right. *"Be diligent to show yourself approved to GOD, a worker who does not to be ashamed, rightly dividing the word of truth"* (2 Timothy 2:15).

Don't forfeit your requirement to personally listen and learn of Him and grow in His grace. By faith, Noah built a very large ark without any rain in the immediate forecast. It required determination and precise attention to detail. Noah listened to God and did precisely what He said to do, to fulfill His future purpose. The story of Noah and the ark is a famous biblical event and is widely known amongst people of the earth. The story is so popular that people, books, and movies have repeated it over and over. Noah built an ark and gathered pairs of animals, both male and female. God sent a flood, and then the floods subsided, giving the earth's future new inhabitants another chance to listen to and obey God. Most people can recite the story without any second thought because it's been repeated so many times. Unfortunately, the story is not an exact replica of God's instructions because it's about what we believe God told Noah. There is very little harm in getting it wrong in this instance because it's not our story. Fortunately, as the real story is recorded, God did not say two of every animal (read Genesis 7). Noah got it right and it pleased God. God is speaking to us, in the same manner. It's probably not to build an ark, but it's something that He has designed specifically for us. We must listen as He speaks and then do as He says.

Listening to God requires a concerted effort on our part. Listening cannot be achieved simply by being in the same space with another person. It is possible to be deaf to what is being said because we are waiting for a break in the conversation to speak. If you really want to know what God wants – ask Him. Unfortunately, it's easier to tell God what we think He wants. It's much more challenging (and profitable) to settle down for a moment and ask God what He wants you to do. Then shut off your mind, stop talking, and wait on Him to answer. As you wait on Him, your strength will be renewed. Trust God to direct your life. Jesus Christ always and only.

We walk by faith, not by sight. Sixteen years into my employment, I received notice that my job would be eliminated because of the company's "right-sizing." As the time drew nigh, my coworkers were pleased that they would keep their job and not concerned that others would lose theirs.

On the Friday before the Monday when separation papers had to be submitted, I received an unusual call from a coworker. He was reaching out to me to let me know that he was not leaving and that because of his choice, I would be let go. I sensed a sarcastic chuckle in his voice, as he delivered his unsolicited message. He asked me what I was going to do at the end of it. I replied, without any uneasiness, that I would trust God as I never want to be where He doesn't want me. Our phone call ended.

Monday, I submitted my separation package paperwork. A couple of hours after submitting it, I got a call from the Friday-chuckling coworker. He called to tell me that over the weekend he and his wife were talking about the package, and she suggested he take the package so they could spend more time together. He submitted his paperwork that day – I withdrew my paperwork.

Some years later, I had a manager who seemed to have angst against me and my on-shift partner. He decided that he was going to do all he could to eliminate our employment at the next annual evaluation. He told most of my coworkers of his devious plan. One by one we received calls telling us of his well-thought-out plan. Others seemed to be delighted that we were going to be fired. I received multiple phone calls and had conversations inquiring about what I was going to do. I continuously replied, "I'm going to trust God."

The Friday before the Monday employee evaluation was scheduled, the manager called to let us know that he would be performing the evaluation next week. The Sunday prior to the evaluation, the company did something unprecedented. They decided to swap the operation manager and the maintenance manager, and they were to begin their new assignments first thing Monday morning. On Tuesday, we got a call from the new operation manager saying that he was coming to the station to complete our evaluations. Then he said, "Look, I have been reading the previous manager's notes and it appears he was going to get both of you fired. I don't see what he wrote attached to the persons I know. Do me a favor and write down all that you have done in the last year so I will be able to justify giving both of you a fair evaluation. We did, he came, and we got an excellent evaluation with a raise.

A couple of weeks later, the company reversed the manager role swap. I retired from that company with 42 years of service. These events exponentially helped me learn to trust God in ordering my steps and not put any weight on the world's thoughts or suggestions.

Be open to something new ...

"Behold, I will do a new thing; now it shall spring forth; Shall you not know it?" (Isaiah 43:19a).

Due to skepticism and cynicism in our world, we learn or are taught that "seeing is believing" – only believe what you can see with your own two eyes. In our faith relationship, we learn that we are blind and that "believing is seeing" – there are elements in our lives that can ONLY be realized when we trust God with the particulars. God controls all outcomes (it's out of our hands).

We do control what we yield. So, it's important to make choices to follow and serve Him and seek His glory in all things. We must choose this day whom we will serve. If we chose to follow Him yesterday, it will need to be renewed today. If we did not choose to follow Him yesterday it will need to be restored today.

While traveling to serve a church member Holy Communion, I was partnered with a fellow deacon, and we were tired on our last visit. We signed in after entering the care facility and talked to the staff. We then prepared to go around the corner to the member's room. About midway to our destination, we were walking by the elevator when its doors opened. A woman and man exited the elevator and came up to us and asked that we go to their loved one's room and pray for them and the family. We said yes

– and off we went. We did eventually reach our intended destination after leaving God's intended "along the way" target. God's timing is always correct. This event required God to regulate and order the timing of our previous communion visits, schedule the delay at the reception desk; position the woman and man leaving a room and riding an elevator, the elevator reaching the ground floor at the precise time two bondservants walked by who were willing to serve God at the moment. ALL GOD.

We have an ability to not only see the glory of God with faith, but with His direction, we can also be the glory of God. We need to believe that He is the Lord of all persons and all moments.

Don't Compete – Don't Compare ...

"What is that to you? You follow Me."

After the resurrection, Jesus had a recorded exchange with a disciple and asked him three times if he loved Him and then gave him instructions. At its conclusion, the disciple was instructed to follow Jesus. The disciple, seeing another disciple not going with them, asked Jesus about him. Jesus' reply was if He decides to do one thing with one disciple, but another thing with another disciple – "What is that to you? – You follow Me."

In order to truly develop our unique relationship with the Lord, we must follow Him as He leads us. *"Whoever desires to come after Me, let him deny himself, and take up his cross, and follow Me. For whoever desires to save his life will lose it, but whoever loses his life for My sake and the Gospel's will save it"* (Mark 8:34-35). As we stand on His battlefield, listen to the Commander.

What Mean These Stones?

Be still and know that He is God ...

I continue to learn that the universe is unfolding as it should. However, often, it's not as we expect. The signs of the times can be daunting (they always have been). His ways are not our ways; His thoughts are not our thoughts. Walk by faith and not by sight. It can be scary, but it will be profitable for both Him and us when we are led by Him.

Don't be consumed with recognition or with being recognized. What difference does it make who gets credit, as long as God is glorified? *"And what does the Lord require of you but to do justly, to love mercy, and to walk humbly with your God?"* (Micah. 6:8). The days may turn dark, and the sun may not shine, but the Son never loses His power or brilliance.

"Praise the Lord! Oh, give thanks to the Lord, for He is good! For His mercy endures forever" (Psalm 106:1).

Praise the Lord all you Gentiles; Laud Him, all you peoples! For His merciful kindness is great towards us, And the truth of the Lord endures forever. Praise the Lord!" (Psalm 117:1-2).

My prayer for you:

Father God, we, Your bondservants, praise You for Your love, grace, mercy, and patience towards us and Your creation. We again place ourselves on Your throne to ask You for the forgiveness of our sin against You and others and to acknowledge our waywardness from Your will for us.

Open our eyes to see Your glory and give us a pure heart to do Your will to enable us to be Your glory. May we feel the promise of Your peace that surpasses all understanding as we trust You to guard our hearts and minds in Christ Jesus.

May the penned words of our minds, the spoken words of our mouths, and the meditations of our hearts, and the actions of our hands be acceptable to You and bring You honor and glory. Amen

What Mean These Stones?

Day 10: GROWING FAITH

Courtney Faith Encheff received her double B.A. from Life Pacific University in Bible and Arts and Letters. She resides in Southern California in her forever home with her husband and three children.

Leading Bible Studies in her community and encouraging others to grow in their faith alongside her brings her joy. Courtney is a professional voice actress, which is her dream job and has voiced multiple audiobooks, animated characters, YouTube channel series, ads, and more.

Some of her favorite pastimes include reading, playing board games, and attending her high schooler's basketball games. Her favorite scripture is "*You will keep him in perfect peace, whose mind is stayed on You, because he trusts in You*" (Isaiah 26:3).

Lack of Faith:

Once upon a time, in a land, not so far away, but long, long ago.... there was a girl, a Christ follower, who wasn't fully following Christ. She loved Him but had not been fully obedient to His way and found herself pregnant at 20 years old. She was attending Bible college at the time and had signed a code of conduct that she would live a life worthy of a leader and as an example in the faith. As you might have guessed, that girl was me.

I was nine days away from leaving on a mission trip to Africa with my school when I took the test that confirmed that I was pregnant. I was in shock. I confided in my best friend who suggested I speak with a couple from her church for wisdom regarding the trip. I wasn't prepared to share the news with the world yet. They suggested I tell the leader of the trip I was pregnant for safety purposes. Because the leader of our trip was the president of my Bible college, I decided to first tell my mom. She then went with me to speak to the President. Due to the contract I signed, there were consequences for not abiding by the rules. As a result, I was to return and answer questions within days of speaking with the school president, in a room with faculty members/teachers, who would then discuss and pray about my situation and call me with the outcome. Typically, a student is suspended for a semester or a year.

I clearly remember being in that room with about eight men and women whom I respected, and whom I knew cared for me. I remember one of them, my previous teacher, asking me a question along the lines of, "Have you heard God say anything to you? And if so, what?" Without a doubt in my mind, at that moment, I clearly heard God speak to my heart…. "Do not marry him." I of course didn't share that piece of information with the room. I ignored it. I told them we were planning on getting married as soon as possible.

I remember my sister calling me when I was at work one day. She told me she couldn't sleep the previous night and had been praying. She told me I didn't have to marry him, and two wrongs didn't make a right. She asked me if I had prayed about it. I hadn't. I had already heard from God that I wasn't supposed to marry him, but I was doing my best to ignore God. Why would I ask God, if I wasn't planning on listening to Him? Then I would be blatantly disobeying. If I didn't ask, then maybe I wasn't disobeying.

My mind was set, and I was going to do things in order. I was going to be married before this baby was born. I was not going to have a broken family. Yes, the relationship was not healthy, but that was just because of the shame. Things would get better, and I would get my happily ever after.

Well, fast forward and guess what? God knows what's best for us after all. Who would have thought? I thought my plan was best for me and boy, was I wrong! God has a way of rerouting us when we don't listen, and ultimately, I ended up divorced.

It was a long road of resistance and trying to make it work, but ultimately, I discovered that what I thought was best for my daughter was really harming her. She needed to see and know what a healthy relationship looked like while growing up in a loving, peaceful home. I learned that my lack of faith did not serve me well at all. I could have saved myself from a lot of heartache had I just been obedient to God's voice at school that day. Even though God's plan may not seem like the best plan, He really does love you. You can also trust that He wants what's best for you.

"For I know the thoughts I think towards you, says the Lord, thoughts of peace and not of evil, to give you a future and a hope" (Jeremiah 29:11).

Little Faith:

Fast forward a bit to when I was in a long-distance relationship. It was perfect as I felt cared for but didn't have to expose my daughter to the relationship. This was the first person I had "dated" since the divorce.

I was at church one night and the pastor was up on the stage. This was the night they were telling the church that he was stepping down from pastoring this particular church. I remember the other man on the stage asking him what was next, and why he was leaving, so he could answer some questions about which the church might be wondering. He explained that he felt God was asking him to step out in faith. He also honestly didn't know what was next, but he felt that God would reveal that in time as he just trusted Him.

Growing Faith

I immediately started crying. Others around me were crying because the pastor they loved would no longer be their pastor. I, however, was crying because at that moment, when the pastor spoke, God was using him to speak to me. I knew in my heart that God wanted me to end my long-distance relationship. I felt like if there were no other prospects, then why end it? It was nice to be treated nicely, but God clearly told me that I needed to trust Him, or He couldn't bring the right guy to me.

Having somewhat learned my lesson of disobeying God's nudge, I ended my relationship on May 9th. Exactly three weeks later, on May 30th, in that exact same church building, I met my husband!

"Now to Him who is able to do exceedingly abundantly above all that we ask or think, according to the power that works in us" (Ephesians. 3:20).

Weak Faith:

Fast forward yet again. I was now happily married and had just given birth to a baby boy! Yet, things were awful with my ex-husband. Once again, I was on the phone with that same sister. She told me she heard a song on the radio, and she thought it should be my anthem. It was called, "Brave" by Sarah Bareilles. I tended to do whatever I could to keep the peace and was not feeling brave at all.

Shortly after, the art director at the church shared a powerful spoken word, titled, "Brave." Then shortly after that, I was at a dance workshop at church and the devotion given was about...being brave. God was repeatedly telling me to be brave.

Once again, in my heart, I knew why God kept telling me to be brave. I was supposed to go to court and make changes to the schedule and court order for the sake of my daughter's peace. But the court is scary, and lawyers are expensive. I felt like Moses, as if I wouldn't know the words to say. Despite having weak faith, I obeyed. I set up an appointment with a lawyer whose fee was $5,000! If it took more hours than the $5,000 allotted, then I would owe her even more.

Rewind three years, to when my husband (who was my fiancé at the time) and I had gotten in a car accident a few weeks before our wedding day. The car was totaled. We spent the next year or so going to a chiropractor, who requested that we work with his suggested lawyer to ensure that he got paid.

Just when we needed it, in God's perfect timing, three whole years later, we got an unexpected check in the mail for $5,000! We did not even know we would be getting money. We were just working with the chiropractor per his suggestion to make sure he got paid. God fully provided the exact amount we needed to pay the lawyer's fee.

Court day arrived, and I was beyond scared. But God! The judge granted every request that I desired. Since then, things have drastically improved, and I have no doubt that God's will was done even through my weak faith.

"You will keep in perfect peace, whose mind is stayed on You, because he trusts in You" (Isaiah. 26:3).

Small Faith:

Fast forward again. My husband and I, along with our children, of course, moved to a wonderful neighborhood. I felt that nudge from God again that I was supposed to lead a neighborhood women's Bible study. Excuses filled my mind. I was already so busy with three children at this point. I needed God to make it very clear if this was what He wanted.

Our neighborhood has a Facebook group where people can ask questions, get referrals, give or sell things, set up playdates, and more. It's such a blessing! One night, a particular question caught my eye: "I desperately need a women's group...is there anyone in the community who has a regular women's Bible study?" Once again, I felt that tug on my heart. I remember thinking, "I think I'm supposed to lead it, but I can't really host with the kids at home and I'm so busy right now." Still wanting God to give me a clear sign, I decided not to respond just yet.

Woman after woman responded to her comment saying that they needed one too, and would love to attend if there was one in the neighborhood. A few said that they would be willing to host but weren't comfortable being the leader. Having literally only one night a week free, I asked God to make it clear to me if this is what He was asking me to step into. Knowing people were busy, they suggested meeting only once a month.

I finally chimed in and asked when they wanted to have this study: on a weekday, weeknight, or weekend. The lady that originally posted stated that she was hoping for Monday nights.... the one night I had free.

We have been meeting in the neighborhood twice a month now for over four years! This group has been such a blessing to each of us and I am so grateful that God planted that seed in my heart and gave me the green light! It has been such a joy!

"... *So continuing daily with one accord in the temple, and breaking bread from house to house, they ate their food with gladness and simplicity of heart, praising God and having favor with all the people*" (Acts 2:46-47).

Great Faith:

Fast forward one last time. My beautiful first-born baby was heading into high school! The time had come to decide where she would attend. We had planned for her to attend a public school with a great basketball program. She's a great starting player.

However, weeks before school began, we got a curve ball thrown our way. Her club basketball coach got a job as the girls' basketball coach at a private Christian high school that is 40 miles away from where we live. He asked us to consider sending her there to get the basketball program off to a strong start.

We agreed to take a tour of the school, but I was honestly thinking, "This is crazy. There is no way I am going to drive 160 miles every day (80 miles roundtrip twice a day) for her to go here. Not to mention, it costs way more than we can afford. I also have two younger children whose school has the same start and end time but 40 miles away."

Once we went to the school, I was slightly more open to the idea. However, we still couldn't afford it. It cost money even to apply to the school.

Rewind about a year and a half.... I had been thinking of ways to help bring some income in since my husband works for the school district and doesn't get a paycheck in the summer. I always had a dream of one day being a voice actress and someone had mentioned the idea of doing audiobooks. I investigated it and discovered that I could record audiobooks from home and get paid for it! My dream wasn't really to do audiobooks, but it was close enough and allowed me to work from home. What I really wanted to do was cartoons, commercials, video games, those sorts of jobs. But the website to audition for those jobs charged an annual fee that was pretty high, and I didn't have the confidence yet to pay that much. After a year of narrating over 100 audiobooks, I felt confident enough to sign up for that website.

Now back to the time of paying for and turning in the high school application... I turned in the application and the following day received a job that equaled the amount of the school's admission application. The next step was to apply for financial aid, which also had an upfront fee. The following morning, I woke up to another job offer. I felt like God was telling me not to worry. This is where He wants her, and He will provide.

Just like when I needed to break up with my boyfriend before meeting my husband, He was requiring me to step out in great faith first and He would provide.

The day before my daughter was supposed to start at her public high school, we made the decision to have her attend the private Christian school. I have a log in my notebook that shows how every time I had to pay for tuition, books, uniforms, sports fees, etc. God provided the money through my voice work. He has been faithful.

This school has been so amazing for my daughter. I have seen her confidence grow before my eyes. She has been the captain of the Varsity basketball team for two years now and has grown in leadership skills. She has an amazing group of friends. She has teachers and faculty members who pray with her and for her and have a personal relationship with her. She is learning God's Word through her Bible classes and chapel, and her relationship with God is stronger than ever.

It is so amazing to look back and see how God was preparing the way. When I started doing audiobooks three years ago, a private school for my daughter was not even a thought in my mind. I needed that year of audiobooks to have the courage to do the voice jobs I currently do, which God has used to provide for my daughter.

It definitely took great faith to sign her up at this school, not knowing where the money would come from, in addition to all the driving I was committing to. Yet again, I have no doubt in my mind that this is God's will for my daughter. I get the joy of witnessing her thrive and grow every day because I dared to believe that God knows best!

"Trust in the Lord with all your heart, and lean not on your own understanding. In all your ways acknowledge Him, and He shall direct your paths" (Proverbs 3:5-6).

In closing, I hope you can see how throughout my life, God has been with me, even when I wasn't trying to listen. He knows us by name and cares about the details, even if they seem small or silly to us or others. He is faithful to speak to us, provide for us, encourage and direct us, and give us peace and hope. He has the plan to prosper us.

This faith journey is far from over. There will continue to be circumstances that will challenge my faith. I pray that I can continually grow in my ability to trust Him and dare to believe when He speaks to me. I pray this for you as well.

"And we know all things work together for good to those who love God, to those who are the called according to His purpose" (Romans 8:28).

My prayer for you:

Dear Heavenly Father, I pray for the readers of this today. I pray they would be encouraged by my stories of faith. I pray that You would open their eyes to see how You have been faithful in their own lives. I pray that they would recognize Your voice and the nudge of Your Holy Spirit.

By faith, they are courageous and filled with faith enough to obey Your Spirit's leading. By faith, they are healed of past hurts and fears that are holding them back from fully trusting You. By faith they know You will use everything for good and in the end, they are victorious through You.

Give them the excitement to walk this journey of life with You by their side. Surround them with godly people who will uplift them and encourage them and pray with them and for them. Open their eyes to see others and themselves the way You see us: with perfect love. Equip them to do good works and fill them with the fruit of the Spirit. Give them a peace that surpasses understanding. Fill them with the joy of the Lord! May they grow in their adoration of You so much that they can't keep silent! Give them a passion for Your Word and for Your people! Bless them so that they may be a blessing to others!

In the name of Your son, Jesus. Amen.

Day 11: MY FAITH TITLE

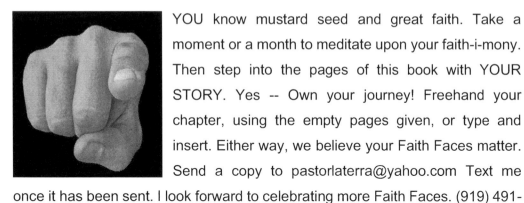

YOU know mustard seed and great faith. Take a moment or a month to meditate upon your faith-i-mony. Then step into the pages of this book with YOUR STORY. Yes -- Own your journey! Freehand your chapter, using the empty pages given, or type and insert. Either way, we believe your Faith Faces matter. Send a copy to pastorlaterra@yahoo.com Text me once it has been sent. I look forward to celebrating more Faith Faces. (919) 491-1553. Woohoo!! Remember to send a prayer at the end. I feel your "come through power" already!

_____

_____

_____

_____

_____

_____

_____

_____

_____

_____

_____

_____

_____

_____

_____

_____

_____

_____

_____

My Faith Title

Day 12: BE NOT AFRAID

Marisa Frech has lived in the desert since 1989 and recently moved to Mountain Center, California. She's been married to Greg Frech for almost 26 years and together they have two children, Karissa who is 24, and Hunter who is 19. She is a lover of hummingbirds, sushi, and Jesus.

Her business, Kreation Succulents was established in February 2016. Her backyard hobby turned into a business quite organically, and she refers to it as a gift from God. With money pooled together from her Bible study group, she arranged a piece to be donated for Southwest Community Church's Annual Luncheon and Silent Auction. That piece was quickly noticed, and a few ladies approached her and asked, "Do you work at Art in Nature in Palm Desert?" She quickly responded that she works WITH art, IN nature... IN her backyard! A job was secured that day, and she has been creating unique arrangements with love and joy ever since.

I'm writing two weeks into my COVID journey. I declared that I have express COVID. Be not afraid, God goes before me! My sweet husband, Greg, and daughter, Karissa, are dealing with the lingering effects of it. I'm still healing and doing my best to provide healthy meals, care, and support. Every part of my body just wants to rest...but...my spirit!!! My spirit is rejoicing at the thought of my sweetest friend, Dr. Pastor LaTerra, celebrating her 40th birthday in Christ! Forty years of walking diligently and faithfully; 40 years of trusting and believing; 40 years of putting on the armor of God and letting the battle belong to Him; 40 years SAVED!

What is faith? Why is faith important? What comes of faith? I am going to do my best to share my faith journey, to encourage and strengthen yours! It is my hope that you will celebrate the goodness of God and see His faithfulness in your life.

Hebrews 11 is THE faith chapter in the Bible. It shares the accounts of many, who by faith, responded to God. Simply stated, Hebrews 11:1 (ESV) says, *"Now faith is the assurance of things hoped for, the conviction of things not seen."* How do you have complete trust in God? In my experience, it takes time. Time to get to know Him in His Word. Time to get to know people and their stories. I do believe that you can have an "and suddenly" experience too! Nothing is impossible with God!

I share my journey; I would like to share a little bit of who I am and from where I came. My name is Marisa, and I was born in Virginia, in the '70's. My dad is a Marine and a retired sheriff deputy. Initially my mom was a stay-at-home wife. She later retired from the Superior Court of California. They both grew up working in the fields and have a unique perspective on life and suffering! By faith, their children would have a better upbringing than they did!

I have an older sister, Yvonndy, who is four and a half years older than me. We grew up in California and Okinawa, Japan. My father did multiple tours, which afforded us the opportunity to travel all over Asia. I have been to Malaysia, China, Hong Kong, Singapore, Thailand, Japan, and South Korea. I had the joy and privilege to travel throughout Europe after getting married! I have seen a big portion of the world and have learned that it doesn't matter where you live, you can find hope and joy anywhere!

We grew up Catholic and attended church with Father Ducci, from Italy, who was filled with the Spirit and made learning about God and His ways fun and exciting! My earliest memories were going to church with my family, singing, and breaking bread after. I had quite an idyllic childhood.

We moved back to California in 1988 and were stationed in 29 Palms. I was in seventh grade and so excited to be closer to my extended family. My uncles, Tom and Bob, were also stationed in 29 Palms! We often had dinners with all the cousins, aunties, and uncles. Life was full, and peace was great. We went to a little Catholic church on base and sang old hymns. My favorite was "Be Not Afraid." I still sing it to this day.

At that time, I didn't fully understand the words or meaning of the song. I just knew it spoke to me and stayed with me. I felt the power and love of God in these words. I felt safe and protected. I felt hope and encouragement. I believed the promises and I made it my song, singing it to myself whenever I was afraid.

Shortly after placing roots in 29 Palms, my parents decided to buy a house in Cathedral City, California. We moved on a cold and blustery day, rare in our desert. It was February, 1989, and I was in another new school. This wasn't a problem for me. I had grown accustomed to leaving and having to make new friends. I always saw it as an adventure! I thank God for my courageous spirit. It has allowed me to accept change and embrace its challenges. Yet again, I held onto the promise of God: "Be not afraid, I go before you always."

My parent's example of hard work and dedication, added to sacrifice and determination, always included hope and faith in Jesus, and helped my sister and me see the possibilities of a life walking with God. It wasn't always pretty or easy, but quite necessary to overcome the trials and tribulations of life.

Boy, oh boy, was I going to be challenged in my faith. On August 17th, 1990, one day before my 13th birthday, my dad was deployed to Saudi Arabia. The Gulf War had started on August 2nd and our lives were forever going to be changed. The fear that gripped my heart was so intense, almost paralyzing. You see, my dad is a Vietnam vet. If I had listened to the statistics, fear, and doubt, I would have been overcome...

God knew what He was doing when He moved us to the desert. I couldn't see it then, but He was truly going before us. Almost every night we would watch the news and see tanks, explosions, and scud missiles. It wasn't good for us to watch, but it was the only way of knowing what was happening in a land far away. This was a time before the Internet and social media. It was very hard to connect with your loved one. We either waited to get a call (usually with a very bad connection, and very short) or we waited weeks for a letter. They call it snail mail for a reason!

At a certain point, my mom realized it wasn't good for any of us to be glued to the TV, watching the war play out. She did her best to hide her fears and create an easy and light-going atmosphere in our home. She encouraged us to live life, eat good food, and have fun. We ate out A LOT! I'm such a foodie and I think my love for food was established during our travels overseas and during the nine months my dad was gone. *"Oh, taste and see that the LORD is good; Blessed is the man who trusts in Him!"* (Psalm 34:8).

By this point, my mom was back to work. She worked for a pest control company, and her coworker was a believer. She would encourage my mom with the Word of God and was a wonderful support in a great time of need. I was in 8th grade, attending Nellie Coffman Middle School. I was on the drill team and doing my best to manage my fear. I was just beginning to learn the power of prayer and sharing my fears and anxieties with God.

A friend invited me to AWANA. It's an international, nondenominational, Bible-centered youth organization. The acronym

AWANA comes from the first letters of the phrase "Approved workman are not ashamed" (read 2 Timothy 2:15).

Looking back, I was in eighth grade, and this organization is for youth from three years old, through sixth grade. I don't know how, or why...but God!! Those nights were filled with fun and friends and Jesus mixed in. Seeds were being planted and through God's faithfulness, He would send many to water and nurture those seeds.

I was taught that when you're feeling down, doing something nice for someone else will help you feel better. I decided to start a support group to process my feelings and help other students do the same. We shared about our loved ones and helped each other to see the good and be the change.

We also decided to collect canned goods, coffee, candies, and notes to send to the troops. We wanted them to know that they were loved, known, and thought about! I was encouraged in my faith and bolstered in my spirit. It really helped to see the love and support of my peers and it helped me feel good instead of feeling helpless. Knowing that God was with me through it all helped anchor my fears and let me trust in God.

I prayed every day! I wanted my dad home. To my relief and answered prayers, my dad came home in mid-May of 1991! He arrived just in time for the end-of-the-year awards. He saw me receive an award for my support group. I thanked God for His faithfulness.

Little did I know that a song, "Be Not Afraid," would stick with me and ready my faith. At that time I didn't read my Bible much, but those words were living and active promises of God. I didn't know that at the time. All I knew is that they comforted me (that's what God's Word does) and made me feel safe.

This song has carried me through for years and now decades. Every time I want to respond in fear, I remember the lyrics. I sing them out (old-school hymnal way...slow and steady...with power) and my faith holds tight to God's promises.

They have carried me through so much. I wanted to conceive and had a hard time doing so! We finally welcomed our love child, Hunter Frech, on August 30, 2002. I had major surgeries multiple times, chronic autoimmune issues...hello, I'm alive and well. Despite challenges in our marriage...we just celebrated 25 years! Even through frustrations in parenting...Karissa, our firstborn, has been accepted into two Doctoral Physical Therapy (DPT) programs and is interviewing with three more. Hunter is now married to our sweet Sophia, and they all love the Lord. I am typing this from our new home, which is a total gift from God, just like the last three were.

When feeling lost and not knowing my identity...to being rooted in the Word, God birthed a business even through that difficult and lonely season. I've found joy and passion, and I know my purpose. I'm blown away by the faithfulness of God's Word and His promises. *"If we are faithless, He remains faithful; He cannot deny Himself"* (2 Timothy 2:13).

The song, "Be Not Afraid," softened my heart. It helped me let God in, to love and nurture my heart. I willingly accepted Jesus Christ as my Savior at Calvary Church of Cathedral City, California in 1992. I have experienced 30 years of His faithfulness, 30 years of trusting and believing, and 30 years of singing "Be Not Afraid!"

Isn't God good and faithful? He is calling you and patiently waiting for you to respond. He can handle your fears, doubts, concerns, and questions. Life will be full of trials or tribulations, but God walks before you. He will lead the way. He is encouraging you to be not afraid!

My prayer for you:

I give thanks for this day and for the time you are taking to read about my faith. It's my heart's prayer that you would be encouraged by my testimony. If you haven't, invite Jesus into your heart and lay your fears at His feet!

What a great exchange. He'll give you the courage and strength to face a new day and new challenges. You'll experience a love like none another. You'll find your purpose in Him and through Him.

I'll end with my favorite scripture in faith that you will respond to God and start your own faith journey! "*The LORD bless you and keep you; the LORD make His face shine upon you, and be gracious to you; the LORD lift up His countenance upon you, and give you peace*" (Numbers. 6:24-26). Be encouraged and be not afraid!

Be Not Afraid

Day 13: FROM FAITH 2 FAITH

 Bishop Kephyan Sheppard is a native of Palm Springs, California, and is the Pastor of Word of Life Fellowship Center in Desert Hot Springs, California. He has earned a Bachelor's Degree in Biblical Studies, a Master's Degree in Divinity, and a Doctorate in Ministry from Next Dimension University, as well as an Honorary Doctorate in Biblical Studies from Bread of Life Seminary in San Antonio, Texas. Word of Life has served over 6,000 meals to the homeless community under his leadership, impacted thousands of families by providing toys for the holidays, along with school supplies, and established a Bible college in the city of Desert Hot Springs.

Furthermore, Bishop Sheppard is a former Commissioner of the city of Desert Hot Springs, an on-call chaplain to the city's police department, a board member to the city's Microloan Program, an advisor to Desert Hot Springs High School's Black Student Union, and the Community Champion for Advancing Desert Hot Springs.

In addition to his work in the community, Bishop Sheppard is an area representative for the Fellowship of Christian Athletes. He covers five high schools and a middle school in the valley, teaching the Gospel during lunch-period Bible studies.

He also serves as a Professor at the Bread of Life Christian University Theological Seminary, Desert Hot Springs Campus. On July 20, 2019, Dr. Sheppard was consecrated to the office of Bishop in the International Churches of Praise and is a member of the African American Joint College of Bishops.

Moreover, Bishop Sheppard is an accomplished musician. He has been playing the saxophone since the age of eight and has recorded three albums (*Kephyan: Revealed*; *90's Love Songs;* and *Beyond 1 and 2*).

From Faith 2 Faith

"For in it the righteousness of God is revealed from faith to faith; as it is written, 'The just shall live by faith'" (Romans 1:17).

Miracle 1- The Lungs

"The effective, fervent prayer of a righteous man avails much" (James 5:16).

I was born with debilitating asthma. While speaking with my childhood doctor, as an adult, it was revealed that my case of asthma was extremely difficult because it was triggered by allergens. The frustrating thing about the allergens is that at the age of five, I underwent a battery of allergen tests which revealed that I was allergic to nearly everything!

Fast forward a few years, and I was rushed to the hospital via ambulance. I remember tubes attached to my body in every space possible, beeping machines, and a medic yelling, "His oxygen levels are dropping!" I remember being placed inside an incubator, feeling an internal chill that nearly frosted my external body. I recall the look of defeat on the faces of my grandparents (who raised me). One year later, my grandparents' hopeless faces were well founded. A medical report delivered a bleak prognosis.

My grandparents were people of faith, pillars of the church and community. Having already experienced the death of one of their daughters when she was young, they were now facing the possibility of watching their first grandchild die. They prayed. In the hospital surrounding my bubble, they prayed. At home, they prayed. At the church, they prayed. God answered in the form of a young doctor who was familiar with my case. To this day, the miracle is unexplainable, but what God did is known and unforgettable. Within 24 hours, not only was I removed from the incubator but also was discharged! The enemy tried to take my young life, but we serve a God of purpose. My life was preserved because of purpose!

Miracle 2- The Disappointment (Hamstring)

"For I know the thoughts that I think toward you, says the Lord, thoughts of peace and not of evil, to give you a future and a hope" (Jeremiah 29:11, NKJV).

I often teach that disappointment occurs when desires are unmet. That is exactly where I was in the Spring of 2000. I was a multiple-year NCAA All-American sprinter who had just run a qualifying time in the 200-meters for the US Olympic trials. Now, the odds were between slim and nonexistent that I would make the Olympic team. These were the glory years of Team USA, the years of Michael Johnson and Maurice Green. However, the honor of being on the track, coupled with the experience that I felt would prepare me for the next stage, was enough to get me excited.

One would say that my running on the track was metaphorically symbolic of my running from my purpose. Well, I hit a wall. While training for my post-collegiate career, I tore my hamstring. As I rolled around on the track, I knew it was over. I cried for weeks. I sat in dark places and even contemplated suicide. My life as I had planned was over. It was at that moment that I met Jesus. Additionally, it was at that moment that I realized I had been in church my entire life. I knew the church well, but never had a true relationship with Jesus.

I knew from a young age that I was called to the pastorate. I had grown up in the church and saw firsthand the scandal and hurt. I observed how the church and its politics destroyed marriages and families. I witnessed how the church kept children away from their childhoods. I wanted nothing to do with the church!

I cried as He healed more than my hamstring. I worshipped as He restored me. I praised as He equipped me. I left that season proclaiming that MY REDEEMER LIVES!

Miracle 3- The Heartbreak (Mother's Passing)

"The Lord is near to those who have a broken heart, and saves such as have a contrite spirit" (Psalm 34:18, NKJV).

Although my mother did not raise me, during my teenage years she became a prominent figure in my life. This was so much so that in my young adult years, she and I became inseparable. I am truly one of those individuals who can honestly say that my mother was my best friend. She had desires to see me get married and for her to become a grandmother. In 2004, her dream came true. My wife and I were wed and called to let her know while she was at her birthday celebration. To hear the excitement in her voice was worth it all.

My mother had been diagnosed with a rare lung disorder in prior years. But through it all, she pressed. She worked two jobs, sang in the choir, and held her household together, all while being bound to oxygen tanks 24 hours a day. She was a model of resilience. Often, we would watch her smile and cook, even while she struggled to catch what appeared to be her last breaths. My mother was called home a short time later. Although I had the honor to spend much of her final days with her, her passing knocked the wind out of me. We knew the prognosis. We understood her time was limited, but the pain was surreal. In my darkest hour, when I was inconsolable, the Lord was close! I am grateful that He is faithful.

Miracle 4- The Healing Part 1

"...For I am the Lord who heals you" (Exodus 15:26, NKJV).

I finally found my bride! The woman that I am certain God fashioned for me entered my life and I wasted no time. As previously stated, I was excited to even let my mother know that we were married. However, all that elation and excitement came to a screeching halt when my wife developed a mass on her neck. We frantically searched for a doctor who could explain the mass, and finally, we ended up at a hospital in Los Angeles. After several biopsies, they determined that she had developed lymphatic cancer. Obviously shellshocked and concerned, we immediately began discussing treatment options and were told that if she didn't start rounds of chemotherapy immediately, this condition could become fatal. Being newlyweds, we rushed into the treatment. However, after a few rounds, my wife explained that she could no longer continue the treatments. We then decided we would stand on the Word of God.

The next few months were filled with moments of anxiety. From a husband's perspective, I had fears and concerns that my beautiful newlywed bride could be taken from me. We had a son, and it was tough to even discuss the prospect of what could happen. Nevertheless, we pushed forward in faith led by the courageous spirit of my wife.

In addition to prayer, we began researching homeopathic treatments and natural remedies. While we are not certain of the "how" we do know the "what!" God healed my wife's body. There is no other way to explain it. The doctors that she had previously seen had no answer! Even at her 12-year check-up, they were unable to detect any cancerous cells in her body. I believe that this trial, the mass, was sent to push us further into our destiny together.

Miracle 5- The Unexpected Gift

"And let us not grow weary while doing good, for in due season we shall reap if we do not lose heart" (Galatians 6:9, NKJV).

For seven years we desired a baby. A few years into our marriage my mother passed away. It was painful to realize we were unable to give her that grandchild she craved. However, we still had the desire to have a child together. We began to seek medical opinions and advice after several years of trying...to no avail. We were told that we were compatible, but the window of opportunity had closed; therefore, we should consider adoption. We were also told, because of the chemotherapy, my wife would be unable to reproduce. Feeling defeated and overcome with grief, we began to look into adoption agencies. But every time we scheduled a meeting with an adoption agency, we argued in the parking lot. One Sunday at church a man of God laid hands on us and let us know that my wife would give birth. From that point on, our faith was restored and renewed, to the point where we went and bought a gender-neutral onesie to bring the miracle baby home in from the hospital. Fast forward 7 years, August 11, 2009. Our baby girl was born, against all odds healthy and strong!!! It wasn't our timing, but God's. To those waiting on a promise, DUE season is on the way!

Miracle 6- The Healing Part 2

"Bearing with one another, and forgiving one another, if anyone has a complaint against another; even as Christ forgave you, so you also must do" (Colossians 3:13, NKJV).

I grew up without a relationship with my biological father. I was raised by my grandparents. I'm so grateful that my grandfather molded me into the man that I am today. For years I had resentment towards my biological father because I knew that he lived in the area and had a family. In middle school, I discovered I had a sister from his marriage. Years later I discovered I had two younger sisters as well. After high school, I made it a point to find him and build a relationship. I was told that he was a chef at one of the major casinos in Las Vegas. So, I moved to Las Vegas after my collegiate track and field career ended. Months passed, and I was told he left Vegas and moved to Miami, Florida. I was crushed, but the anger overwhelmed the heartbreak.

Fast forward several years later, I am now a happily married man, and I am traveling on the road to a weekend getaway with my wife. My phone rang from a number that I did not recognize with a Miami area code. I answered, and the voice on the other side of the phone was that of my father. His words were, "Son, it's your dad, I know you don't know me…but I need you." As we conversed, he disclosed that he was dealing with a rare form of cancer. He needed to move back to California because his wife had left him, and he was homeless in Miami. Without question, I went into action. We located and furnished an apartment for him. We set up specific doctors, so forth, and so on. But after his return to California, he vanished once again. Eventually, he invited me to lunch to clear the air. We met at a local Applebee's and over lunch discussed life. The things that he said and the things that he shared hurt me to the core, but by the grace of God, I was able to keep my composure.

Some years later he would make that call once again, letting me know that he needed me. This time he was dying. I slept with him in the hospital, and we shared laughter. He told me about his life growing up, and how much I reminded him of his younger self. He told me he loved me and that he was proud of me. There is something about the affirming words of a father and the healing those words promote. He apologized. At that moment, I made the decision to forgive him, because at that moment I was reminded of all the times that I stood in need of forgiveness. Today, I am grateful that although he's no longer with us, our relationship was salvaged. I am appreciative of the fact that I was able to share the Gospel with him before he left this earth. I am grateful to know that my father loved me.

Miracle 7- The Launch

In November 2011, we were in flux. We realized our season had ended at the ministry where we'd served for years, and it felt like we were in the wilderness experience. We tried to attend several ministries, and God would not let us get comfortable with any of them. It was in the middle of December of that same year that God spoke to us and told us it was time to plant a ministry in the city of Desert Hot Springs. If you know anything about the Coachella Valley, you know the reputation of the city of Desert Hot Springs. Reminiscent of Jonah, I did everything I could to plant a ministry in any other city except for the one to where He'd assigned us. However, obedience has its rewards. It is through obedience that we can experience the hand of God in our endeavors.

What began as a living room ministry with six adults and a few children, evolved into a ministry that has impacted the region, growing tremendously, and pointing many souls to Christ. After our living room, we transitioned to the senior center, worshipped in storefronts, and even at least a couple of properties.

Next week, our ministry will officially celebrate 10 years. In that period, God saw fit to grace us by allowing us to purchase our own property with three acres of land attached to it. This miracle speaks to obedience and faith.

As previously mentioned, Desert Hot Springs is not the most desirable place to serve in the Coachella Valley. I'm reminded of the scripture that asked, "Can anything good come out of Nazareth?" when they were told that's from where Jesus would come. I reflect on that scripture and smile because we are living proof that God can do something great during seasons of chaos and turmoil. Whatever your assignment is, even if it's uncomfortable, please understand God is in the midst of it.

Miracle 8 – The Healing Part 3

I am HEALED!

The Apostle Paul mentioned a thorn in his flesh to the church in Corinth. In the writing, he wants us to focus on the grace of God to sustain us even while dealing with thorns in our lives. For years, I've dealt with a physical thorn. Coupled with my asthma, I have also developed a sinus issue. The sinus issue made it impossible to pass air through my nostrils for nearly six years. Yes, for six years, not only could I not breathe at 100% capacity, but I was unable to pass oxygen through my nose at all. The miracle in that is for six years I preached every Sunday, recorded two albums on saxophone, and lived a life that did not appear to show an ailment at all.

After several surgeries that seemingly did nothing to resolve the issue, I was referred to a specialist. The specialist had an interesting last name… Church. We discussed my situation and the previous surgeries. Then he looked me in the eye and said, "We are going to get this corrected. It's a miracle that you've been able to function at a high capacity with these issues." For the first time, I went into surgery without any anxiety. The peace of God literally had overtaken me. I remember joking around before anesthesia was administered, watching the doctor come in and grab everyone by the hand for prayer. I remember the presence of God in prayer. As I slept, the Lord used that doctor's hands to successfully remedy the issue I suffered with for over six years.

Post-surgery, I opened my eyes and of course, I was hungry, but I was grateful because I was able to breathe. I was excited to know that I would be able to have a sense of smell again, and I was all smiles.

Weeks later I sat back and reflected on the healing journey. Tears rolled down my face. While many think the miracle was simply a successful surgery, I began to praise God for the miracle of sustaining me while medically I shouldn't have been sustained at all.

Miracle 9 – The Assignment

"It is good for me that I have been afflicted, that I may learn Your statutes" (Psalm 119:71, NKJV).

In Late February 2021, Covid-19 touched our family. I remember the fatigue I felt, and I assumed the lung issues were merely seasonal asthma issues. Valentine's Day after service, I was told that I didn't look healthy. The next day I went to urgent care and shockingly collapsed. Somehow, they were able to lift my large frame and seat me against the wall until the paramedics arrived. Upon arrival, they informed me that I needed to be rushed to the emergency room immediately. The trip in the ambulance was filled with anxiety. I must be honest with you and tell you that I wasn't sure what was going on. I couldn't breathe, and I felt like I was losing consciousness by the minute.

After reaching the emergency room, they ran a battery of tests. They discovered that I had Covid-19 coupled with double pneumonia. The doctor informed me that it didn't look promising, and while trying to be strong, I was told to make a phone call to my wife that I never thought I would have to make. I was told that I would be there for nearly a week, and the first night was critical as it would determine if I would need a ventilator for the remainder of my stay. I don't remember much about my surroundings, but I do recall asking for the television to remain off and the phone to be unplugged. I knew that this would be a time of intense prayer.

Something amazing happened the first night. While I was praying for healing, God was giving me an assignment although I didn't understand it at first. Then the Holy Spirit helped me realize because God was giving me an assignment, healing had already been completed. On the second and third nights, I began to rejoice and write, because He truly was speaking. That time in the hospital allowed me to hear clearly, without distraction, the voice of God concerning the next phase of my assignment. Although I was extremely uncomfortable and, in some pain, I was still at peace because I knew He was there with me.

Here's the miracle. I was at home with six months of oxygen supply, because patients that had the type of case that I had usually needed six months of oxygen support before they could start to move around freely. But God! On the third day, I removed the oxygen mask and was able to walk outside. To this day, the nursing staff continues to marvel at the fact that after one week we were able to call the oxygen supply company and ask them to retrieve their equipment. DON'T TELL ME WHAT GOD CAN'T DO!

My prayer for you:

Heavenly Father, I thank you for every mountain and trial that You've allowed me to overcome. It's because of Your hand in my life that I can share these testimonies of miracles and victories. I pray that the words that I have shared will be an encouragement to all who read them, an encouragement to keep the faith.

Regardless of what they go through and how unfair life can seemingly be if they just keep their FAITH in You, they too can be victorious. Father, show them that You are the God who heals, restores, and beyond.

I pray this in Your darling Son Jesus' name, Amen.

Day 14: DARE TO BELIEVE

Pastor Crystal Mance is a daughter of the King, life coach, mentor, teacher, preacher, conference speaker, project manager, entrepreneur, and accomplished author writing her first debut non-fiction book entitled *R.E.S.E.T.: Releasing Every Situation Encourages Transformation.*

Crystal is an Executive Assistant/Project Manager at the University of Pennsylvania. She has a Master's Degree in Life Coaching and Biblical Counseling from Integrity Bible Institute.

She is a passionate and fun-loving woman of God who loves connecting with people and sharing nuggets from her life experiences. She is an encourager and enjoys seeing the Lord transform the lives and hearts of people through her transparency. Crystal has ministered to women around the world and challenges others to embrace who they are in Christ and fulfill their earthly life purpose. She has been married to her husband, Darryl, for 10 years and is the mother of two adult children. She is also Godmom to many.

For more information and to book speaking engagements or life coaching sessions, please submit all inquiries to Crystal Mance at resetexecconsulting@gmail.com

It's 2022 and here we go again, taking a leap of faith in the one true and living God. When I think about it, my entire journey has been a faith walk. It's been one of standing on the promises of God and standing firm in what I know and believe our God to do and be. He has never failed, He has never let me down, and He's always been by my side.

Since I was a young girl growing up in the Church of God in Christ, I remember hearing the Word of God and thinking about God deeply. I want to know Him. Little did I know, not only would I get to know Him, but I would get the opportunity to grow in Him, and also grow in my relationship with Him. Hebrews 11:1-2 (Amplified Bible) reminds us; *"Now faith is the assurance (title deed, confirmation) of things hoped for (divinely guaranteed), and the evidence of things not seen [the conviction of their reality—faith comprehends as fact what cannot be experienced by the physical senses]. For by this [kind of] faith the [a]men of old gained [divine] approval."* As I process this passage of text, I see my life and faith walk on full display. For years, I believed God to continue to manifest miracles in my life and in the lives of my family members. As I write this chapter, I see the hand of God in every area of my family's lives.

As I continue to grow in the Lord, my faith and relationship with Him grow. Even in times of fear, I hold firm on my faith in God and His promises for His children. To be honest, I am somewhat of a literalist. I'm determined to believe the Word of the Lord and how it applies to His children. So where did it all start? How did I get here, and why is my faith in the Lord so strong? I'm glad you asked.

What does faith look like to me? As I said previously, I remember believing God for some great things even at a young age. While my relationship with Christ was certainly not where it is now, I have no doubt that it was the Lord who brought me through to this place. As I continue to grow from faith to faith and glory to glory in the Lord, my faith continues to strengthen and is at times unwavering. God continues to use my life's journey to show others that He is real, He is faithful, and He is a loving God who is still very interested in blessing His children.

In 2007, while in worship service at the F.O.R.T. as the pastor was preaching, I clearly heard the Lord say it's time to go home. Now in my mind, I thought, "Yes Lord, I'm going home as soon as the service is over." But that is not what the Lord was referring to. You see, Pastor Hollmon was preaching from Deuteronomy 6:8; "You've Been Here Long Enough."

While I was listening to the message, it never dawned on me that God was telling me I had to move back to Philly. As I was driving home, the Lord said, "Not to your home here, but it's time to move back to Philly." Now at that time, Philly was the very last place I wanted to be. I moved to Houston with my son in 1993 and made it my home. So, when I heard the Lord's instructions I thought, surely, He couldn't be telling me to go back, and if so, why?

Going back to Philly meant I had to quit my job and find a new one, find a place to live, and a new church. Well, as I'm sure you're aware, God doesn't give you all details of the assignment. He just expects us to obey His instructions and get moving. After a time of prayer and fasting, I began packing and asking God, "Did I hear You clearly? Am I moving according to Your will, and in Your season?" Only for the Father to come back and tell me, "Yes," time after time again.

At some point, my faith began to kick in. I knew I couldn't rely on a man to give me the answers. What I wanted and for which I had been searching could only be found in God and in my obedience to Him. So, in faith and with my Sista-friend, I packed up, rented a moving truck, and headed back to Philly! I rented a Penske truck and took that long 26-hour drive back. With my faith in tow, we traveled the highways and made our way back. I tell you; I was afraid, nervous, and not sure about anything other than the instructions the Lord had given me.

Wait, let me go back a bit. During my time of praying and fasting, I told the Lord, "If this is You leading me back, then please make it clear. Where will I live and work? What church will I go to, and how will all of this come to pass?" I had to learn that God doesn't lay out the full plan, so we don't get ahead of Him. He gives us a nugget of what we need to get us moving forward.

The Lord gave me specific instructions, and I followed them to the letter. He instructed me to call a girlfriend of mine who lived in her home by herself in Norristown. He said, "Call her. Tell her you are coming back and need a place to stay. She will say yes." By faith, I made the call and she immediately said, "Yes."

Back in Houston during my time of praying and fasting, God told me that I would have everything I need, and everything was already in place. I had to move by faith in the season that was in front of me. Not in the season to come, but in the now season by faith in Christ. But I digress.

While I didn't understand God's plan and was afraid to follow what the Spirit of the Lord placed on my heart, I dared to believe that God would do and had already done just what He said. So, as I said, God provided a safe place for me to stay. Shortly after my arrival, He led me to my church home, and right after that I got a new job making more money than I've ever made in my life. It was by faith that I met my husband and purchased my first home.

By faith, I had to be obedient to the Father and know that it was His voice that I was following. It was by the leading of the Holy Spirit that I moved back to Philly, to grow for His glory and to serve in His Kingdom. I know it can be scary at times, but what do you have to lose? The Father already knows your beginning from the end. He knows the plans He has for you. So why not trust Him, why not step out on faith? There's absolutely no failure in God, and I'm here to tell you He has not failed me once. I've messed up and didn't obey Him plenty of times but bless God for His grace and mercy that allowed me to get up and try again.

As I write my chapter, my husband and I are now in a new season of 'Dare to Believe,' as God, through the leading of Holy Spirit, moves us to Atlanta. With so much on the table in my natural eye, God is yet still opening doors, creating opportunities, and making ways. He continues to grant us favor that surrounds us like a shield. We 'Dare to Believe' that God is not a man that He should lie, nor the son of man that He should repent. He is faithful, true, and holy.

Now again, I must be honest that after being in Philly for 15 years, I've watched God do many miraculous things in the hearts and lives of His children. Yet so many people still don't believe Him, believe that His word is true, nor believe that He truly is an awesome and amazing God. I 'Dare to Believe' that God uses us as examples in the earth to show others of His goodness, His love, His unmerited favor, and the blessings He has for His children. While they may look so very different for each of us, we are very clear that it is only God.

So let me go back a bit further. In 2007, when I arrived back in Philly, I began to see the manifestation of God's promises. Everything I dared to believe God for began to unfold right before my very eyes and in my heart. The Lord was establishing a deeper relationship with me. I was hungry and desired to go deeper in Him. Even my understanding of the Father and His Word began to explode in my heart.

When I returned to Philly, I returned to my hometown, where I grew up. So, it wasn't like I'd never been there before. It was a familiar place and home for much of my extended family on my paternal and maternal sides of the family. Yet God chose to bring me back. I remember crying to God, "Why am I here? Why do I feel so alone, and what are You doing?" As I visited different places, trying to reacquaint myself with the city, I felt like I had never been or even lived here before. I remember crying out to God, "I feel so alone, and no one is here with me!" In His still soft voice, I hear, "I am here. I am with you. You are covered." I cried for hours after hearing the love and comfort of the Spirit of the Lord in my heart.

After hearing the Lord's voice in my heart, I began to move forward in Him, wherever He led me. While the road before me was a bit blurry with my limited eyesight and vision, I dared to believe that the same God who spoke to my heart, would cover and keep us safe during our 26-hour drive. He is the same God who knows and has plans for my life, plans to prosper me, not harm me, and to give me a hope and a future.

When I was a little girl, we used to come up with crazy ideas and then say, "I dare you to do this or that." We would then say something like, "I dee double dog dare you," to add sauce to it. That was almost like the challenge to do the thing, only to get caught, get in trouble, and even sometimes get away with it. Back then, I was bold and tenacious and would just do the thing without even thinking. I was always the one to go for the challenge and get caught or get in trouble. As I got older, I would shrink back from that boldness, and be more concerned about what others would think or say. Isn't it amazing how God puts things before us and swings the door of blessings and opportunity wide open and yet we shrink back because we are worried about what others will say or think? The boldness I had as a child had all but withered away into oblivion. But as I spend time with the Father reading His word, I get filled with boldness, strength, and vigor. I stand boldly for the Lord and share about His goodness, grace, and mercy, which is available to all.

Little did I know that a daring little girl would grow up to be a daring woman of God and daughter of the King, who isn't afraid to step out on what the Lord lays on her heart. She dares to believe that if God said it, He will certainly do it and complete a thing.

I also had to learn that as God is leading me to the promise, tests and trials will also come along to try to distract, discourage, and get me off course. They are sent to redirect my focus from what's in front of me to what's around me and what's happening to me at that very moment. But

I've learned that no matter how big the storm is, I must keep my focus and my eyes on Jesus, who is calm in the midst of the storm. I've learned that there is victory in speaking to the wind, waves, the noise of the storm, and those things swirling around. I keep my eyes fixed on Him.

Many years ago, a movie called *Tornado* came out at the movie theater. The movie was about a team of people who chased tornadoes so they could understand them, determine from where they came, how they were created, etc. In the latter part of the movie, a big storm hits the area where they were. As they were rushing to find shelter or safe passage, one of the team members happened to look up into the eye of the tornado. There they noticed the sun, a beautiful blue sky, and birds, but the circumference of the storm was a swirl of destruction, filth, dirt, and loss. You see, daring to believe the promises of God and see them manifest in your life doesn't mean you won't have problems, tests, and trials. As a matter of fact, He says in John 16:33 (Amplified Bible), *"I have told you these things, so that in Me you may have [perfect] peace. In the world you have tribulation and distress and suffering, but be courageous [be confident, be undaunted, be filled with joy]; I have overcome the world." [My conquest is accomplished, my victory abiding]."*

So, you see Jesus already knew that we would have tornados, trials, tribulations, and distress in our lives, but we should be encouraged that He's got it all under control. Having this assurance from Christ, we should live in perfect peace, and dare to believe in the Father as well as His blessings for our life. Keep your focus on the eye of the storm where the peace of God rests, rules, and abides, and allow the Father to bless you in that space.

Now let me be clear, it took me a minute to get to this season of my life and I no longer need someone to dee-doubled-dog dare me to continue. I am determined to believe that God is always with us, and He will never leave my side. To get to this place of 'Dare to Believe' faith in the Father, I had to lean in and be consistent with reading His Word and spending time with Him. I had to learn to trust that God's way is the best way and that He is always on point with His plan for my life.

In 2007, as I was packing up my place, crying, still fighting through the negative thoughts, and wondering if I was really hearing from God, I walked over to the large mirror in my bathroom. I remember saying to the Lord, "Here are my hands, I'm going to take Your hands as you lead me to where You're taking me. I ask that you please never let go of my hands." A very strong presence of the Lord came over me and God has kept His word in doing just that. As we took that journey, praising the Lord all the way back to Philly, God was with us. I felt His hand guiding us all the way.

All my life God has been and continues to be so very faithful to me and my family. The love and blessings of God continue to encamp round about us. God's goodness and mercy continue to follow us and be with us all every day, and we see evidence of it all around us. God's blessings and faithfulness are not just for us, they are for others to see as well. The blessings and love of God don't just affect the recipients of His blessings, but they flow down to others. Others then get to experience Him as well. As a result, others begin to believe, see, and want to know how we did this or that. We quickly reply, "It's only the goodness of God and His promises towards those who believe in and love Him." Resting in the love and grace of God pushes me to 'Dare to Believe' that God will continue to keep His Word towards us.

So, as I write this nugget my husband and I continue 'Dare to Believe' in what God has assigned for us to do as He relocates us to Atlanta. He is opening doors of opportunity and blessings. When the Lord laid the move on my husband's heart, I had so many questions, concerns, worries, and maybe even a few doubts. But God took my heart and mind back to

2007 when He relocated me from Houston to Philly. He reminded me that He was with me then and is with us now. He comforts my heart to 'Dare to Believe' everything, and I mean everything, has already been worked out. Even as I write this, the favor and blessings of God continue to unfold right before our very eyes. So many things are moving. Relationships are being healed, and others are seeing and hearing about the manifestation and blessings of the Lord through our testimony. We 'Dare to Believe' that God has great plans for us in Atlanta. Our path and plans have already been laid out by a wonderful and awesome God who loves us very much. As we continue to pack up this home in preparation for our new home, new land, new season, new relationships, and all God has for us, we stand strong on our foundation and 'Dare to Believe.'

Tornados, tests, trials, tribulations, and distractions come to get us off course. Yet, my husband reminds me, "Babe, that's God's business. We must continue to stand on our faith and 'Dare to Believe' that He saw this coming, and this too shall pass." We are determined to continue to be a witness for the Father, as we continue to 'Dare to Believe' Him for every season of our lives. The past two years have been extremely hard for so many people around the world. However, in the midst of it all, we must still 'Dare to Believe' that God is in full and in complete control. The Father knew the pandemic would come and go at some point. But during it all, when the infectious cases were high and so many people were getting sick or even passing away, God was still with us, leading and guiding us through.

I challenge you to 'Dare to Believe' in the one, true, and living God. He is the God who never goes back on His promises, never goes back on His Word, and is always with us every step of the way as we journey through this life. I challenge you to open your heart and 'Dare to Believe' Him for whatever you feel He's placed on your heart and watch Him do it.

I need you to know He's not a genie in a bottle that you just tell Him what you want. You must put in the work with prayer, fasting, reading His Word, and being obedient to what He tells you to do when He tells you to do it. Daring to believe doesn't mean you're waiting for others to validate what God told you to do; it means trusting Him to know He knows the plans for your life. He knew you and loved you before the foundation of the world. If you'll just 'Dare to Believe' His blessing and promises apply to you as well, they will manifest.

I'm not going to dee-double-dog dare you, but I ask that you open your heart to believe that God is real, Jesus died for your sins, and the Holy Spirit is with you everywhere you go. I challenge you to allow the Lord to transform your heart and mind as you begin to 'Dare to Believe Him' for whatever He lays on your heart and watch Him move.

My prayer for you:

As I close, I ask you to recite this prayer with me: "Father, in Jesus' name, I invite You into my heart to transform it with Your love, peace, and healing. Teach me how to let go and trust You and the plans You have for my life. While I don't understand, and I can't see where You're taking me, I desire to 'Dare to Believe' that You only want the absolute best for me. So, help me to be consistent with You, to focus on You, and to keep You first in every area of my life.

Father, there are so many distractions and things that get me off course. Lord, I desire to stand on Your Word and believe in Your promises. Help me to only believe in You and not fall for the distractions, the nay-sayers, and lies of the enemy. You are the Great I Am, the one true and living God, and I desire to stand boldly on my faith and 'Dare to Believe' You and Your Word.

Thank You for walking with me on this journey and even when I mess up, help me not to focus on where or how I messed up, but to remember that Your grace and mercy are with me always. Father, I love You! Today, I open my heart to hear You as the Holy Spirit leads and guides me to 'Dare to Believe' and trust in the plans You have for me and my family.

I pray and ask these and all things in the blessed name of Christ Jesus my Lord, Amen.

Day 15: A PUNCH IN THE FAITH

Glennette Jermaine Brown is a mother of three, Bernard Jr., Nicholas, and Anna Nicole, and also the grandmother of Makayla. She was born and raised in Philadelphia, Pennsylvania, and currently resides in Southern Florida.

The Lord Jesus became her Christ and King at the age of 16, as she confessed the Lord Jesus with her mouth and believed within her heart that the Lord God raised the Lord Jesus from the dead. She was filled and sealed with the power of the Holy Spirit and is a learning, serving, teaching, and thankful disciple of Christ. Glennette is both a licensed and ordained Evangelist (2003) and Minister (2011). Glennette loves her devotion time with the Lord, time spent with her family, serving the community, cooking, writing, sharing laughter, and exploring the natural landscape. Secularly, she works in finance for nonprofits and ministerially serves as the administrative assistant to the senior pastor of St. John Missionary Baptist Church, one of the oldest and largest African American churches in Palm Beach County.

She is a product of Glenn and Geneva Squire's imperfect and beautifully blended family, and one of 14 siblings. Her brothers are MacCurly, Charles, Julius, Pernell, Terry, and Adam. Her sisters are Rodella, Deborah, Cheryl, Vanessa, Juanita, Edwenia, and Leslie. She is the youngest and eighth daughter, her parent's new beginning.

She is also a product of seeds sown of faith, hope, love, joy, generosity, kindness, truth, laughter, and perseverance. These seeds were planted and began to germinate within her, long before she knew she had them or needed them. The Lord is so good. It is a refreshing perspective for her to have learned and come to understand how our dearest Heavenly Father, the Lord Jesus, and the Holy Spirit have predestined strategies for each of us to sow seeds of faith, defend our faith, and offend the enemy of our faith, in and by our faith in Jesus.

As I reflect on my life to date, I wonder from where all this fight stemmed. Absolutely, yes, it is through the testimony, power, and examples of faith through the Lord Jesus and His Word. He is the Living Word! This empowered fight for faith also stems from examples of people who've sown seeds of faith every day. I am directly connected to people like that, and I'd like to share how the Lord used them to lead me to love, learn, and lean my life godward.

My mother is a wife, grandmother, great-grandmother, auntie, former dietitian's assistant, 1st lady emeritus, singer, and super stylish woman of God. She is embattled with Alzheimer's now, but I am super convinced that although she may not be able to speak when she sees me...she knows me... "Glennette, my baby." Those were the last words she spoke to me before becoming non-verbal. I am also super convinced that Jesus knows, and still cares for her. It doesn't matter what science or society says. My faith in Mom is unwavering. I trust God. Do you know why? Because we are still connected. She is and will always be my dearest love, the wonderful woman who gave me life, love, and lessons.

My mother, who unwittingly shared with me her courageousness, her dimples, her smile, her tone of voice, and her love for cooking, creating, and writing, is the Lady Geneva Squire, affectionately called, "Muh." It was my Muh whom the Lord, in His abundant kindness and forethought, used to plant the seed of intimacy with Him in me, especially in the kitchen. Thank You, Jesus!

As a child, I remember playing spaceship (my head is always in or above the clouds) under the kitchen table or rolling the throwaway dough from Muh's homemade pie crust as she was stewing, sautéing, mixing, sprinkling, baking, frying, roasting, and creating delectably delicious food, cakes, and pies for her family, friends, and whoever else was blessed to place their fork from her plate to their mouths.

Muh was always welcoming me into her space. Although I would be in her way, she never shooed, hurried, or pushed me away. Wow, the patience she had with me! I need to make a note of that.

But, most of all, I remember the tears flowing down my mother's beautiful brown, trembling cheeks with deeply soulful, soft-sounding unintelligible utterances emanating from her heart, while the harmonious voices of gospel singers wafted through the air. Their melody filled our home with polyphonic affirmations of Jesus' knowing, caring, understanding, and fixing it. I had no idea what Muh was saying or why she cried. Now I know and completely understand that she and Jesus were having a private conversation. Everything she needed, He already knew, was present with her, and willing and able to see her through. I hold to that, even in her present state. The words of the old song, "For Jesus remembers when others forget," ring true.

Now, each time I enter my kitchen, my secret place, especially when I encounter a circumstance, the Holy Spirit reminds me of what God's Word says. He recalls the memory of how Muh demonstrated how to defend against a punch in her faith.

Yes, I, too, proclaim Jesus to the circumstance while I am talking to Jesus about the circumstance. Sometimes I do so through tears, sometimes with laughter, but always in and with the offensive weapon of faith, coupled with what I know. What do I know?

I know Jesus knows. I know Jesus is present, I know that Jesus already has the defeat strategy. I know that fear and faith cannot dwell in the same place. I know that I do not employ or house fear, doubt, or worry. I know that a stance of belief in God's written Word worries worry, and makes doubt fear. I know God wins. I know God will bring us through. I know Jesus has a purpose for everything, and I should be giving thanks and thinking on things that are lovely, honest, pure, praiseworthy, and good reports. I know that it is my duty to do my part, by praying, planning, and being flexible to God's master plan. I also know that sometimes I punch in my own faith. Yes, sometimes the issue is you. Pray through that!

My daddy, the late Overseer Glenn J. Squire, was my first love, teacher, and disciplinarian. He is the one whom God chose to lead me to the munificent and magnificent love of Jesus. He's also the one whom God chose to plant the seed of faith in Jesus within me. That seed is growing, grooming, and guiding me in life's walk of faith with Jesus.

The Lord Jesus used my daddy to also sow seeds of ministry in my heart. Yes, he was a pastor, preacher, prophet, and teacher, but most remarkably, Daddy exposed me to ministry outside of the four walls. Daddy reflected Jesus to people by serving as the block captain and beautifying the community, in meetings, and by encouraging home ownership. He impacted police clergy, BBQing ribs and chicken outside of the church, playing checkers in the park, eating breakfast at a local eatery (where his picture is still on the wall), "canning" on his walks (picking up aluminum cans for recycling), and bringing unity within his family and in the church's kitchen by feeding any and everyone who came into the dining room. It was a space lovingly termed, "The Beanery." I mean the beans, chicken or pork, rice, and whatever God supplied smelled so good.

The postal workers, city workers, and passersby would come in and sit side-by-side to enjoy a bowl or a plate of food along with a song and some kind words from God's Word from the heart and mouth of this man. He was and is still affectionately called, "Reb" or the "Porch Pastor."

Reb counseled many at the dining room table over coffee or while relaxing on the front porch of our home. He laid hands on them and prayed with them through their circumstance. Their status didn't matter, they were people…White, Black, Asian, Latino, Hispanic, rich, poor, full, hungry, addicted, newly cleaned, troubled, hurt, in spiritual turmoil, or even lost.

Oh! The praise reports! "Reb, they dismissed my case!" "Reb, I got the job!" "Reb, I'm clean, and I've been clean for 10 months!" "Reb, I am healed!" "Reb can you marry us!" Some joined the church. Some joined other churches. Some never joined a church but would always stop by and pay homage to Reb.

People would donate money, clothing, and food. Oh, and they'd also donate bags, upon bags, of aluminum cans! Sidebar: the generous can drop-offs were not, I repeat, were not my favorite part, but the lessons gleaned of reciprocity and appreciation shown were well received. His presence in the community is truly missed. My daddy taught me without words, how to perfect your gift, whether you have a little or lot, entrust it back to God, and be a blessing to others by sowing the seeds you were given to sow. Love others no matter what, trusting Jesus. Stand on His Word to defend and offend each punch in the faith! Sing Daddy, "Whisper a prayer in the morning, whisper a prayer at noon, whisper a prayer in the evening to keep your heart in tune."

My prayer for you:

Dearest Heavenly Father, Glory is Thy Name! I love You and I am so grateful to You for Your many blessings and acts of kindness. I am so grateful to You for Your Holy Word and the power of Your Word. I speak, Lord. I sing, Lord. I pray, Lord Jesus, Your Word over my life, the lives of my children, my family, my community, my neighbor, and whomever You lead to read this prayer. Thank you, Jesus, for bringing laughter into my soul. Thank You, Lord, for each seed planted within me. Thank You for Your Holy Word that filters and uproots any negative, ungodly, weed seed that would desire to grow in place of complete trust and obedience to You. Thank You Lord Jesus for health and walking with me through hard things and bringing me into my promise. *"Even when I walk through the valley dark of death, I'm not afraid of any evil, because You are right there with me; Your rod and Your staff protect me"* (Psalm 23:4, Free Bible Version). Thank You for Your trustworthiness. *"Those who live under the protection of the Most High are kept safe by the Almighty"* (Psalm 91:1, Free Bible Version). Thank You for being my safe place. *"Like a loving father, The Lord is kind and compassionate to those who follow Him. For He knows how we are made; He remembers we are only dust"* (Psalm 103:13-14, Free Bible Version). Thank You for knowing me. Thank You for Your gentleness with me. Thank you, Lord Jesus, for helping me fight the good fight of faith with praise before the manifested response to my request.

Lord Jesus, I give back to You every gift You have placed inside me. Guide me in how to grow, multiply, and trade my talents for Your glory and the growth of the Kingdom. Guide me to be an example of love and faith to those to whom You have called me to be an example of how to defend against a punch in the faith too! Lord Jesus, let my heart and mind be open and focused on Your wants so that the light of Your Kingdom will allow those in dark places to catch a glimpse of You and cause an unquenchable desire for You to be ignited within them. Lord, to You I entrust these words, these gifts, and these people. Thank You! I love You! In Your wonderful name I pray. Amen!

Day 16: FAITH STEPS

Kirk and Adrienne Williams have been married for nearly 23 years, and have four beautiful children (Jasmine - 31, Dante - 28, Kira - 17, and Caleb 15). After meeting in college at the Indiana University of Pennsylvania, they were married and moved to Las Vegas, Nevada in 2000.

While raising their children, Adrienne obtained her Master of Clinical Speech Pathology, and eventually founded Let's Talk! Therapy Center, a multi-disciplinary clinic that provides speech, physical, occupational, and Applied Behavior Analysis (ABA) services to pediatric and adult patients. Let's Talk! Therapy Center has two locations and over 40 employees. Under Adrienne's leadership and vision, it is recognized as one of the best pediatric therapy companies in the state of Nevada.

A native of Las Vegas, Kirk worked in the college access industry for 14 years and became a national speaker and author with his first book, *College Path*, being published in 2005. An entrepreneur at heart, Kirk created several companies, including TWG Consulting, the LIVE INSPIRED brand, ACCESS College & Career Fairs, and most recently, Inspired Life Memorials & Cremations. Kirk and Adrienne are faithful members of Church Las Vegas (LV) with Pastors Benny & Wendy Perez, and have served as leaders of the Marriage & Family Small Group Ministry for over 10 years.

HER Story – Adrienne:

Adrienne's faith definition: Simply put, taking God at His Word. How? Faith comes by hearing and hearing by the Word of God. People often speak about taking leaps of faith. What looks like giant leaps often begin with a baby step. To help you appreciate where I am, I must show you where I have been.

At the age of 14, at a youth camp, I decided to follow God for myself. It was there, at youth camp, that I first encountered the presence of God. Months later, I began high school. In this new world, I made several new friends. None of the friends with whom I engaged at school were involved in my church nor walking with the Lord. I soon discovered that it was a difficult walk, to walk alone.

Fast forward to senior year. I found myself pregnant, lonely, rejected, and dejected. I was 17 years old; still, only a child turned suddenly into an adult.

Rumors have a way of spreading fast. However, in a small town, they spread like wildfire. Before I knew what was happening or even knew what to do, rumors of my pregnancy spread throughout town, which eventually led to my mother finding out about it in church. Her anger, hurt, and embarrassment now infiltrated our every interaction.

By the age of 20, I had two children and an extremely dysfunctional, ungodly relationship. I had totally walked away from God.

One day while working, a high school friend informed me that one of our former high school classmates had returned from college and was now saved and wanted to invite some friends to a Bible study. I accepted the invitation partially because I wanted to be there, and (quite honestly) because it gave me an excuse to have a babysitter who didn't come often. Much to my surprise, just as Jesus met me at the youth camp at the age of 14, He met me at Bible study at the age of 23. I gave my life back to the Lord.

During these weekly Bible studies, Dara would often invite other college friends from Pennsylvania to come to Virginia to preach and speak to us. On one night in particular, a guest speaker by the name of Earl prayed for me and told me that God was going to build my faith by answering my prayers. So, with baby steps of faith, I prayed. I began reading my Bible. I was so hungry to learn the Word of God that I ended up reading the Bible cover to cover. I grew in knowledge and understanding of God's Word and His promises. The more I read, the hungrier I became for the things of God. I craved His presence. I was able to stand on His promises because I now knew what He promised! I learned that "*So then faith comes by hearing, and hearing by the word of God*" (Romans 10:17). I saturated myself in the Word of God. I memorized encouraging verses. I believed what He said!

I began to put my newfound faith to the test. I began to ask for big, important things such as money to pay the rent or electricity bill. I also asked for small secret things, "Lord, please do something today to remind me of Your love for me." I told God that by my own choices, I felt like I missed out on my dreams. I asked God to allow me to go away to college as I had always dreamed. I also spoke candidly to God and told Him that I want to fully surrender to Him. But it was too hard of a walk to walk alone.

Shortly thereafter, I was invited to Pennsylvania for a weekend revival. I could not believe my eyes! The entire church was filled with college students my age! They were on FIRE for God! I had to be a part of this community. I asked God if He would please allow me to be a part of this church.

I applied to the university, sight unseen, without even knowing what majors were offered! I was immediately accepted. Knowing very few people there, I packed up my life and moved my children to Pennsylvania. I was now a full-time mother AND a full-time college student in a brand-new town with no family and all new friends. Most importantly, God granted my requests. He allowed me to be a part of the church I so longed to be a part of.

Before I knew it, everyone I knew was a follower of Christ! I held tightly to the words Earl had spoken to me. I challenged God by asking increasingly greater requests. My God supplied every one of my needs! Although we were receiving public assistance, my children were well provided for. They had great friends, and great schools, and were happy and thriving. I earned my bachelor's degree and was on the path to a promising career as a Speech-Language Pathologist!

God continued to build my faith by answering my prayers. My responsibility was to stay in constant communication and relationship with Him! You must pray the prayers in order to see them answered!

Times were often tough being a single parent and a full-time college student. Not only did I have to attend class and fulfill class requirements, but I also I had to attend school functions, parent-teacher conferences, and birthday parties. I constantly reflected on God's track record. He never failed me. He always came through. At times I had to wait for my answers, but He never let me down!

My greatest dream of going away to college was fulfilled. My heart still longed for something more. I loved being a mother. I loved being a college student. I also longed to be a wife. The Word of God says if you *"Delight yourself also in the Lord, and He shall give you the desires of your heart"* (Psalm 37:4). Psalm 34:10 tells us that "*... those who seek the Lord shall not lack any good thing.*" Hebrews 11:6 taught me that "*He is a rewarder of those that diligently seek Him.*" I knew my desire to become a wife was a good thing. I believed God wanted to give me the desires of my heart. I knew I was seeking him diligently. So, I asked! God delivered! I have now been married to the most wonderful husband for nearly 23 years!

What I have learned over the years are a few key things:

Faith, like a muscle, must be exercised.

Faith is an action word. Simply believing is not enough. (Faith without works is dead).

Constantly learning God's Word is essential. You cannot stand on His promises if you do not know what was promised.

Remember God's track record. Remind yourself of the good things He has done.

Sometimes God says no. In those times, be thankful. He knows what we don't know. He sees what we do not see. His plans for us are good and His ways are perfect!

HIS Story – Kirk:

I was familiar with people staring at me, but this time it wasn't the same. As an All-American college basketball player for Indiana University of Pennsylvania, (IUP) I was used to the spotlight. I have performed in front of thousands, conducted numerous media interviews, and was very used to people watching and staring at me...yet this was different.

Fresh off the plane and visiting my then girlfriend at the time, Adrienne, I found myself in a church service in the town where I played my college ball. Flying in from Vegas to the east coast, I was headed to Philly for a pro basketball tryout but decided to take a detour and visit my girl in Western Pennsylvania first. The church service was packed, and Pastor Melvin Jenkins (PJ) was on fire and preaching his heart out. Mid-sentence, PJ stops suddenly, stares at me for a few moments, then goes back to preaching as if he never stopped. "That was weird," was my initial thought, but then I just figured PJ must have recognized me as a basketball player from the university because I did frequent his church while I played (I wasn't quite walking with God at the time).

A few minutes go by, and PJ stops his sermon again and stares at me, but this time he is pointing at me. Now it wasn't just PJ looking at me; the whole packed congregation was staring at me; all eyes on Kirk! Just slightly different from when many of those same individuals were watching me play basketball at the arena down the street. "You think you are here for one thing," PJ says, "but God has you here for something completely different." That statement, or really a prophetic declaration, would become one of the pivotal, foundational pillars of my adult life. At the time, I didn't know that.

Faith is about making choices, and taking positive steps forward because of those choices, even when it makes absolutely no sense to us as natural, human beings. In the Bible, God told Abram to pick up everything he had, leave his home and everything that was familiar to him, and he would be blessed. God didn't tell Abram where to go until he started walking. Abram made a choice to follow God's instruction, despite not knowing where he was going or how God was going to sustain or bless him.

God told Noah to build a structure that no one had ever seen or heard of for an event that had never happened before. God gave Noah enough instruction to do what He wanted but did not give the entire full picture. Noah decided to trust God, despite his sure lack of understanding. Come on, God told Noah to build a boat for rain that he had never seen before!

Faith steps really are about TRUST, as my wife Adrienne mentioned. Do you trust yourself more than you trust God, or vice versa? The kicker for all of us, even for our Biblical examples of Abram and Noah, is that God doesn't share the whole enchilada with us at the beginning. He gives us just a little light...just enough for us to decide to take one faith step forward. That's the trust aspect. Can you truly trust that God is leading you down the best, safest, and most prosperous journey for your life, even when you can't see when you are going one step at a time?

From the time I was in the seventh or eighth grade, I planned out my future as a professional basketball player. I knew the path I was going to take, and I was on it. I would get good grades and graduate from high school; play college basketball for four years and make my entry into the NBA. For all intents and purposes, my plan was coming to fruition. I was the Nevada High School Basketball Player of the Year and obtained a full athletic scholarship to play for the University of Colorado. I transferred to the Indiana University of Pennsylvania during my junior year and led IUP to the NCAA Final Four. I obtained several offers to play professionally. Despite a few hurdles, I was still on track to obtain my goal.

But soon after that "staring" incident at church, I had an encounter with God. I can't fully explain it, but it was as if God was speaking directly to me audibly. It was a moment when I heard God clearly tell me, "You will be wealthy, but you won't get there with basketball." My choice, my decision was at that moment. Was God really speaking to me or was that the pizza and beer I had last night? I was 23 years old, and my professional career was just getting started. It didn't make sense to not pursue this dream I have had since middle school, especially when I was so close. I had no indication of what I would do without basketball, nor what God wanted me to do instead. I had to make a choice, and I chose to take my faith step by retiring from my pro-ball pursuits and walking towards what God had for me instead.

That faith step was made over 25 years ago! Those years offered numerous opportunities to trust or reject God's Word on my faith journey. My choice has been challenged, and yes, I certainly questioned whether God chose what was best for me. I have numerous friends who played in the NBA or professionally overseas. Over the years, they all have asked why I didn't play, because my skill and ability were at THAT level. My response has been simple, "Because God had a different path for me." Sometimes you must remind yourself that God's plan and purpose are not only good but absolutely much better than yours. The Bible in Proverbs

16:9 (New King James Version) says, *"A man's heart plans his way, but the Lord directs his steps."*

As I glance back at that one faith step, I can see that God's plan was very good for me. I also see the blessings I have obtained are numerous: my wife of 22 years, Adrienne, four healthy and awesome children, a bachelor's and master's degree, a long career as a college access professional, two budding small businesses (that is a whole other faith step story), and so on… That is what I obtained by taking that one faith step years ago and continuing to trust God with other faith steps throughout the years.

The one thing I have learned (and I exhort you to come to this realization sooner, rather than later), is to trust and view the journey God is taking you on as your success, not the actual goal you hope to attain. The blessings that you are trusting and believing God for may not necessarily happen in your lifetime, but they will happen in your lifeline. God is a legacy-builder and generation creator. His desires for you and your family are great. It starts with one step of faith! It continues with each faith step you take on the journey.

Abraham had to trust God's Word when He told him that he would be a father to many, even though at the time he did not have children. Abraham and his wife Sarah were well beyond their child-birthing years. Abraham knew he would not live to see the promise to fruition, but his job was to take each faith step and trust that God would do what He said He would. For me, God told me I would be wealthy, but not through basketball. While that statement helped me to make a detour in my life's journey, for all intents and purposes, I have not become financially wealthy. At least not yet. Do I believe I will be? Absolutely! God spoke that to me, and various prophecies over me have confirmed it. However, I must understand that it may not happen in my lifetime, but I trust God that it will happen in my legacy, and I am good with that. My job is to take each faith step towards the promise and count my portion of the journey as success. Ultimately, walking in a relationship with God Himself is the prize of success. Each step of faith is an opportunity to build that relationship with the Lord.

As you take your own faith steps, my hope and prayer are that you will truly understand that God is good! He wants the absolute best for you. Even at times when it doesn't feel good; when you can't really see nor understand what you are supposed to do, go ahead and step forward anyway. Trust that God is with you, guiding you, walking each step with you, and will work everything out for your good, because He is just that good.

Our prayer for you:

Father, in the name of Jesus, we thank You for all things great and small. We ask You to bring supernatural courage and confidence to the reader. In You we will put our complete trust as we take our baby steps of faith toward Your plan and purposes for our lives and legacy. Let each baby step of faith lead to a greater realization that Your way is better than ours. We pray that those steps grow our trust in You towards even greater leaps of faith on our success journey.

May we hunger and thirst for Your Word. May we learn Your Word and stand on Your promises. As we walk out our faith journey, may we remember that You are with us during every step. Help us hold onto all the good promises You have given us, especially during times when You seem far away or in times of challenge.

We know Your Spirit illuminates our path. Lord, give us clarity of purpose on where You want us to go, and with each faith step, we believe, God, that You are the prize! Walking in a relationship with You is greater than anything we could hope to attain.

Faith Steps

God, You are great and faithful. Every word You have spoken has come to pass. May Your Words take root in our hearts, grow, and blossom. We thank You for all You have done, are doing, and will do in the future. For every faith step we take, we honor, praise, and thank You because we know that You are with us, guiding us, and leading us into greatness. May Your name be gloried in our hearts, minds, and in every FAITH step we take.

In the name of Jesus, we pray, Amen.

Day 17: FAILING FORWARD

Dr. Walter A. Rogero, II has more than 22 years of pastoral experience. He's served churches on Martha's Vineyard, Massachusetts; Arlington, Virginia; Tulsa, Oklahoma; North Florida; and Rural Arkansas. He holds ordination with the Assemblies of God and has served in the Assemblies, the United Methodist Church, an independent church, and most recently, the Disciples of Christ.

Walter holds three degrees from Oral Roberts University, Tulsa, Oklahoma: Doctor of Ministry, Master of Divinity, and Master of Arts in Missions. Additionally, he holds an undergraduate degree in Music Education from Stetson University in Deland, Florida.

Walter's doctoral work focused on creating a religion and science dialogue in the local congregation. Walter has served as a senior program associate in the American Association for the Advancement of Science's Dialogue on Science, Ethics, and Religion's Science for Seminaries Program Phase I; also as an advisor for Phase II of this program. He has presented at national conferences on developing meaningful faith and science dialogue.

Walter also has professional experience in education, the arts, local government, and business. He is a flute player, as well as an avocational composer. He currently resides in Mountain Home, Arkansas, where he consults and serves as a hospice chaplain.

Have you ever felt a black pit open in your stomach? With each step, you felt smaller and smaller. Have you ever been in front of a group of people and forgotten what you were going to say? Have you ever led a project that was falling apart? Even when you were waking up in the middle of the night in a cold sweat, you couldn't figure out how to fix it!

Have you ever felt like a failure? Do you have a place in your life today that you don't want anyone to know about? And if they did, do you feel like people would say you can't be part of the family, the business, the friends' group, or the profession to which you have devoted your life?

When I was a kid, I had a hard time with handwriting. Now, I wanted to write well, but no matter how hard I tried, I just couldn't make the words and letters look right. In fact, my handwriting was so bad that my third-grade teacher (out of sheer frustration, I'm sure) would send me to the principal's office to scare me into doing better. I still feel the sheer panic of being sent to the principal! As I walked, it was as if the pavement was a rocking ship, and I was about to be cast down into some hole. I could feel my body shrinking with each step; then came the office. Sitting in the reception area was like waiting for the doctor to administer a shot. Underneath was a roiling terror, and behind the terror was the fear that I, personally, was a failure. No one else was sent to the principal for their handwriting, and the message I received was clear, if unintended: "There is something wrong with you. There is something bad about you. No matter how hard you try, you don't measure up."

I wish I could say that I never felt that feeling again. But that terror—hidden under a smile and a carefree attitude—followed me through my schooling. It would leap out in sixth grade when my teacher gave me one weekend at the end of school to complete the semester's assignments, which I'd put off for months, or repeat the grade.

That weekend, fear rode and whipped me mercilessly as I shook and worked feverishly. Failure would lay his cold hand on my back again when I simply could not do Algebra in ninth grade. I was sent to summer school. Then, at the end of my 12th grade year, fear and failure would settle over my future choices when I was denied military service and lost my scholarships and my planned direction.

Anyone who has ever felt the cold dread that there may be something intrinsically wrong with them, knows that the first human instinct is to hide that issue as deeply as possible. Anyone who has done that knows that brokenness only grows in the dark. Perhaps that's why we laugh at Al Franken's old Saturday Night Live "Daily Affirmations" skits where he earnestly repeated to a mirror: "I'm good enough. I'm smart enough... and doggone it, people like me!" We know better. We know that affirmation for what it is—an act attempting to cover a gaping hole at the center of our own personhood.

In college, it looked like I put the trials of my early education behind me. I became an outstanding student and eventually completed a doctoral degree. But in some ways, I was simply overcompensating to cover the perceived failures of my early schooling. In any case, my life after school has been as marked by failure as anything else.

For example, in my first church, I barely managed to draw a scant 15 youths to my ministry. In my second, I was rejected by my co-leader and was so despondent that I debated whether to even come back to the area after visiting my parents for Christmas one year. In my third pastoral assignment, I struggled to be accepted, I was passed over for promotional consideration when the senior pastor left, while maintaining a youth group of eight-to-fifteen. In my fourth church (and my first senior pastorate), I failed to produce adequate housing for my family and ultimately left because I was worn out and my marriage was hurting. In my fifth, I presided over the death of a congregation and spent months going to work and wondering why I was bothering to show up. Then in my sixth, and last church, I was unsuccessful in helping it embrace a common vision. We signed a no-fault separation agreement.

In ministry, we run the danger of comparing our current state with that of our peers. Many ministers, though they may not admit it, are fighting the sense that they simply don't measure up or have what it takes. That danger is not only for ministers, of course. No matter how hard we try, we never actually keep up with the Jones's. When we have the thing, we think we want, we just start looking for the next thing when we're running from a sense of failure or trying to prove to ourselves that our life matters. No accomplishment is good enough. No matter how hard we work, we never look as cool and happy as our friends on Facebook or Instagram; we never "arrive." Or at least if we do, we barely get to savor arriving before we're into the next thing. That's because truly "arriving" doesn't exist if it doesn't exist inside our lives already. We're all looking for happiness, and the harder we look the more happiness eludes us. The reason for that is that happiness is not something that we can find, it's something that sneaks up on us when we're doing other things. By the way, your friend's perfect Internet photos were staged.

If we are not careful, anyone can view their lives through the lens of it only being a string of failures. The best, kindest, and most sensitive of us are especially prone to this. One of my early spiritual mentors used to say: "people have failures, people are not failures." I have had to remind myself of that truth many times through the years.

It's been said that the difference between a wealthy person and a poor person is that the wealthy person earns (at least) one dollar more than they spend and the poor person spends (at least) one dollar more than they earn. It's also been said that the difference between success and failure is that success stands up one more time than it falls down. I've attended conferences where the leader proudly proclaimed that we're allowed to quit on Sunday night as many times as we want if we start again on Monday morning. The United States culture values the person who makes it on their own, who pulls themselves up by their own bootstraps. But the truth is that sometimes, we don't feel like spending wisely.

Sometimes we don't have the heart to get back up. Sometimes after we quit, we walk away—never to return.

Motivational speakers love captivating audiences with stories about the value of failure. They will say that Abraham Lincoln failed something like 18 times before being elected to the White House and lead our nation through the Civil War. They will tell you that Steve Jobs had a disastrous couple of years between founding and returning to Apple (NEXT computers, anyone?).

Motivational speakers will tell us that the most successful people fail a lot. In fact, they indicate that if we are not failing, we are not growing. There's a lot of truth in this (even though some of the motivational stories may need good fact-checking!)

We are not always inspired by stories of failure; though. Sometimes we are overwhelmed by them. Some people have a hard time believing they can succeed. Sure, they like the stories, but they don't see themselves as another Abraham Lincoln or Steve Jobs. Maybe they're in a particularly bad spot right now, a hole of some sort, emotionally, relationally, physically, or spiritually. Maybe they had someone who told them things (or did things to them) in their formative years that left them feeling worthless, unlovable, broken, wrong, or incapable. Maybe they've just had a series of events that make them question if things could ever be different.

This chapter is for the person who feels depressed: who wakes up and wonders why they should get out of bed, who goes to work and wonders if anything they do makes a difference. This chapter is for the person who wears a mask to hide their flaws, but they are so tired of hiding things that they are just about to give up and say, "It's not worth it anymore."

If I was writing to someone else, the kind of person looking for a motivational speaker, the kind of person who just wants to adjust their mask and prove to the world how worthy they are of respect, then I would go back through the ministry experiences I listed earlier and share another perspective on all of them. I would share that in my first church, where I barely managed to keep a scant 15 youths in my youth ministry, I built strong relationships. I grew the youth group and have people in the congregation still asking about me almost 25 years later. If this were about tooting my own horn to motivate, I would share that in the second church, where I was rejected and despondent, with the help of others I grew the ministry from 15 youths to over 200 and developed a team of 25 leaders who carried the ministry for years after I left. See, if I was writing to stir people to success, I would list all the accomplishments that would overturn the statements I made earlier. But the truth of the matter is, those aspects of my church work where I felt like a failure were every bit as real to me as those that I can cite as a success.

In their 2007 book, *Overcoming the Dark Side of Leadership*, Gary McIntosh and Samuel Rima tell us that it's the negative things, the kinds of things that can lead to big and spectacular failures, that drive successful people. What is more, it seems that the bigger the skeletons someone has in their closet, the greater their potential for either huge success or catastrophic failure. But some of us really only have little skeletons in our closets, (and in our pantries and attics, and the other nooks and crannies of our lives). Some of us are not trying to do great things. We're just trying to make it by, and we're having a hard time even doing that.

However, no matter what our dark side consists of, and no matter how success-or-failure-oriented we are, it is dangerous to reject the parts of ourselves that do not match whom we think we should, ought, or must be. It's a fearsome thing to shove down those parts of ourselves that we think of as failures. Because, like the tears we don't cry when we need to mourn, they have an ugly habit of cropping up in some other time or place where they bring havoc and wreckage into our lives.

So, though we may have failures and though we may not be failures, it is critical that we embrace our failures along with our successes. When we fail to accept the failures that are part of our story, we give them the power to affect our lives.

Accepting our failures becomes easier with time. That is because time allows us to make sense of our failures. Of course we had to fail there, we might say, because if we hadn't failed there, we would never have met this person or had that experience or opportunity. It is much harder to accept our failures as we are having them when things don't make sense and we don't understand where they may lead. Being able to do that becomes easier with practice, but it only becomes possible when we come to see ourselves as loved regardless of our issues and failings. Maybe that's why grandparents, as a class of people, are so important to small children. I know my own grandmother, especially, played an important role in making me feel loved when I was little. Of course, she's not around anymore, and many of us either never had grandparents to fill this role, or don't have them now.

In the final consideration though, our grandparents, teachers, parents, or mentors will always fail us if we look to them for our value. That's because they are finite and only have so much love or capacity to give care.

One of the most compelling things about Jesus Christ is that He described God in terms of love and acceptance that were almost unfathomable. He spoke of God as his Abba, his "daddy," and He shared what this meant through His actions and through stories meant to help His hearers understand. Allow me to paraphrase one of the clearest pictures He ever gave of what that loving and accepting God is like.

Once upon a time, there was a punk kid who told his dad that he wished he was dead, so he could have the insurance money. In fact, even though this guy was a complete jerk about it, he managed to convince his dad to sell half of the family's property so he could leave and live the life he wanted to live. After listening to this for some time, the kid's father ultimately did what he asked, selling half of the family's property and giving the kid half of all he owned.

Well, at first, he thought things were great! The kid moved to Las Vegas, rented a penthouse apartment, bought some high-fashion clothes, and was hanging out with a fun group of friends. He threw the best parties and spent every night with a different prostitute, was high every day on a new type of drug, and he only rented luxury cars when he wanted to go out. Of course, it didn't take long for his cash to start drying up.

After a couple of months, he was evicted and was flopping at friends' houses until even his friends moved on. He sold everything he owned for drinks or drugs. Then he was out on the streets. He started going to the day-labor pool, and most days got to work at a chicken processing center. His job was removing the entrails of the chickens by hand, and he was expected to gut 1000 chickens a shift. One night, he was so strung out, and so hungry that he started putting the stuff he pulled out of the birds into his pockets, so he'd have something to eat later. When the company caught him, they fired him on the spot. That night, when the fix started wearing off, and he saw what he'd stuffed in his pockets, the thought came to him: "my dad hires people to landscape for him. Maybe he'd let me do that if I begged." So, he started walking back to his dad's place.

Now, as badly as he'd behaved, his dad had never stopped missing him. He was always looking down the road, hoping his son might come back. One day, as he was looking, off into the distance, he saw his son. This dad went tearing down that road to meet him, threw his arms around his smelly, dirty neck, and cried. The kid started to tell the dad the speech he'd been preparing for the days he'd been walking. "Dad, I've really failed. I've failed so badly that I don't deserve to even be a landscaper for you. I really hope you'd just give me the chance to do at least that, because I am a failure and I need some way to at least eat," the son said.

Now, we all know the rest of the story. The father responds, "Don't be silly! You're not a failure. You're my son! Get a shower! We're going to the finest restaurant in town!" He dialed up the family and told them to put their best clothes on and get ready to go out because they were going to have a party! They did. He told the boy he could have his room back and that he would always love him. That dad assured his son, no matter where he'd been, no matter what he'd done he was fully reinstated because he'd come home.

Of course, that's a paraphrase of the story generally called the Prodigal Son. I'm sharing it in this way, because Jesus was telling people that is what God is like. When we turn to Him and are ready to own the failures of our lives, He covers those failures and uses them to make a new chapter in our story. Although I can't confidently say that every failure will advance our lives. I can say that most do. When we turn to God we fail forward.

Can I tell you another story? It's about my dad. Before I do, I want you to know that my dad has always been my hero. He's my friend today. I can't tell you how grateful I am for him. Even so, I don't know about most of what he did when he was younger. I do have a few glimpses though, and this is one of them.

I remember a night, many years ago now, when one of dad's old buddies was at our house. During the conversation, to which I was not paying special attention, my dad said something that immediately drew my attention. I do not think I will ever forget it. He looked his friend in the eye and said to him, "The only thing I remember about that night, is that every time I stood up, I pointed myself toward the truck so that when I fell down, I would be that much closer!" Apparently, they'd been out drinking. The image of being so drunk that he couldn't walk was so unlike the man I knew. I hardly could believe I'd heard that story right. But as I think about failing, I think there's a lesson there too.

Sometimes, the events of our lives are so overwhelming that we really can't walk. We can hardly even stand up. Maybe the failures we are experiencing are so catastrophic that we don't know how we can even live with them in our lives, much less face them or accept them. We want to run from them. We want to hide them from ourselves, from other people, and even from God. We think they are so bad that God Himself could never accept someone who had them in their lives.

That's where the parable that Jesus told comes in. Jesus was telling us that no failure we ever have can keep us from God's love if we will just turn to Him. My paraphrase may seem over the top to you, but it actually does not fully capture how scandalized Jesus' hearers would have been by the behavior of the young man. Yet, Jesus clearly said that despite the son's brazen and abhorrent behavior, the moment he turned and moved toward the father, that is God, the father himself came running to accept, love, and reinstate him to his sonship.

You and I will have failures, but we are not failures. Successful people fail a lot. But this is not a message about worldly success. Instead, can I encourage us to allow our failures to point us to God, even if the best we can do is aim ourselves in His direction so that when we fall down, we'll be at least that much closer to Him?

See, today I'm a hospice chaplain, and I visit people who are dying every day. I've come to realize that the only failure that is a true failure is the one that we allow to drive us farther from God instead of closer to Him.

For it is the person who turns to Him, who will one day be embraced and hear, "Well done!"

My prayer for self and...you:

Father, I've failed again; in things I've done and in things I refused to do. My failures so overwhelm me that I don't know if I can bear their pressure. I fear falling under their weight. Thank You for strength to stand and the courage if I fall, to fall toward You, even into Your arms.

Thank You for Jesus, whom You sent to show the way, and to be the way, the truth, and the life. Let His truth dwell in me richly. May His life fill mine to overflowing. May His light be my guide. In it, may I be utterly and wholly redeemed and restored.

Help me to see myself as You see me. Help me to know that I am loved despite my failures and sins. Help me to accept my broken parts along with my whole ones. Help me to believe that all things will truly be well and that in You, I have a hope and a future. Give me eyes to see and ears to hear. In You, I am freed from the chains that so easily entangle me. Your wisdom, with which You created the Heavens and the earth, now pours over my life. Fill me with Your Spirit that I might encourage and strengthen those whom You place in my path. Help me, when I fail, to fail forward, to fall towards You, and to be healed of my wounds that I may heal the wounds of others. Bless me that I may bless those around me. Make me Your instrument of peace, life, and light. Make me well. Make me whole. Let me know Your love in a new way. I mandate to live in that love, so all else fades. I am Your child, and You are my Father. My success is but to reflect You in all things and all times. Therein, I meet failure with grace and in grace to grow, and in growing, diminish that I may put on Christ and become truly myself in Him. Make me the person You have made me to be and let that be enough!

In Jesus' name, Amen.

Day 18: SPIRITUAL OPPORTUNITY

Dara Gagnier obtained her Master's Degree in Administration and Leadership from Pepperdine University in Malibu, California. She is an experienced leader who is a leading innovator in forward-thinking education. Dara founded a private school that focuses on providing accelerated and creative learning opportunities for students.

Dara is a real estate investor and a spiritual leader who advocates for bringing the Lord into every aspect of daily life. She resides on the east coast of the United States and enjoys reading, writing, travel, sports, time with family, and the great outdoors.

"Mom, you got a text message," my daughter announced as I was going about my business. I went to where my phone lay on my desk and checked it. The message was from a good friend of mine from college, someone whom I considered to be a great woman of faith and a person who was currently in full-time ministry in California. My interest was piqued, as over the years our demanding schedules didn't allow for frequent communication, though we always kept in touch enough to maintain a stoked fire of friendship. Contact between us usually meant we had something of significance to relay. At first glance, the message appeared to be a long one and read as follows:

"GN (Good News) Dara, The Word declares you have not because you ask not. I'm asking for $1000 towards my daughter's surgery by faith happening later this month. I believe God for this surgery to bring about the results necessary for her spiritual life to escalate THEN for the torn ACL to heal completely, by His Word and power through the skilled surgeon and the medical team. She has a yearlong recovery. No basketball...But God!! Now hear me, my joy. I'm walking in complete applied faith for the $23,242.09 surgery to be paid in full before surgery at the end of this month. We personally have $10,507.08. Talk it over with your husband, my joy, and get back with me to the extent of your faith partnership, above, at, or below the faith driven ask."

It was a request for money and the amount specified to me specifically was $1,000. This pastor was the mom of a young girl who was a basketball super achiever. Her daughter had sustained a serious injury to her knee and was now in need of an involved and expensive surgery.

I considered the message I had received. My first reaction was wanting to immediately help this friend. However, as I thought over the request for a bit, my analytical mind kicked in. Was there insurance? What about Medicaid? Could they apply for that, and have it cover the needed surgery? What about a payment plan? Couldn't they go forward with the surgery, put down the lump sum of money they had as a first payment and then arrange to pay off the rest monthly? Many ideas of how they could, should, or would be able to proceed without financial help from outside individuals crossed my mind. As a "problem solver," I briefly and intellectually worked on solving the problem of the large medical bill alternatively to what my friend had asked of me. While considering the many avenues from where this money could come, besides me, the intellectual man began to slowly give way to my mature spirit man. The mature spirit man began to remind me of the vital lessons of the ways and methods of our precious Lord and Savior, Jesus. It was as if I heard the Lord say, "Consider this situation based on what you know about ME and from what you know about how I operate." I then began to think in that better vein.

After all, it was not normal or typical thing for this particular friend to request money in the first place. In fact, it was downright unusual. Unusual! I had learned that unprecedented, or unusual happenings were very often the Lord breaking into my life circumstances with His plan, purposes, or direction. When that occurred in my past experiences, I learned it was best to pay attention and go with His flow.

The words of a testimony I had heard from an associate pastor's wife in my church then came immediately back to my mind. She had shared with the congregation about a need that had been brought to their family from the local community. Someone needed and had requested help with a utility bill. When she and her husband discussed it, her husband specifically said to her that he believed this situation, the request for the money to meet a need, had come specifically to them for a reason. He remembered how the Lord is a master orchestrator and how specific He is in His ways and designs for all things concerning our lives. She went on to explain that the pastor realized that the need came specifically to them for a reason, so they decided to give and meet the need. This blessed both the person with the need as well as those giving to meet it. The happy ending to this testimony was that the Lord went on to richly meet and provide for a financial need that they, the associate pastor and his wife, had. As I put that testimony on replay in my mind and also considered the very concrete giving lessons the Lord had taught me over the years through my relationship with Him, I recognized this request for the $1,000 was brought to ME, SPECIFICALLY, FOR A REASON.

Interestingly, the request came at a time when my finances were a bit tight. This is typical of how the Lord works. I didn't necessarily have the requested amount readily laying around in liquid cash per se. Many years previously, my husband and I decided we would aggressively pursue financial freedom through real estate investment. The path had been a trying one for various reasons. However, we were at a stage where we were finally "breaking through" in our local market. Still, when we were between property projects, disposable cash could still be a bit tight. My friend's request had come at just such a time. We were focused on obtaining a value-added real estate project, and we didn't have our next property that met our criteria nailed down just yet. Finding a fixer for just the right price was always a challenge. The market was super-hot in our area then, and there was always a lot of competition.

These circumstances, however, did not stop me from giving and meeting my friend's request. After all, I had long ago learned how to believe the Lord for a need to be met and had no problem jumping off the cliff, so to speak. This was a spiritual skill I had acquired over the years, even when I wasn't quite sure how my own future needs and endeavors (I always have major, creative projects going that require money) would be met. But Jesus had always proven Himself as the ultimate safety net and provider and I knew He would work it all out.

Once I made the decision, I forwarded the money to my friend. The giving was from a sincere heart as I truly wanted to follow the Lord and do what I felt was the right thing spiritually. I also gave because I sincerely wanted to sow into my friend's life. So, I was not giving with the motive to "get" anything. After all, it was basic Christianity 101 to know that when you give, the Lord always takes care of you. I was therefore secure in knowing that it was "more blessed to give than to receive." I knew my future was already well provided for, in Him.

Lately, however, the instructional points of the "giving" lessons were being refined and taken to another level. Some of those key points shown to me were:

The Way of the Lord is specific and orchestrated.

The Way of the Lord will require something of you first, in faith (it won't be convenient or easy).

The Way of the Lord brings the opportunity to you.

The Way of the Lord deems that within the opportunity, He is truly trying to get something to you.

The Way of the Lord has you walk in His way, which is giving selflessly, without expecting anything in return.

The Way of the Lord has your jaw-dropping, in awe, at His amazing way when you see the end result.

The Way of the Lord brings you abundance because you are a test passer/seizer of spiritual opportunities.

The Way of the Lord, through His giving opportunities reinforces the intimacy component of trust and delight in your relationship with Him.

After seizing the spiritual opportunity the Lord presented to me, and meeting my friend's request to give the $1,000, as is His way, the Lord amazed me. Prior to this request for giving, there had been a fixer property that had been advertised directly by an owner on an ad website. I had contacted the owner immediately and had given him an offer on the property. The market was super-hot, and he wanted to wait and see what other offers he would get. He quickly received other offers. Through conversation, he let me know he had other offers and wanted to know if the amount we had offered was our bottom line. I looked at the numbers again and decided we could ink our offer up just a bit on this lower-dollar house by $5,000, but no more.

In a kind manner, I made it clear that we took pride in the fact that we pay truly fair prices, and that the property just wasn't worth any more than that in its current condition. It turned out he wasn't interested in our offer and therefore didn't accept it. He had other offers for higher amounts. In the end, he made it clear that he had decided to go with one of those other offers and that we would not get the house. This all took place over the course of several weeks.

Isn't it amazing then, that after I followed the Lord's leading, seized the specific spiritual opportunity being offered to me, and gave my friend the requested $1,000, the seller of the fixer-upper who had previously rejected our offer contacted me? It turned out, the other folks who had promised him more money were just wannabes and ran him all around and were never able to come up with the money and make good on their offers. He was therefore happy now, to accept our original, previous offer. The deal we had known to be a complete "No Go," and considered "completely dead," was suddenly resurrected! Wow! I wasn't expecting that. Yet, how typical this was of the Lord. While all the basic and amazing tenants of giving were present in this situation, like giving in obedience and then receiving an incredible harvest, there was a much deeper work being wrought through the "giving challenges" brought my way.

The work was one of reinforcing special depths of the intimacy and trust in my up close and oh so personal relationship with the Lord. A work where there was a profound knowledge of His character and how much I could truly trust Him, rest in His loving arms, and depend on my Abba Father. These spiritual opportunities allowed me to build a deeper understanding of the true love and fidelity of my oh-so-personal Lord and Savior. A lesson, that if I choose to cooperate with His leading, was always constantly reinforced by the Master Teacher and Lover of my soul.

Often, when a need or a request to give comes a person's way, the focus is on what will be taken or extracted from them. It goes without saying, however, that the Lord truly is never ever trying to EXTRACT from you for the sake of taking away. He logically and reasonably requires of you saying, "Learn of my character, learn of my love, and learn of what a true love relationship is like where there is complete trust and complete provision." When He requires something of you, He has truly planned something to come your way in the future to take you to the next level; but you have to pass the giving test, so you can be confident and enthralled in your love relationship with Him.

The bigger of what is required of you, the bigger the outpouring He wants to bring your way, both in harvest and relationally. In my case, the harvest was our next real estate investment deal, which came with a financial blessing. The harvest was also a blessed reinforcement relationally, one of the most beautiful love stories in the world.

Often, the spiritual opportunity to give is a concrete indicator of a specific thing the Lord wants to do in your life. It's rather interesting then, that I was recently contacted by my same dear friend, to contribute this chapter to a book she was assembling.

Many years ago, the Lord put it in my heart to write books. I have multiple specific ideas for books I want to write as part of my spiritual and natural legacy. A few months ago, I had prophetic dreams that had a very clear message. It was time for me to get those books written that were in my mind and spirit.

However, for the books to emerge the way I would like them to, I would need a special sort of both natural and spiritual provision from the Lord. After all, writing and publishing a book is quite an undertaking. But how could that provision come to me?

Could it be that my friend's request to give a chapter to her literary project is a divine setup for the provision I will need to bring my own books to fruition also? Here, again, we had an unusual and unprecedented request coming my way. These are hallmarks I've learned to pick up on throughout life's journey as indicators that the Lord wants to do something specific for me and also for the person making the request. It is noteworthy that this request came to me now, and that my "requirement" is to help someone else get their book done, right when I am about to enter a season of getting my books written. It's amazing how the Lord works.

As is usually the case, the request is not convenient or easy. My time is far more valuable than my money. As a wife, mother of three children, a spiritual leader, an entrepreneur and investor, time is a most precious commodity. Therefore, the requirement in this scenario of dedicated and uninterrupted sacrifice of time is a very significant one.

However, I have learned the ways of the Master, and now notice the obvious hallmarks of His operation present in this scenario. I know in the end, it's a divine setup, and while meeting the need of my friend's request, He's also trying to get something to me. I also recognize the scenario is prime to reinforce deep truths in our relationship. Could it be that this current request for giving on my part, is the very ingredient needed in the recipe that will prime the pump for the provision (spiritual and natural) that I will need to accomplish the tasks of writing my own books? I dare say it could be so. More importantly, however, I know this "giving" requirement scenario, as it is walked out, will only serve to build a stronger, better, and deeper relationship with Jesus.

I am reminded of a real life, tangible example that duly illustrates this principle. Years ago, there was a conference I really wanted to attend that was literally on the other side of the country. Though money was extremely tight in that season, somehow, I had been able to register for it and pay the fee months prior to attending. The time came for the event, but the problem was that I was completely broke. How on earth could I go to this? What about the plane ticket and ground transportation once I got there? What about a hotel room? How would I pay for meals? I had two choices. I could stay at home and miss the conference I had already paid to attend, or I could go on faith. Again, my rich history with the Lord let me know that I could depend on Him. I moved forward and began to plan to attend. The Lord provided for the plane ticket I needed. Once I arrived at my destination though, while continuing to depend on the Lord, I was also completely dependent on my husband who was back home, to come through for me. He was working on something and once the money came through from it, he would put it in my account immediately. I would then have access to it and be able to pay for what I needed. Well, the Lord came through for me throughout the whole conference. So did my husband. He did what he said he would do and was able to get me what I needed within 24 hours after I arrived on site.

This situation served as a major 'Miracle Grow' in our relationship. His coming through for me in my time of need let me know that I could trust my husband. It also let me know I could count on his word. It let me know he cared about me and my well-being, wanted to be sure I was provided for, and that I was a priority to him. It let me know that I had a true friend and someone in my corner that I could really count on when it mattered the most. As a result, my love, trust, and intimacy increased with my husband, led to strong bonds in a beautiful relationship. I was a proud and adoring wife because I was able to count on him to be my hero when I really needed one.

The same thing happens when we participate in the giving challenges the Lord brings our way. It provides us the opportunity to go deeper in our relationship with Him as we are the recipient of concrete proof of His faithfulness, goodness, richness, trustworthiness, and awesomeness! He is the ultimate hero we can count on when we really need one.

What about you? Is there a spiritual opportunity before you that you are contemplating seizing? Have you had any unusual or unprecedented requests come your way? Are the requests for giving your time, money, talents, or attention hard or inconvenient? Will you seize the spiritual opportunity and pass the test? Will you accept the invitation to go deeper in your relationship of trust, dependence, and intimacy with the God of the universe who truly and purely loves you? I hope you will say, "YES."

My prayer for you:

Dear Lord Jesus, You are an awesome God who always wants to bless us and build a beautiful relationship with us. May I begin to recognize Spirit-led requests for giving as divine appointments and opportunities from You. May I realize that You are always moving and working and trying to usher me into the next experience You have for me, but I have to trust You first and pass the test. May I know in what You require of me lies the seed for a great harvest, great blessings (for others and myself), and most importantly, for a great and deep relationship with You.

In Jesus' name, Amen!

Day 19: PERFECTLY IMPERFECT

Heather Harrison is discipleship pastor at Church 212 in Palm Desert, California. As discipleship pastor, she oversees Life Group Ministry as well as assimilates individuals into the family of Church 212. She began her faith journey when she was 16 years old after the Lord Jesus pressed upon her stubborn heart to surrender. Following that miraculous search and rescue, Heather vowed that whatever she would do and whomever she became would be for Him—a life lived in eternal gratitude. This response led Heather to be married to Daniel Harrison in 2009. They have two story makers together, a son born in 2012 and a daughter born in 2015, whom she homeschools.

Heather holds a Master of Arts Degree in Pastoral Counseling: Church Ministry and Discipleship from Liberty University. Her passion is to disciple, nourish, and equip mankind to live a life in companionship with God.

Pastor Heather is passionate, pragmatic, and an open book. You can email her for speaking engagements and ministry impact: heathermarie@church212.com

What if I told you that your brokenness was inevitable? I have heard many people attribute their hurts, habits, and hang-ups to childhood trauma and wounds; and while I believe them, I share my testimony with them and assure them that a perfect childhood may have made things easier in life, but it surely wouldn't have saved you from brokenness.

I had the closest thing to a perfect childhood. My father adored me. My mother was my best friend—but still my mother. My older brother was my personal terrorist, who went by the unspoken Law of the Elder Sibling. (This law states that the role of a personal terrorist solely belonged to the oldest sibling and any violators would therefore be prosecuted under their executory judgment.)

I grew up in the same house from when I was four until I married. The neighborhood was what it should be—safe, full of play, running in and out of one another's houses, squabbles, and feuds. There was never a romance. We only saw one another as brothers and sisters. We have all grown up and now congregate regularly at our parents' homes for our children to play together.

I made straight A's and befriended all my teachers. parent-teacher conferences looked the same: Here's samples of Heather's work; she has a great attitude; here's an example of that; and then "I wish we could clone her." (I'm serious. This was a phrase used among teachers throughout the years.) I received awards and honors in scholastics and my extra-curricular activities in sports and theater.

I never lacked a friend. I couldn't tell you about the formula for this except I believed in order to have friends, focus on being a friend to others. In the middle of playtime at recess, if I saw someone regularly by themselves, I would branch off my group and go befriend them and invite them into my group of friends. I was never an underdog, and I couldn't let anyone in my sphere of influence consider themselves one, either. I was perfectly set up to thrive in life.

Perfect. Now, there's a word. I heard it all my life from nearly every authority. It was either said of me or over me: "Heather's perfect," or "Heather, you're perfect."

Perfect. Every time I heard it, my heart would clench in hypocrisy. I would one day come across the verse that says, "For the Lord does not see as man sees, for man looks at the outward appearance, but the Lord looks at the heart" (1 Samuel 16:7). My soul would sing that day.

My outward appearance yielded "perfection" in the measure of man, but my heart was hateful, and my mind was torturous. Unsolicited, evil thoughts plagued my mind, leaving me in tears as a child and would continue to torment me into adulthood. Violent images would loop through my mind, and I couldn't stop them. I didn't know when they would come, and I didn't know when they would release me. I'd come to my mom and dad, sobbing, unable to escape. "Imagine them in your hand, Heather, and blow them away." I didn't have that amount of breath in my lungs.

I looked on the cruelty of my peers and the hypocrisy of my elders with contempt, and hate germinated in my heart. It only grew stronger and stronger, snuffing out any hopeful outlook I had of the future. I hated my own kind. The injustice, the oppression, the clawing to the top mentality, found even in the youngest of my friends and continuing into those who were to instruct me in the ways of the world left me heartsick.

When I became a teenager, the sickness manifested itself through depression. I remember isolating at any moment I could, withdrawing from conversations and people emotionally and physically. I began to hear voices that weren't there, each different and each calling my name. There was one time, during the day, that I turned around after another voice called my name down the hall of my high school. There stood a shadowed figure at the end of the hall. I normally saw these shadowed figures in the dark at night, so seeing this one in the day alerted me that my depression had reached new heights. I turned and rounded a corner. As I was making the turn, I saw the shadowed figure make steps to follow me, juxtaposed to the hall. The depression left me numb and I began to idealize suicide. I remember rationalizing my ideations—If this is life, I don't want anything to do with it. Those who kept me afloat in life were my family. But being the youngest in the family, I assumed that one day I'd be left to maneuver in this world on my own, and frankly, I didn't see the value in that, so why waste any time?

This pit of despair was the one out of which not even my self-control could pull me, nor the accolades of man, nor the romantic promise of the future. There was no promise until I heard a voice that triumphed over the tormenting ones and my own! It was the voice of the Lord.

At that time, it would come as no surprise to you that I was dabbling into dark material through the media of reading. It seemed that the fictional narratives to which I turned kept getting darker, and I have no doubt that was a stimulus in driving me further into my pit. One day, one of the friends from which I had isolated found out where I was hiding during lunch hours on our large campus, and she asked if I wouldn't mind if she joined me.

Deep inhale. "Sure," I said on the exhale.

She noticed the book in my hand and began a conversation about reading. She asked if I had heard of a certain book series. Knowing she was a Christian because of how vocal she was about it, I grimaced and said, "I don't read 'fluffy' books." She pressed on, saying I should give it a shot and if I didn't like it, all I had to do was give it back to her. That was something I would commit to.

The next day, she handed me the book. When I decided to open it and read it, on the inside I found a scripture. I wasn't expecting to see it, so it caught my attention. It read, *"Would not God search this out? For He knows the secrets of the heart"* (Psalm 44:21). I hadn't heard anything like this before. I know now, upon reflection, that my soul leaned in with interest at this seedling that had entered my heart. I had no idea what it could do, what it would do.

I enjoyed the story. It was unexpected and strange. But what was stranger was after every time I picked up the book, I found myself turning back to the front and reading that scripture again and again. It was as if it drew me to itself. That's when I heard Him for the first time. His first word to me:

"Surrender."

It wasn't audible but it was clear as day. I knew it was the Lord; my soul knew it very well. But He had used a word that was the very word I was fighting against. My depression had been beckoning for me to surrender to it, and so I was fighting the temptation to give in to its fullness through suicide. This voice, though, cut quick to the depth of my heart. My first response to Him was, "Absolutely not."

When it comes to fight or flight, my natural response is to fight, and I was in fighting mode. Albeit, internally, but that is where the battle was. After my response, His voice went away.

Until He would speak again.

"Surrender," He would say. "No!" I mentally retaliated.

He never changed His mind. Not once. He didn't explain Himself. He didn't elaborate why I should surrender. He didn't promise any benefits. In His holiness and glory and authority, and by His grace, He demanded my soul to surrender to Him. It wasn't oppressive or even forceful. He was gentle, persistent, and kind. He was patient, and never compromised His authority. Again, after I rejected Him, His voice went away.

These events would go on for an unknown amount of time. When you are depressed, the time seems to blur all together. However, I knew it wasn't extensive because I don't think a soul could last that long trying to fight off the Lord's pursuit. You either harden or you melt in the Potter's hand.

One night, while I was finishing up the book my friend had loaned to me, I turned to the scripture again before closing it for the night.

"Surrender." Again, His patient, persistent, and unrelenting voice commanded me once more. Except this time, I couldn't reject Him. I couldn't tell you what was different about this time. It was like all the others, except perhaps I didn't have the strength to go on anymore. I truly reached the end of myself. I didn't know what to do!

I defaulted to what I had seen in the movies. I got out of my bed, kneeled at my bedside, propped my elbows on the mattress, and froze. I didn't know what to say. All I had to say was, "Okay God... I surrender." And in that moment, it was as if a wet blanket was peeled off my back. So much so that I turned around to see if I was still alone in my room. I was—physically. Bewildered, I climbed into bed, rolled over to turn out my light, and muttered, "Well, that was weird," as I made myself lie down and sleep.

To my amazement, the next morning when I woke up, I felt fully A L I V E. I had felt cold, numb, and dead inside for so long! That all had melted away with this now all-consuming fire inside of my belly. I can't explain it to you any other way. I knew in that moment that it was Jesus who had rescued me out of that miry pit. I knew it was Him! My eyes had brightened, and I had become a new creation. My soul fully knew it well!

On that day, I vowed to Him from a heart of gratitude, "Whatever I become and whatever I do will be all about You! My life is Yours!"

He has been my constant companion the rest of my days. He has delivered me from returning bouts of depression. He has led me through a life of abundance. He has mended my broken heart time and time again. He has delivered me from death. He has called me out and called me up from sins to which I had run. He has redeemed me and continues to redeem me.

This is my testimony: The world promises brokenness because it is broken. Your brokenness was inevitable, but your brokenness is redeemable. He is the living and active God, and He is pursuing your soul, too, because God matters, people matter, and you matter. He is faithful and He is to be trusted.

Amen.

Psalm 40 (English Standard Version) is my prayer for you:

I waited patiently for the LORD; He inclined to me and heard my cry.

[2] He drew me up from the pit of destruction, out of the miry bog, and set my feet upon a rock, making my steps secure.

[3] He put a new song in my mouth, a song of praise to our God. Many will see and fear, and put their trust in the LORD.

[4] Blessed is the man who makes the LORD his trust, who does not turn to the proud, to those who go astray after a lie!

[5] You have multiplied, O LORD my God, Your wondrous deeds and Your thoughts toward us; none can compare with you! I will proclaim and tell of them, yet they are more than can be told.

[6] In sacrifice and offering you have not delighted, but you have given me an open ear. Burnt offering and sin offering you have not required.

[7] Then I said, "Behold, I have come; in the scroll of the book it is written of me:

[8] I delight to do Your will, O my God; Your law is within my heart."

[9] I have told the glad news of deliverance in the great congregation; behold, I have not restrained my lips, as you know, O LORD.

[10] I have not hidden Your deliverance within my heart; I have spoken of Your faithfulness and Your salvation; I have not concealed Your steadfast love and Your faithfulness from the great congregation.

[11] As for you, O LORD, you will not restrain Your mercy from me; Your steadfast love and Your faithfulness will ever preserve me!

12 For evils have encompassed me beyond number; my iniquities have overtaken me, and I cannot see; they are more than the hairs of my head; my heart fails me.

13 Be pleased, O LORD, to deliver me! O LORD, make haste to help me!

14 Let those be put to shame and disappointed altogether who seek to snatch away my life; let those be turned back and brought to dishonor who delight in my hurt!

15 Let those be appalled because of their shame who say to me, "Aha, Aha!"

16 But may all who seek you rejoice and be glad in you; may those who love Your salvation say continually, "Great is the LORD!"

17 As for me, I am poor and needy, but the Lord takes thought for me. You are my help and my deliverer; do not delay, O my God!

Day 20: PARACLETOS

Sandra Perry is a servant of God. Southern California has been her home by way of Compton and the Los Angeles areas where she grew up. Sandra is a graduate of Dorsey High School in Los Angeles. She holds a Psychology Degree from the University of Phoenix and an Organizational Leadership Degree from Azusa Pacific University. Sandra currently resides in Moreno Valley, California, where she works as a Business Process Specialist. She has been married for close to 35 years to a wonderful husband. They have three remarkable children ages 32, 24, and 17. They are the loves of her life. Sandra enjoys reading and writing, and dabbles a little in sewing every now and then. Her goal is to develop an entrepreneurial passion within herself and have a successful business whereby she can give back and bless others.

By faith, I was able to overcome the effects of mental illness. Through the power of God and faith in Him, I can say, *"God is our refuge and strength, a very present help in trouble"* (Psalm 46:1). We are not exempt from the struggles and journey of life with all of its twists and turns, disappointments and triumphs, challenges and provisions. But God has provided all that we need to overcome all in this world. We have a helper (Paracletos) that is available to lead us to a sure triumphant end. My journey to the finish line is not complete but thank God, I experience His manifested presence daily and I know His power is available to me every moment.

Even when I hadn't acknowledged God or fully understood His availability to me, His grace and mercy covered me. Fond memories of my mom often flood my thoughts and though much of my struggle stemmed from her experience, one thing I know is that she consistently pressed in to God. She continued in God's direction, and He met her there. She prayed and God moved, *"The effective, fervent prayer of a righteous man avails much"* (James 5:16). I have learned that my experience, though painful, is to ultimately bring glory to God, this is the pleasure I feel in sharing. By faith, I dared to believe God wanted to talk to me. By faith I accepted Christ. By faith, He is transforming me daily. Though the tempest rages around me at times, the Lord has allowed me to navigate to a place of peace and rest by faith.

My Story

From the time I can remember, I was only aware of myself. The external around me was drowned in the background as if I needed some attention but was never able to find anyone available. My mother, bless her heart, struggled with mental illness. I am told she had a nervous breakdown and was placed in a mental facility when I was very young. She apparently was released without much help to resume life and care for her children. Mental illness wasn't talked about back then, nor was there any follow-through in caring for those who experienced mental health challenges. I don't know much of the details of her experience, but I do know my experience with a mom who suffered from extreme depression.

In retrospect, my encounters with my mother's depression started at a very young age. My earliest memory was of me franticly shaking my baby bottle, hoping that someone would come to my aid. I remember uttering the words, "Somebody is going to hear me." I also vividly remember attempting to change my own diaper at times because my mother was too busy fussing at other people to worry about me. Looking back, I laugh because I probably should have saved myself the trouble by going to the potty anyway. But deep down, I just wanted to be seen. The memory has stayed with me all these years as if to allow me to recall it, not for the neglect but for the marked process of time.

I have memories of being placed on the front porch alone while mommy was inside lying down. I remember the feeling of extreme terror as the garbage truck approached with its extremely loud motor getting closer and closer. What was a child to do at about four years old? I ran off the porch to hide behind the bushes while crying. I was saved as my dad happened to pay us a visit and swooped me up in his arms. I remember, because he asked my mom why she had left me out there, a scared little thing behind the bushes. Now, this might all sound innocent enough but very traumatic to a 4-year-old, and it caused one of the loneliest feelings that lingered for years.

That porch was a childhood place I would rather forget. I was often left out there alone, just sitting in the sun as it beat down on me. My brother was six years older and was usually playing marbles in the backyard with his friends. The porch was hot, but I dare not ask or try to sneak in as that would be met with a redirect back to the porch. I was kind of afraid of her; she was often upset and yelling at someone, and it was best to not be noticed. This experience eventually created an internal vacuum that sucked me into my thoughts. I was often thinking, imagining, and caught in my thoughts. I found it easier to dialog with my thoughts and feelings rather than with people. That porch was a place where I felt abandoned, lonely, and rejected. However, this was where I learned to be comfortable with my thoughts and become very introspective.

The first day of elementary school had come. I was going to school and some of the kids walked together in a group. My brother told me, "Now listen: I am only going to show you the way to school once. After that you better remember." It felt like a long way to school. I tried to remember which way we were going. We finally made it to school and my brother took me to my class. I was excited! I did wonder why some of the kids had moms take them to school. Some kids were crying, and their moms looked sad. I didn't have a mom with me; it felt strange.

The teacher gave all the students a book. It was called *Janet and Mark*. She asked all of us to read individually. Some of the kids read the book aloud, every word; most could read a few words; but a few didn't know any of the words. I was in the latter group, to which one boy in class blurted out, "You guys are in the stupid group." The teacher threw a stern look and–said, "That wasn't nice." The other kids laughed and giggled. I had a very sinking feeling about this school thing.

The next day my brother turned to me as we left the house and said, "Ok, now you are going to lead us to school."

I was so nervous and terrified. He put me in the front and he and his friends lingered behind. I knew the general direction, so I started walking. After a while I looked back and they had disappeared. I remembered wanting to cry as I approached a street and needed to turn or go straight, but then I saw some other kids walking. I recognized one that I saw the day before, and somehow within me I knew they had to be going to school too, so I followed. With much relief, I made it to school! After that, my brother told me, "Great! You know your way to school. You can walk by yourself because I am going to walk with my friends." Here, I learned to be resourceful, look for clues and pay close attention.

I spent many days in class worried and unable to concentrate or learn because not only was I not receiving the support I needed at home from my mother, but I also had to remember my way home lest I wander and end up in a scary place. I didn't progress much and was the last one in the class out of the beginner books. As a result, I felt isolated, even in the middle of school with all the children.

During that time, I decided that I was going to have to figure it out on my own. I have to say here, that though I didn't know it, there was an inner equipping that caused me to develop a mind to figure things out. It was leading and I was following.

Later, we moved from Compton to Los Angeles, and I became a latch-key kid (I wore a key around my neck to let myself in the house). My brother was busy with his new friend, and I was left alone. I was instructed to walk to school and back with some of the neighborhood kids. I wasn't allowed outside so I was alone again. It was during this time that I realized my life was different from the other kids. I could look outside from the window and see them playing outside.

Some of the women on the block would sit for coffee just across the street. Everyone knew that family. They had a giant covered porch and perfectly manicured lawn that the old man would take care of daily. That porch was much different from the porch I remembered sitting on. Theirs seem to be a happy place where the ladies would gather and laugh. Though I don't remember why, for a short period of time I was allowed to go to their home after school and play. One of the ladies on the porch, while I was there, said, "Honey, why don't you ask your mom to come and have coffee with us sometime." I did get the nerve to tell my mom this, to which her reply was, "They're just a bunch of nosy gossipers." Though the thought of her visiting seemed pleasant enough, somehow, I knew it wouldn't be received. I was glad to get out without any harsher words from my mom. Here I learned how to carefully think through all the possibilities before giving information.

Mental illness manifests in different forms. My mom also suffered from obsessive-compulsive disorder (OCD) and our home had to be spotless, extremely clean, and if it wasn't she would be triggered and fuss all night. I seriously mean she would fuss non-stop into the evening. My brother and I quickly learned to make sure every nook and cranny were clean before she arrived home from work. This created in me a bunch of nervousness, feelings of anxiety, fear, and an obsession to please for fear of consequences. My mom's daily routine was to catch the bus to work, (she didn't drive) come back home, inspect the house, cook dinner, and then off to the room with the door shut. There was no real communication. We knew what was expected and my brother and I just did it.

Once we tried to go to bed without cleaning the kitchen. We were awakened in the middle of the night to my mom fussing and we were made to clean the kitchen; all the while she ranted. My brother tried to backtalk, and it was met with the cast-iron skillet right to the noggin. He fell to the floor, and I think he was disoriented, but I was busy wiping that kitchen into shape without a word. We went to bed, but mom fussed until I can't remember. I tried to go to sleep but her voice was not one that could be ignored. We never did that again. No matter how tired or sleepy we were, the kitchen stayed clean.

Despite the ongoing struggles that I faced at home and at school, my mother made sure that we always went to church on Sundays. Growing up in a Christian Baptist church, I just remember being there for so long! From Sunday school to evening service we would be there, so at a young age, Sundays were always a love-hate deal for me, as you may imagine. Considering that my mother was still battling depression and could snap at any moment, I was always on edge, trying not to do anything that would cause her to fuss. My brother would often trigger my mom to fuss, and I just didn't understand why he would do that when he knew the consequence of not being ready: my mom would fuss.

Now we lived in LA, but our church was back in Compton. My dad was the faithful chauffeur and companion to my mom. He would show up around an hour before church and sit and wait for us. He was patient, always joyful, and in a good mood. Sometimes his presence would make my mom nervous, but she didn't quite fuss as much with him around. Even if she did, he was able to calm her down, at least most of the time. I felt a sense of relief with him around. So, I had resolved to get dressed and ready, do my necessary chores, and sit on the couch downstairs with Daddy while the other two, my mom and brother, ran around frantically upstairs to beat the clock. My dad was the time clock and after a while, he would say in his kind voice, "Chris, Doll, it's time we get going."

During that time, I had resolved that if I ever had a family, no fussing would be allowed. I wanted to be like my dad — calm, cool, and positive. I started to spend a lot of time with my dad back then. He would come and take me with him. He would take me fishing and we would sit in the quiet and just enjoy the silence with nothing to do. We would also go out to the country area and hunt for rabbits. He taught me to hold a rifle and shoot. Sometimes he would just drive around and visit people or the pool hall (billiards, they call them now), and then we'd get ice cream afterward.

My dad was my serenity place in the middle of life, but somehow, we never talked about my mom during those years. I think he knew what I was dealing with and wanted to offer me some support. I guess he did the best he knew how without overstepping my mom. You didn't want to push her; there could be an explosion. So, everyone around seemed to know there was something wrong but no one, I mean no one, challenged her or mentioned anything. I learned it was best to just please and accommodate what she wanted, and all would be well. I learned to twist and bend and do whatever it took to make her happy and keep her from having an episode of ranting.

In those young church years, we had a Sunday school class and we learned about the Bible. It was the only time in my reading that anything in the Bible made sense. I enjoyed answering questions, although most of the time I would rather just listen. My brother was the smart one, so he always got the questions right.

One year I felt the need to raise my hand and to be baptized. Something in me wanted to. Everyone seemed to be excited. I was excited too. I thought it meant something different would change for me, but it didn't seem to do that at all. My mom continued to be the same and my life continued to be the same. I didn't understand. What did being baptized in the name of the Father, Son, and Holy Ghost mean anyway?

One thing was for sure, we never missed church. Rain or shine we were there, and I was made to participate, though I didn't mind. In the choir, on the usher board, in Sunday school, and whatever they needed help with, I had to participate. I didn't like the Easter poems though. I could never remember them and always muddled through. My early years made me feel invisible, as if I were just there, but I also felt compelled to be better.

During high school, I was strongly encouraged to get a job with my sister at a grocery store chain. I had learned to drive; my mom always had a car in the driveway but could never drive. It worked out for me, and it was a welcomed relief to get away. So, I went to school during the day and worked in the evenings. I liked having my own money to get what I wanted, but my grades started to decline. I was also asked to work a lot of hours beyond my schedule until there was no real time for fun or any friends. It was kind of okay because I had been accustomed to being alone anyway.

At a point, it started to become overwhelming to keep up with school, homework, and working a practically full-time job. I got up the courage to ask if I could quit the job. It was a trigger that sent my mother into a frenzy. She said no, as I needed my little job to take care of myself. I didn't even realize at the time she was struggling financially and needed me to help out and take care of my own basic necessities. That subject was never discussed with her again. The demands of the job started to become overwhelming, and I was drained. I worked whatever schedule they gave me without any questions, even though I saw other workers demanding to be off some weekends. I was too afraid to demand anything for fear that if I got fired, my mom would be upset.

I did manage to graduate from high school and receive my diploma, but what next? College was never the answer for me, and to be honest, I never even knew that was something I should consider doing. I felt trapped, I wanted out of that store but didn't know how to go about doing that.

I felt that if there was an answer, God knew what I should do. Now I really didn't have a relationship with God, but I often tried to read the Bible, which made no sense to me at all. One day I even sat in the middle of the bedroom floor and cried, which I rarely did. I was tired and I felt I wasn't on the right path, but I didn't even know how to fix it. I had this overwhelming urge that God wanted to talk to me, but I couldn't hear. So, I told him, "God, I know you want to say something to me, so I am listening. Please tell me."

Shortly after that time, I met my now husband (let's just say, Tony). He was in school, had a nice job, and attended church right in town. Through some pre-ordained circumstances, we had to go to Tony's church. It was a little storefront church with not many people, but I was surprised to see him leading the few people in worship with a hymnal. I had never seen something like this before, but I sat down, picked up the book, and will never forget reading the words of amazing grace. If you are at all familiar with the Black Baptist church, you would know that they sing this song with such passion (that is what we will call it) that you'd hardly get the real meaning. It is more like an emotional experience. I had a completely different feeling as I connected with the words in that hymnal. The pastor's teaching was very simple, and I understood it in a different way. I called it teaching and wouldn't call it preaching because there was no moaning or crooning, though he was passionate. In the end, he took us to Romans 10:9-10, and there was a revelation that I hadn't known. I was thinking that I had never confessed salvation but was afraid to state that publicly for fear of judgment or looking stupid for never having seen this before.

Later, Tony and I talked about it, and I received Christ as my personal Savior. There was a difference. It was as if I had been reading the Bible with a blinder on, and it was suddenly removed. I began to have an insatiable urge to read the Bible now and spent many morning hours just reading. I felt this was what God wanted to tell me months earlier. I also became angry that I hadn't gotten this information at the church I attended all those years. I felt like it would have saved me a lot of painful experiences. But I finally began to reconcile that feeling. I was going to see to it that no child would find themselves ignorant of the truth. During this time, I learned that without the revelation from the Holy Spirit, we can be blinded by the things of God. *"All things that the Father has are Mine. Therefore I said that He (the Spirit) will take of Mine and declare it to you"* (John 16:15). I can say with confidence that God has been at work in my life both to will and do of His good pleasure, and I am glad.

Through my unfortunate childhood traumas, I developed some faulty views of myself that others were oblivious to. One of my big hurdles was internal storming (a disturbance of the internal atmosphere) that caused me to be self-conscious, a people pleaser, anxious, and continually disappointed in myself. It all stemmed from the trauma of neglect that no one knew about because it was overlooked or simply because no one was looking.

Now, however, I had become saved and married. But without marital counseling, inevitably I carried this baggage and pain of living with someone with mental illness into my marriage. I was always trying to please others, always trying to do my part no matter the inconvenience, difficulty, or cost. I faced many painful experiences in my marriage simply because I didn't know how to have boundaries; I didn't know how to just be me.

There was no known way of respectfully declining any invitation that lacked peace or caused pain. Simply put, the expectation was to fulfill every request at all costs. There was no space for self-care or preservation; not because there was an external restriction but an internal paralysis to do what usually comes naturally for most, self-preservation.

But God is faithful, despite no marital counseling, God sent the Paraclete to help. Now I wouldn't recommend relying on God's grace, but if you find yourself struggling, His grace is sufficient. "*But He has said to me, 'My grace is sufficient for you (my lovingkindness and My mercy are more than enough-always available-regardless of the situation); for (My) power is being perfected (and is completed and shows itself most effectively) in (your) weakness,' Therefore, I will all the more gladly boast in my weaknesses, so that the power of Christ (may completely enfold me) and may dwell in me*" (2 Corinthians 12:9, Amplified Bible). Even in my weakness, God has caused me to overcome by the blood of the Lamb and the word of my testimony.

I didn't know how to tap into all that God had placed in me and use it for His Glory. My Imago Dei was off, but God would not leave me there. He is showing me day by day what He has placed in me. Even when it is hard to see His hand at work, I walk by faith and not by sight. "*For we walk by faith, not by sight (living our lives in a manner consistent with our confident belief in God's promises*" (2 Corinthians 5:7, Amplified

Bible). Without faith it is impossible to please God; so, I choose to simply believe His Word over what I see, feel, or experience in the natural.

God has created me to bring Him praise. If I say my life or even my circumstances were a mistake, I take away from the detailed work that He did when He created me in my mother's womb and equipped me for all that I would face in this life. He knows the beginning from the end, every detail of my life; the path that I take. "*I will give thanks and praise to You, for I am fearfully and wonderfully made. Wonderful are Your works, and my soul knows it very well*" (Psalm 139:14, Amplified Bible). The enemy tried to steal my identity, but it is found in Christ.

My mom died at 91. She experienced depression for many years but was never truly able to find someone close enough with whom to share what she was experiencing. By faith, she still got up every morning and went to work. By faith, she prepared meals. By faith, she provided for her children to the best of her ability. God's grace covered the rest, as she had many church friends over the years who were there for her in other ways.

Though it didn't seem like it at times, she loved, loved her children, grandchildren, great-grandchildren, and great-great-grandchildren, and knew them all by name. Even with the presence of depression, there wasn't much she wouldn't do to try and help any of us. She was a major part of my life as an adult and helped me in many ways. We had a good relationship during my adult years, and I learned how to love unconditionally through her life.

She always pressed in to God, and He sustained her life. She is at rest and at peace with our God, no doubt. Though she was not emotionally present for me in my younger years, she made sure we had a stable address, food on the table every night, good clothes to wear, and the ability to get where we needed to go. God covered the rest and is still covering. While in the hospital, not able to really talk, she was mouthing words to which my niece asked, "Grandma, are you praying for me?" Her answer was, "I am praying for all of you." I believe He honored her faith prayers.

My prayer for you:

This prayer is for those who are depressed or dealing with mental illness. Whether it is a family member that you are trying to help or a friend who is experiencing mental illness, love them and do what you can without judging or trying to fix them. Get them as much help as they are willing to receive but remember to trust God to do what you can't do.

Father, we confess You as Lord of our lives. Thank You for Your Word. We can study it and discover that we have been made in Your image. You took Your time to create us with individual personalities and gifts. Though they may seem flawed to others, You see beauty. Father, strengthen us for this journey of life because we run this race to win the prize. If we get knocked down, we will get back up in faith, believing that You have a plan for us, to give us a future and provide hope.

You are a God who sees all, the beginning to the end. When our faith is failing, send Your Word to our spirit and provide Your Holy Spirit to be our helper. Show us how we are wonderfully made so that we may find joy in being used by You no matter what our mental and emotional challenges might be. Send those to us who can support us in the natural, those whom You have gifted with knowledge and wisdom to help. Let us not be too stubborn to receive help when we need it. Open our understanding so we know what to do and how to do it. Give us Your peace that surpasses all understanding. Give us patience with ourselves and others. Let us allow Your grace to be sufficient in every difficult situation.

Let us not be ashamed of who we are for we are all naked before You, but we are clothed in Your righteousness. Our life is not hidden from Your sight, and you have accepted us as Your sons and daughters. Keep us in all our ways and send Your angels to have charge over us. Help us find rest for our souls in You.

I rebuke and destroy every principality, power, and ruler of darkness that would set itself up against the true knowledge of God, and we take every thought captive unto the obedience of Christ. We dismantle every yoke of bondage that the enemy has tried to attach to Your people, God. We take the powerful Word of God, and we swing it like a sword at all foul thinking that the enemy has tried to subtly use to deceive us.

Father, we don't pretend that we haven't faced difficulties in life, but we lay it all before you; we release every burden now. Help us to renew our minds by spending time in Your Word, God. Father, we submit and surrender our bodies as a living sacrifice to You. We seek Your face, Lord, and we know that everyone who asks receives, who seeks finds, and to everyone who knocks, the door is open. We trust Your process, Lord, and wait on the manifestation of our victory.

We ask that You heal our minds and bodies right now, Lord, and we believe that we have received what we have asked of You. We now rise up and walk out our faith with peace and anticipation of the manifestation of what we have petitioned and received from You. Father, help us to live each day one at a time, dependent on the Paraclete. In the mighty name of Jesus, Amen.

Day 21: A WALK OF FAITH

Bishop Claude Robert Barnes was born June 23, 1941, and is a native of Wilson, North Carolina. He graduated from the Charles H. Darden High School, later attended Fayetteville State University, and is a graduate of Palmer Theological Seminary in Philadelphia, Pennsylvania.

Bishop Barnes became pastor of the Church of Faith, Inc. in 1974. Under his leadership, the Church of Faith, Inc. dedicated the current edifice on May 14, 1989. Bishop Barnes celebrated his 48th Ministerial Pastorship and his 22nd year as a Bishop on June 25, 2022. This progressive and forward-looking ministry Is dedicated to serving God and mankind. The vision for the Church of Faith is to "To Exalt the Savior - Equip the Saints - Evangelize the Sinner."

Bishop Barnes has birthed several pastors and is the General Overseer of two associate churches, Life Empowerment Church, under the pastorship of Pastors Marcus and LaTerra Ruffin, (Moreno Valley, California), and Church of Faith, Inc. II, under Pastor Welton and Minister Sonia Barnes (Garner, North Carolina).

Having worked for the Philadelphia police department for 20 years before retiring, he received numerous accommodations from the city of Philadelphia and community groups for his work in the Community Relations Division. Bishop Barnes continues to work tirelessly to bridge the gap between the police department and the community. He has created several community outreach programs, such as the Church of Faith Community Development Corporation, which is involved in developing new housing in the Mantua section of West Philadelphia, and ongoing community health fairs to address the disparities that exist within the African American Community.

Bishop Barnes is a member of the University of Pennsylvania Advisory Board and serves as Vice President of the Mantua Civic Association. He is a great teacher and writer who has made his material available to all who ask.

Bishop Barnes has been married to his wife, Doris, for 60 years. They are the proud parents of Brother Michael Barnes (deceased), Pastor Anthony Barnes (wife Crystal), Sister Doris Barnes, Minister Reginald Barnes (wife Guylaine), and Sister Crystal Barnes. They are also the proud grandparents of Nychelle, Janae, Tevin (wife Alyssa), Kristoni, Gabrielle, and Alexander.

A caring man of God who works continuously to improve the quality of life for his fellow man, Bishop Barnes is a man of integrity, a teacher, a mentor, and a pastor to other pastors. He is highly respected by his peers and loved by all. He asks the question, "What is our purpose in life after God has given us His very best, other than to be a servant for our Lord? Nothing else in life matters."

After sixty years as a Christian, I am still amazed, honored, and grateful that God would select someone like me to be a Christian after all the things I did with my life before salvation. I came from what they called a dysfunctional family of eleven; my parents were separated. After high school and one year of college, I left home and went to Newark to live with my older brother, James. After a short time, I left and went to Philadelphia where I lived with some of my schoolmates. I found a job and continued in my sinful life.

Eventually, I met my wife, Doris Woodard, who also lived in Philadelphia, at her brother-in-law's house, Earl Rountree, with whom I played football in high school. What is so amazing about meeting my wife in Philadelphia is that we had attended the same high school and the same social events. I even delivered the newspaper to her father's house; yet we never knew each other. After one year of getting acquainted, we were married. I became the chef at the Stanton Dinner Restaurant where I worked, but my lifestyle had not changed.

Then the hand of God began to work in our marriage. My wife became a Christian and joined the Church of Faith with her aunty, Ossie Woodard, where Elder Robert McBay was the pastor. Her decision to give her life to Christ and change her lifestyle surprised me because we were partners in sin.

In hindsight, her decision to become a Christian was the beginning of my "Walk of Faith." It wasn't long before I followed her and joined the church, giving my life also to Christ because of the tremendous differences I saw in her life.

Elder McBay was a man of great faith. He was a father to me, which I never had. There was a vacant property adjacent to the church owned by the city of Philadelphia, which he wanted in order to enlarge the church. He said the Lord told him that the city was going to give him the property, and that is what happened a year later. I helped him add a new addition to the church. The pastor taught me how to do plumbing, roofing, construction work, and how to make cement. My faith was growing, although I was not totally aware of it. Church was something new to me, but I was obedient to the man of God.

I was soon ordained as a deacon and also given the responsibility of a trustee. This was a new responsibility for me because I went to church when I was in North Carolina, but it was spotty at best. This was all new to me and I was fearful, but I didn't want to let the pastor down. By this time, I was growing in my walk of faith.

I wanted to become a policeman, but I was now familiar with the city of Philadelphia. I went to the Lord as I had seen Elder McBay do, and God granted me my prayer request. In November 1966, I became a Philadelphia policeman, where I worked for 20 years. I spent the first 10 years in the 17th police district.

In 1974, the Lord called Elder McBay home, and to my surprise, the Elder Council asked me to be the pastor. When I took the pastoral position, I was not aware of the tremendous responsibility the job required. With my love for Elder McBay, the church, and my overall concern for the members of the church, I wanted to be in a position where I could protect them as Elder McBay had done. By faith, I believed I could do it.

The song titled "Sovereign" has encouraged my walk of faith. It declares that God can do what He wants to, whenever and however He wants to. Because He is Sovereign, my walk of faith has been strengthened. Let me share with you one reason.

Before the pastor was called home to be with his Lord, I wanted to go to a special unit in the police department called "Community Relations," but you had to be recommended for that position, and I didn't have anyone to do so. So, I went to the Lord and told Him about my situation and that He was the only one I could depend on. I told Him about it daily. One night on my way home from the 4 pm to 12 am shift, I was crying out to the Lord. When I got home at about 12:30 am the phone rang, and it was my pastor, Elder McBay. He said to me, "Son, the Lord told me to tell you to stop worrying Him about what you are asking Him to do. The Lord said He heard you and He is going to take care of it." This was making my walk of faith stronger and stronger. I now realized that I had a relationship with God that I was not aware of. The more I trusted Him, the stronger it became.

I had been sharing this desire with my partner, an older Italian officer, who lived in South Philadelphia. The next day I came to work, and we were on patrol, he asked me, "Do you have a minister's card?" I said, "Yes." He asked me to give it to him, as he had a friend who owed him a favor. So I did, and a short time later when I came to work one night, I was told, "A transfer has come down for you and you are to report to the Community Relations Unit tomorrow at 8 am." When I arrived the next day, I introduced myself, I was given my assignment, and I wasn't asked any questions. I never even knew who gave me the recommendation. All I knew was that I was a lightweight fighter in a heavyweight fight. But in my walk of faith, I have been introduced to a Savior who has never lost a battle, and He takes care of His own.

I love what Paul said in Romans 8:28: "*And we know that all things work together for good to those who love God, to those who are the called according to His purpose.*" Now God knew that when the pastor died, I needed to be at church on Sunday. Guess what, I now work 9 am to 5 pm and am off on the weekends. I can wear a suit and tie, drive my own car, and the city pays for my gas. There was no doubt in my mind that God had called me and had a purpose for my life.

"Walking by faith and not by sight" is a life journey. The process is like learning to walk for the first time as a child. I cannot remember my own experience, but I've learned the method from watching my own children. The child learns to turn over first, then to crawl. Next, the child learns to hold on to something to balance themselves, and finally begins to take steps. Once they have confidence, they then turn loose and begin to take steps on their own and from there they begin to walk.

I can identify with this progression from the time I became the pastor of the Church of Faith. I had only been ordained as a deacon but never as a minister. There were other ministers and preachers that I believe were more qualified than me. Then the elders of the church, Elder Gwendolyn Tunewald and Mother Louise Littles (Granny) told the church that the Lord had revealed to them that I was to be the next pastor. The year was 1974, after the death of the late Elder Robert McBay. I never considered the responsibility of my new position because God had given me a "servant's heart." I had to preach and teach Bible class as I learned this walk of faith.

I learned that "one day at a time" was the best way to proceed, having no prior experience in church affairs nor Bible experience or seminary training. The just must live by faith. The Holy Spirit instructed me for the first time to take an easel, a marker, and the books that I had, which were few, to begin to teach the book of Genesis. This was strictly a walk of faith. God taught me how to study, and as I learned, I would be able to teach and preach because the Holy Spirit would have something to work with.

There have been many challenges in my walk of faith that God has allowed, to test my walk. The Lord put in my spirit to build a new church sanctuary and to renovate the existing building. I responded sincerely but the means to accomplish this feat eluded me. We have a very small congregation with limited income.

What seems impossible for man is an opportunity for God to accomplish His purpose. We started a Church Building Fund drive. To my surprise, one member allowed us to use $10,000 to deposit in the bank to receive the interest. That was a tremendous blessing. Within a few years, we were able to raise $90,000, which opened the doors to negotiating with the banks. Now my walk of faith faced its greatest challenge.

We had begun our Church Building Fund drive on March 4, 1985, with what seemed like an impossibility, but *"By faith all things are possible"* and I believed it. The Holy Spirit led me to tell the members that our fund drive would have to be outside of the church. The Lord had given one of the church members, Sister Dorothy Fralin, $10,000 that she would allow the church to deposit in PSFS bank and use the interest for our building fund. At that time, the banks were paying 12%, which was a blessing.

We also needed an architect and a contractor to apply for the loan to accomplish the task. God gave us an architect who was willing to work within our budget. I had no idea what design we wanted; therefore, we told him what we needed. He came up with a design that the members enthusiastically accepted. We were given a price tag of $ 300,000.00 for the drawing. This was a tremendous amount for our small congregation, but by faith, I believed it could be done.

When God is in the plan you can walk in your blessing. He will go ahead of you and make your pathway straight. Our contractor was a Christian and God gave us favor with him. We never signed a contract; it was only a handshake. I couldn't believe what we got for the money we had. The contractor zoned the church heating and air-conditioning system. We needed three and only had the money for two. The contractor gave us the third one. In May 1989, we marched into our new church. It was beautiful and I sat down and cried, and I gave God praise and thanks for what He had made possible.

There were other experiences that occurred in my life with which I struggled. I was consecrated as a Bishop on June 25, 2000. My struggle was with the title, "Bishop." There has been so much abuse of that title that I didn't want any part of it. Then the Lord showed me according to scripture that it was biblical. When I read Titus 1:7-9 and 1 Timothy 3:1-7, I received peace of mind and no longer felt ashamed of the title.

The Lord reminded me of the work He had anointed me to do, which was the work of a Bishop. I helped to establish several churches by assisting with their legal papers and the by-laws required by the Internal Revenue Service to get their 501C3. I had hand-written papers on biblical theology and had my secretary type them into the computer for me. My daughter-in-law, who works for AstraZeneca Pharmaceutical Company, had a college professor who taught a religious credit course for any worker who wanted to earn college credits. My daughter-in-law made them aware that she had already taken a religious course at her church. She was told that if they could see the curriculum, they might consider it. When she presented the church's curriculum course on biblical theology, they gave her four credits.

The curriculum has been used to train many pastors and ministers who started a church or a ministry. I have many other Christian biblical subjects that God has gifted me to write that have benefited many, and I don't mind sharing them. If you were to ask me how I did it, I couldn't explain it. All I can recall is the urge to write, and most of my work was done by pen and paper.

That anointing is no longer present, and that urge to write has gone, but my walk of faith with the Lord has been greatly enhanced by my experiences with my Lord and Savior. Is there room for spiritual growth? Absolutely. I face challenges daily, and the pathway to greater faith has been laid. All I must do is stay the course that God has designed for me. *"In all your ways acknowledge Him and I will direct your path."*

I am a prime example of what God can do for a man or woman who is fully yielded to Him. He will give you all the tools you need to accomplish His purpose and goals for your life. I was given a saying by the Holy Spirit that makes sense only to me. "I know that I know, but what I know, I don't know, but I know that I know." God gives gifts to His servant to be used when He anoints the individual to use them. I believe that the scripture teaches, "When you open your mouth, I will speak for you and through you."

God will also bless you financially, but you must put His agenda first. Scripture says, *"Go into the vineyard and work and whatever is right I will pay you."* He has promised to supply our needs, and God cannot lie. Please do not try to help God by getting ahead of Him; He is the

One doing the blessing. If God has given you a promise concerning future blessings, wait on it. He will give it to you when He knows you are ready to receive it, and it will not be a stumbling block to you. These can be trying times and your walk of faith will be challenged. Ask God for patience and wait on the blessing, by faith!

My prayer for you:

Eternal God, my Lord and Savior, I come to Your throne of grace, acknowledging You, the One who is worthy of all the praise, glory, and honor that is due to Your holy and righteous name. I pray that You will continue to bless and protect those whom You have sent out into the sinful world to do faith-driven kingdom work. Make the body of Christ aware of the nearness of the end of time, of Your imminent return, and of faith as the vehicle that pleases You.

Give us the strength and wisdom to resist the influence of society in Your churches. Give our pastors, ministers, and teachers the courage to stand for the truth, and preach and live the word of faith, even when it is not popular to do so. Let us teach and not entertain the flock You have given us to shepherd, feeding them the Word of God through faith, so that they might be able to stand against the influence and trickery of Satan.

Keep Your leaders humble and supplied with what is needed to grow and prosper the flock. Then, the congregations will bring glory and honor to Your name.

Lord, we thank You for this day, for this time, and we submit our prayer requests to You. We are fully persuaded, by faith, in the wonderful name of our Savior, Jesus Christ, Amen.

Day 22: BEFORE MY MOTHER'S WOMB

 Ronald Covington was born in North Philadelphia. He is the faithful husband to Josette and together they have two amazing sons, Manny and Chris. Ronald is a graduate of the Indiana University of Pennsylvania (IUP), and holds a Bachelor's Degree in Accounting. IUP is where he gave his life to Christ (1991). Ronald is currently a Sunday School teacher at Seeds of Greatness Bible Church in New Castle, Delaware. He lives by this life scripture: "A man who has friends must himself be friendly" (Proverbs 18:24).

One of my earliest memories of God was seeing our family Bible at my grandmother's house. I was around age four or five, and to me it was huge. And at age 50, it's still huge ☺. (I teach Sunday school, and I take this Bible to church with me and use it.) It had my grandpop and grandma's names as "This Bible belongs to" and it had our family tree in it, though the branches were not completed. I was fascinated as a child, looking at the pictures depicting the major stories of the Bible, as well as the historical maps. I remember my grandmother showing me the Lord's Prayer, Matthew 9:9-13, and I would spend many days trying to remember it by heart.

Around Easter every year, I would watch *The Ten Commandments* with her. I was fascinated. I think I actually used that word as a kid. Ok, maybe not. But I was in awe, scared, angry, elated, and cheered when I watched this movie every year. And when God parted the Red Sea! Are you kidding me!? As you know that movie is four hours long and was shown as a two-part series. And each night for two hours I didn't move. It's the only time I can remember sitting still for that long as a kid.

On Saturdays when we would be cleaning the house, my mother would have music playing, some R&B as well as some spirituals. I remember James Cleveland's "I Don't Feel No Ways Tired." I don't remember what I was going through at age six, but this was one of my favorite songs. Whatever I was going through, God didn't leave me. Another favorite song, one my mom would sing to me, was "No Charge" by Shirley Caesar. On Sundays, my mother would take my sister and me to church, Open Door Baptist Church, off 26th and Columbia Avenue in Philly, and I always liked hearing the choir sing ☺. Occasionally, I would hear something the preacher said that would get my attention. At bedtime I was taught a traditional prayer, "Now I lay me down to sleep, I pray the Lord my soul to keep. If I die before I wake, I pray the Lord my soul to take."

Fast forward, as a parent, when my two sons were young, we prayed a little differently. I would have them tell God something that they were grateful for, and we would call our family, aunts, cousins, friends, etc. by name and ask God to bless them. Throughout my childhood, I knew about God. I was exposed to the things of God. I understood the fear of God. And I understood how to respect God. But I didn't know Him just yet.

"I am with you always, even to the end of the age" (Matthew 28:20b). These words were written before I knew this scripture even existed. My childhood was a little tumultuous. Therefore, my point of reference was from what I thought my childhood should look like, what my family life looked like, what my environment was like, and what I saw on TV. I had the perfect idea in my adolescence of what my life was supposed to be. Having a vision is very important. I believe that God's gifts start to be revealed and developed according to His plan, in childhood. Therefore, those who raise us must have a certain level of obedience to God because they can affect how long and how easy or difficult the journey

of His plan may be. Psalm 139 covers the whole journey, from before being in our mother's womb to life everlasting; preferably, life everlasting with God, for those who accept Christ as their Savior. In summation, in part of Psalm 139, David says, "*If I ascend into Heaven, You are there; If I make my bed in hell, behold, You are there.*" So, currently, and looking back retrospectively, I can find myself in this passage.

The story has it, I wasn't a planned birth, and on top of that, my mother had her tubes tied. The medical term is tubal ligation. Yet I hear God saying to me, "*I knew you before I formed you in your mother's womb*" (Jeremiah 1:5a, New Living Translation). This is a story I overheard as a kid. Back then you were not allowed to be in the same room when grown-ups were talking. Moving on, my parents separated when I was five. My mom raised my sister and me. We were very poor, oftentimes living with other relatives. The longest I lived at one address was three years, including up until the year I got married, in 2000.

I was very shy, had a speech impediment, and wore corrective orthopedic shoes. That was probably the worst. You know, sneakers were everything as a kid. I had low self-esteem, though my mom continued to tell me she didn't make junk and neither did God. It took me a few years to get it, but now you can't tell me I'm not pretty. So, part of why we moved around a lot as a kid was because my mother had faith that there was always a better opportunity somewhere and she was going to give her children the best opportunity she could for them to succeed. I directly benefited from her faith in God and her faith in my sister and me.

I remember closer to my teenage years, I started to dream bigger. I started to use faith in the guise of dreams. I say this because I didn't fully understand the spiritual aspect of faith. But God knew what He was doing, without me being aware that He was involved. I remember saying I didn't want to be a statistic, a negative statistic labeled on so many from my environment. I didn't know it then, but I do know now, that those statistics are misleading and have a lot of systemic biases in them. But either way, I wanted something better than the limitations my environment offered.

As a kid, I always wanted to play football, but I didn't like vegetables. But my mom said if I wanted to be a football player, I had to eat vegetables. James 2:17 says, *"Thus also faith by itself, if it does not have works, is dead."* Now she didn't give me that scripture, but she taught me the principle. So, I started watching football on TV when I could and found friends who wanted to play in the yard. I wanted to go to college because I wanted to play football. I started to understand that I needed to be a better student in school if I wanted to go to college. I started to follow a dream and take steps in pursuing that dream. I started dreaming about cities I wanted to visit. I started dreaming about the kind of car, the kind of house I desired, and so forth and so on. I've made a list of things and it's still growing, although a lot of them are being checked off.

Continuing with my childhood journey, I attended three different high schools in three different states in four years. I started off my freshman year in Illinois, where I did get the chance to play organized football for the first time. I made the freshman football team. For accuracy purposes, I think everybody who tried out did. But I did win a job as a starter.

Then in my sophomore year, we moved back to Philly, right before school was about to start. My mom didn't want me to go to the traditional neighborhood schools, and the other schools where you had to apply for admittance had closed their registration. So, after fighting for a month or so and getting turned down by those schools, she was running out of options. At the time, unbeknown to me, my father was living in New Jersey. I was presented with the option of living with him and going to a better school. Now I hadn't seen my father since I was maybe eight. What a challenge presented before me. Again, God's hand moving presented decisions that would navigate my path of faith. I chose to go live with him, with the thought of the opportunity for reconciliation because I despised my dad for not being a part of my life. God presented an opportunity for forgiveness. I was not saved yet, by the way.

I did great in school. In fact, that's when I realized I wanted to be an accountant, which is my current occupation. But my relationship with my dad did not go well at all. I ended up leaving during Christmas break. There were difficult challenges, dysfunction, hurts, disappointments, ideals, mapped-out vision, step-by-step plans, my own inadequacies, self-pity, anger, anger towards God, questioning God, why me? I even got mad at my mom and thought, "Why did you even marry him?" though I was smart enough to never say it to her. Through all of that, God never left me, whether life was good, or I felt like I was in hell.

It may sound like I was about to close, but nope. I have more.

That which we need faith for is based on our deficiency on what we cannot obtain on our own merit (see Hebrews 11, The Message Bible). This is where we cannot compare faith with other faith. "*For I say, through the grace given to me, to every man that is among you, not to think of himself more highly than he ought to think; but to think soberly, according as God hath dealt to every man the measure of faith*" (Romans 12:3, King James Version).

What I lack I need faith to obtain. If another person already has what I lack, there is no need for their faith to obtain that which they already possess. What I have found out, is that clichés don't have the same power as the Word of God, though we have been guilty of quoting them and believing that they do. They don't because most of them are in contradiction to the Word of God. Culturally, we have sayings that are used for inspiration and encouragement.

"So then faith comes by hearing, and hearing by the word of God" (Romans 10:17). The late '80s and early '90s were very exciting and inspiring for me. Culturally, I was starting to see more African American TV shows and movies. To me, my generation had one of the greatest music eras ever. We had the benefit of my parent's generation of great music. And then we had the birth of hip-hop. My music tastes also started to mature. I started enjoying jazz. I had a whole new world that I was exploring and man those were some great times.

I am now at my last and final high school, a performing arts school that encompassed two other disciplines, college-bound academics and nursing/health disciplines. My exposure to the performing arts was profound from the music concerts to the dance ensembles, plays, and talent shows. The talent shows... By my senior year, this shy, awkward kid with low self-esteem was part of a group that sang with the background music, in case I missed a note. We had the whole dance routine down. There were five of us, named "Picture Perfect," and we did three songs off the New Edition's album. I was Johnny Gill, by the way, the newcomer to the group.

By the way, this school didn't have a football team, but I ended up running track. I graduated from high school and was on my way to college. I wanted to go to Penn State and still play football, even though I hadn't played since my freshman year in high school. My thought was, I'll try out for the team once I got there. But God had a different plan. My counselor forced me to listen to her and apply to the Indiana University of Pennsylvania (IUP). Lo and behold, they were the only school that offered me a 4-year academic scholarship. So, I was off to a school that I'd never heard of before nor did I know where it was, except when a group of students came to my high school to share their experiences, right before graduation.

But I'm still excited about going to college. I'm there with a small group of friends. Somehow IUP was able to recruit 10 or 12 of us. I was assigned a roommate, which happened to be a guy from my high school. We didn't have the option of choosing whom we wanted to room with, so I had no idea who it was going to be. Anyhow, I was feeling a lot better about life. I joined the track team, then about 140 lbs., and put playing football to the side. I explored the different activities they had on campus.

This part is a little fuzzy to me, about the actual encounter, but I think at an event I heard the choir sing, the IUP Voices of Joy. There was an immediate connection. Then at some point, I found out that they sang at the local church, Victory Christian Assembly, not too far off campus, and they provided transportation there. I went a few times. I really liked listening to the choir and then when the preacher, Pastor Melvin Jenkins, preached, there were a lot of times I felt inspired by his message. Now for the record, I went to church as a child, but as I got older, we went less frequently. I'm not sure why, but we just didn't go. In my freshman year, I would go to church every so often, but not frequently. But there was a common theme. I would go to church, leave inspired, but soon after church was over, I would feel empty.

Now, college brings on a new set of challenges and struggles, and a lot of these were new to me. No one in my immediate family had gone to and finished at a university. Though I had a scholarship and a meal plan, I was still poor. I was trying to balance being an athlete and a student as well as wanting to be involved with the social life on campus. Over the next two years, I would do well academically one semester and struggle the next. I would go to summer school to make up for the bad semesters. I was assigned mentors with the scholarship, which helped me tremendously, one of them being Lael Jenkins, the pastor's wife.

God's hand was navigating my life, though I never knew He was involved. Because God is the author and finisher of my faith, it started well before I knew Him. All along, He has placed people in my life that I never knew. He allowed me to be in circumstances I would not have ever chosen, and when I have been wrong, He has given me opportunities to get right. All these things were being used to reflect His goodness towards me.

"Lord, I believe; help my unbelief!" (Mark 9:24b).

In my Junior year, I have now started to go to church more consistently. Academically, I'm about the same. Athletically, I'm doing great on the track. In my mind, I'm the man. Socially, in my mind, I'm the man. Herein lies God's perfect timing. I am hearing God's Word now on a more consistent basis. Though my life seems to be at the best I can ever remember, God's two-edged sword is cutting through all of it (read Hebrews 4:12). I am starting to have a different feeling now, no longer a feeling of emptiness, but a pulling. From what I understand now, there was a conviction of the sin in my life, and I needed to decide about the words I heard coming across the pulpit from Pastor Jenkins. I'm around Christian friends more often and I'm seeing a difference between them and me. Though I have this satisfaction from what I have accomplished, being "the man," I did not have the joy that I saw in my friends who were saved. I knew of a lot of their struggles and hurts and all the things I mentioned before, but they had this joy that seemed to always anchor them. A few days leading up to November 24, 1991, I remember a friend, Cyd Wilson, just talking to me about God and salvation. I remember the internal struggle, which I now understand was the fight for my soul.

Friday night is when we had Bible Study. Pastor Jenkins strategically chose Friday night to teach God's Word as a counter to the parties that were happening in and around campus. This particular Friday night, November 22nd, there was a call for those who wanted to accept

Christ and to get baptized. I remember the strong unction to raise my hand the first time he said it, but I didn't move. Then the unction got stronger the second time he said it, and this time I raised my hand! I remember he prayed for us and gave instructions for the upcoming Sunday to be baptized. That Sunday, November 24th, 1991, all the candidates who raised their hands were in Pastor Jenkins's office. He explained the purpose of baptism and asked if there was anyone who hadn't said the confession of faith, and I said I hadn't. I don't remember if anyone else said they hadn't, but I followed his lead in confessing Christ as my Lord and Savior! Before and after the confession, Pastor Jenkins was singing "The Potters House" by Tremaine Hawkins.

My declarative prayer for you:

Faith is what God says makes you righteous with Him. Do not despise the day of small beginnings because they are the foundation of a greater end. I pray that you know that God can use everything in your life, both what you perceive and what may very well be a bad situation to benefit you, for your good. Be open with God. Tell Him everything. He's your closest friend and yearns to commune with you. When you need help, ask the Holy Spirit, whom God has sent as your helper. When you make a mistake, even purposely, go to God and ask for forgiveness. He is faithful and just to forgive you of all your sins. I pray that you be kind and love as Christ asks us to. And lastly, I pray that you see people and situations the way the Lord sees them.

In Jesus' name, Amen.

Before My Mother's Womb

Day 23: WE STAND

Todd and Raquel Koos were married in Tulsa, Oklahoma (2003). Raquel has her undergraduate degree in French and German from Oral Roberts University. She received her Master's Degree in Teaching English as a Second Language (TESL) from Oklahoma State University. During the COVID-19 pandemic, Raquel decided to continue her education and passion for health and fitness by gaining her Certificate in Nutrition from Precision Nutrition (Certified Nutrition Coach). She also became a Certified Personal Trainer (ACE and NASM).

Todd holds a post-graduate degree in Physical Therapy from the Mayo School of Health-Related Sciences, his Master of Divinity from Oral Roberts University (ORU), and is a Fellow of Orthopedic Manual Physical Therapy (FAAOMPT).

Together they reside in Charlotte, NC, have four children (Caris, McKenzie, Joshua, and Zoe), and own two companies, The Physical Therapy Center, LLC, and The Fitness Process, LLC.

Their favorite scripture is from Psalm 84:10: *"For the LORD God is a sun and shield; The LORD will give grace and glory; No good thing will He withhold from those who walk uprightly."*

An older man of God who had a powerful, miraculous ministry was asked the secret of his success by a young Bible college student. This General in the faith slowly opened his Bible, pointed to it, and said in a clear loud voice "Believe it." In Hebrews 12:2 (The Passion Translation), we are admonished to *"look away from the natural realm and fasten our gaze onto Jesus who birthed faith within us and who leads us forward into faith's perfection."* As followers of Christ, be encouraged that destiny awaits, no devil in Hell can hold you or the ones you love from the work God has ordained for you/them to do from the foundation of the world (read Ephesians 2:10).

On April 11, 2018, our eldest daughter, Caris Ann (Grace, Grace), tore her ACL and medial meniscus at gymnastics practice. This was a devastating blow to her athletic endeavors. In the previous year, she had won the floor exercise at the Eastern National Championships, and according to her coaches, she was well on her way to winning another one, mere weeks away. Unfortunately, it wasn't the first challenge we've had to walk through with our beloved Grace gift.

Having married in our 30's, we were excited to have children, "as many as we could before we turn 40" was our theme. So, when our first was a miscarriage, we realized how precious children are as well as how badly we desired to be parents. We desperately longed for a child. So, like Hannah (read 1 Samuel 1:9-28), we got serious about seeking and asking God for a child, something we had not done previously. After becoming pregnant again, I (Raquel) went to my first few prenatal visits in a high state of anxiety. Oh, to have put into practice then, what I do now, namely to "pour out all your worries and stress upon Him and leave them there, for He always tenderly cares for you." My angst was so tangible that my OB-GYN would give me an ultra-sound almost every visit to set my mind at ease. Praise God! The baby was alive and (literally) kicking, and the pregnancy was going well. That is of course until it wasn't.

Week 37, three weeks to go, and Todd and I are going to the last prenatal visit before Caris arrives. Oh, happy day, we had the nursery prepared!!! We blissfully walked into the office for a quick routine check, just like the others, and then we were planning to go to lunch. During the visit, my doctor told me that I was exhibiting symptoms of pre-eclampsia, which is "a potentially dangerous pregnancy complication characterized by high blood pressure. It usually begins after 20 weeks of pregnancy in a woman whose blood pressure had previously been normal. It can lead to serious, even fatal complications for both mother and baby" (Mayo Clinic). It was a surreal time, no lunch, no three more weeks.... we just headed to the hospital and prayed.

After a few hours of being hooked up to machines, my doctor arrives and tells us to prepare ourselves because I was going to deliver the baby that night. Even though it was totally unexpected, we weren't fearful. We were trusting God that Caris was healthy, and I would be as well. We are what the typical person would call "health nuts," so even before pregnancy, it was going to be "au naturel" with the birthing process...Period. That is until the pain hit, and then it was like Mike Tyson once famously said, "Everyone has a plan till they get punched in the mouth." Labor pains changed my plans. The epidural was a godsend.

As my labor started in earnest, the doctor noticed that whenever she told me to push, the baby's heart rate would go down. Knowing my desire to have a natural birth, she did everything she possibly could do to fix the problem. However, the umbilical cord was wrapped around Caris' neck, and it was a very dangerous situation. I needed an emergency C-section. This was definitely not a part of my plan! But once again, God's grace had gone before me as a simple epidural turned into heavy sedation and now at 37 weeks instead of the normal 40, I gave birth to my baby girl weighing in at 3 lbs, 11 oz and 17 1/2 inches long. At that size, my poor doctor thought she had made a miscalculation in my gestational schedule. But by God's grace, baby Caris was very healthy and passed all the Apgar tests normally given to newborns. She came out of the womb fighting and hungry, and I remember one of the nurses calling her feisty. For the next several days, Caris would live in an incubator in my room and be bottle fed by her father as I recovered. It was during those early days in the hospital that God highlighted Psalm 66:12 (The Passion Translation) to me during a morning devotional.

"We've passed through fire and flood, yet in the end you always bring us out better than we were before, saturated with Your goodness."

This verse became an "anchor" for my soul. And exactly seven days after we were first admitted, we took our baby home weighing a "whopping" 4 lbs, 2 oz.

Jumping ahead 11 years, several sprains, bruises, and now possible concussion later, Caris and I are at a sports doctor awaiting the results of her brain MRI. Thanks to a rigorous gymnastics schedule, this was nothing new. What was unexpected however, was in addition to a concussion, her right sinus, behind the bone of the normal sinus, was totally compacted. So, we started concussion therapy with our ophthalmologist, as we awaited treatment and then surgery for the sinuses. Additionally, the doctor found that Caris was near-sighted in one eye, and far-sighted in the other. I had never heard of such a thing. How could it even be possible? Throughout her gymnastics career, especially the previous 2-3 years, this girl had been landing on the beam and flying from one bar to the next, and double back flipping and twisting with little to no depth perception and impaired vision. No one ever questioned her eyesight, not even the coaches! No wonder she could never catch a ball when her father threw it to her! The fact that she had excelled in gymnastics was a miracle in and of itself, let alone at a high level. Within the space of a few months, Caris had concussion therapy, vision therapy, sinus surgery, and new glasses.

In April 2018 when the first ACL tear occurred, we prayerfully opted to do stem cell treatments to regenerate the ligament. We wanted to give her body a chance "to heal" without an invasive procedure at a young age (now 13). After 15 months of declarations of God's Word, fasting and praying, we received a prophetic confirmation that we should "speak to the dry bones as they will grow sinews and live again." Indeed, several treatments later, our miracle was confirmed. The ACL regenerated, and Caris was allowed back in the gym in early July of 2019.

Our faith was through the roof! Caris' faith was through the roof! She was progressing again, getting stronger, and preparing to compete! We had won the victory, to God be the glory.

But yet again, on December 9, 2019, just 3 weeks from competition, the regenerated ACL rupture tore. This time, we opted for surgery. She was crushed and we were dumbfounded, but we trusted ourselves to God all over again. Her recovery began again in early 2020 during the shutdown. Caris diligently did her rehab and healed physically, emotionally, and spiritually. All this while, the 2021 competition season drew near. She progressed well and made it to the season in great shape, but as the season progressed, yet again, there were some issues with the knee. Caris persevered and successfully completed her season, winning the following: Level 9 NC State Meet (VT, AA Champion), Southeast Regionals (VT, UB, FX, and AA Champion), and Eastern Nationals (VT, AA Champion).

Although we were celebrating God's grace and another championship run, the pain she was experiencing, even at Nationals, forced another MRI, and unfortunately, the need for another surgery. She underwent a medial meniscectomy of the right knee in May 2021. So, if you are counting, she has had six stem cell procedures, and now two major surgeries. Now, following another bout of diligence in rehab, hours of practice, and preparation for her first full Level 10 season in 2022, it became evident only three competitions in, her knee was simply too unstable to compete. Caris needs surgery number three.

At this point, what do you do? How do you proceed? For us, we set our hearts to praise God, to acknowledge His goodness in everything, and to continue to "believe" that God's hand is upon our daughter, whether competing or not.

We prayed and discussed with Caris next steps...... surgery again. She has a dream, feels that God has spoken to her about her future... that she will, indeed, overcome and compete at the collegiate level. Today, we are doing as the old General in the faith told the Bible college student to do, "Believe it."

We continue to trust God that "*even when our path takes us through the valley of deepest darkness, fear will never conquer us, for you already have!*" (Psalm 23: 4, The Passion Translation). We are contending for healing and wholeness in every area of Caris' life. Having done all, "*we take faith as our wrap-around shield, for it is able to extinguish the blazing arrows coming at us from the evil one!* (Ephesians 6:16, The Passion Translation) and WE STAND.

Our prayer for you:

Lord, we thank You that we don't have to be anxious about anything, but by prayer and supplication with thanksgiving, we can make our requests known to You. So, we praise You that You are merciful and gracious, slow to anger and abounding in steadfast love and faithfulness. We thank You for perfecting everything that concerns us, and for being touched by the feelings of our infirmities. You lead us in the way we should go and guide us with Your eye upon us. Thank You that as we walk (are led) by Your Holy Spirit, we hear Your voice saying, "This is the way; walk you in it."

We obey Your voice and a stranger's we do not follow. You are our Savior and have redeemed us from the curse of the law so that the blessing of Abraham can be ours. Abundant life is our portion in Christ Jesus. You even said that healing is the children's bread, and that by Your stripes we are healed. We thank You for that provision and receive it by faith and contend for it by faith for our family.

We Stand

Day 24: FROM FAITH TO FAITH

Jaime and Maria Bikis have been married for 28 years and have two children, Sara (27) and Ryan (25). Maria began her career in X-ray and mammography and now is the owner and sole proprietor of La Dolce Vita Pastries & More. Jaime is the Supervisor of Expanded Learning with Desert Sands Unified School District. They are rooted and grounded at Love of Christ Community Church in Indio, California, where they are active elders. Jaime teaches Bible study and is part of the leadership team and men's ministry. Maria is the president of the women's ministry, leads the "Love" fundraising group, and is a greeter. Jaime and Maria continue to fight the good fight of faith that has transformed their lives.

In the beginning.... Jaime's story

For as long as I can remember, I have always had faith. I remember as a small child kneeling around my mother's bed with my brothers and sister and my mother would lead as we all recited the rosary. I did not understand what we were doing as a family, but my mother's faith was on full display. As a child, I believed in my mother's God because I believed in my mother. I did not know who God was, but I knew her and trusted her even though her God seemed so far away.

My story is a familiar story of how a faraway God not only knew me better than I knew myself, but He came looking for me! His love never relented in His pursuit of me. Compassion came after me! The Author and Developer of faith found me in my mess and refined me into the believer that I am today. I now have a personal relationship with the God of my mother. I also know that I know that He will never leave me nor forsake me, and I can access everything in the kingdom by faith.

I was a rebellious and impetuous teenager growing up in the Midwest. All my physical needs were met. I had clothes to wear, shoes on my feet, and food on the table. However, it did not satisfy. I wanted what I wanted, and I wanted it now even if I did not know what that was. Although the family unit remained intact, there was always strife above and below the surface. The home was marred by sibling rivalry and marital discord. Let me just say, it was not abusive, but it was less than tranquil. I sought the company of friends outside the home as much as possible, but my friends were all in a similar dilemma. We were rebellious and prone to fight any authority whether at home, at school, or in the community. During this time, I began experimenting with tobacco, alcohol, and marijuana, not knowing of their devastating effects on a young and impressionable youth.

Seed Time

One evening my friends and I were hanging out, looking for marijuana. We started to hitchhike, and two African American men picked us up in a Fleetwood Cadillac. We thought we hit the jackpot! For sure they were going to share their stash with us, and the night was about to get so much better. Much to our surprise, these well-dressed men in pompadour hats shared the Gospel in an honest and loving way and held our hands as we recited the salvation prayer. As we exited the car, I knew something was different. I felt it. I did not know what I felt but it was real. My friends laughed it off and went on their way, but the course of my life would not be the same.

God planted the seed in me at 16 years old. Afterwards, I tried to do the right things. I stopped using. I went to church with my mom, but it did not feel like it did in the car. I faced ridicule when I encouraged my friends to stop using. Having no root system, it was only a matter of time before I was back hanging with those same friends and same bad habits. A seed sown without the proper nutrients will not produce. But from that point forward, the still small voice was there.

I spent the next 20 years running from that voice. As if I could get far enough away from God that He could not find me. However, the God of all truth knew exactly where I was despite trying to hide myself in the garden. Do you know that you cannot hide from God? Love is always waiting for us no matter where we end up.

I met my help meet, Maria Carbone, while I was running from Jehovah Rapha, my provider. A long-distance relationship developed into the bond we now share today. We were married in just a few years and the children quickly followed. Our children have brought so much joy to our lives. However, I knew there was more. There was a deep longing in our hearts to be filled. It was time. It was time to stop running. It was time to start listening to that still small voice. Shhhhhh. Be still. Listen.

Casa Carbone.... Maria's Story

I grew up in a wonderful household where food was our love language. Mom was always cooking and preparing for weekend gatherings in the backyard or the basement of our home. We were a close-knit family and well-connected to our Italian community. My parents were first-generation Americans. They came through Ellis Island to America, the land of opportunity. My parents were hard-working, blue-collar citizens, living the American dream. We never lacked, as dad worked many long hours to provide for and save for the future. He was a planner and a saver, and that legacy is still alive today. We were so busy accomplishing the dream that church was on the back burner. I recall going to Sunday school because I had to in order to receive my First Communion, then Confirmation. It felt like an obligation, not a desire to learn. Why would I want to know of a God who brought me fear, doubt, insecurities, and shame? So, when I completed my "obligations" to the church, I ran from God and into the world. I was a bird released from its cage without any direction or purpose for 22 years. Moving from one unhealthy relationship to another, I began drinking, using drugs, and making one bad choice after another.

I left home to visit my brother in southern California and that is where I met Jaime. He was sweet and kind and was more than happy to be my personal tour guide during my visits. When he came back east to meet the family, I knew he was the one. He later proposed to me on a bluff in Sausalito overlooking San Francisco through the Golden Gate Bridge and we were married the following year. Being the mother of two beautiful children, was more than I could have dreamed of but there was more. With God, there is always more. God was (unknowingly to me) always there to pick up the pieces. He is so merciful! I cannot ever repay Him for all He has done for me and in me.

Baptized by the fire!

Maria and I had been married for about nine years. Money was tight and communication was even tighter. Even though our needs were met, our souls were empty. I had my agenda and I expected Maria to adhere to it. We were living in a mobile home, and we would take our young children to the family community pool. That's where it all began.

We made several acquaintances during this time but there was a connection with one particular family. A single mother and her two boys who were the same age as our children were always at the pool and grew fond of each other. In casual conversation, the mother shared that they needed a place to stay for a few days. Maria and I felt led to help and offered our pull-out sofa for her and the boys. It was all we had to offer at that time, but we were happy to do so. She and her boys were grateful for the help and in turn, she began to share the Word of God with us. Not overtly but in a way where we wanted to know more. God was drawing us in.

Well, a few days turned into several weeks. We came to know a different side of God through her life. She lived by faith. Complete faith. She trusted God to meet her family's and her every need and never doubted that a faithful God would always fulfill His promises in supplying those needs. She shared many testimonies of how a supernatural God would manifest in her life bringing supernatural supply.

One evening after the children went to bed, she shared the Gospel and led us in the Salvation prayer. I remembered the prayer from the backseat of that Cadillac, but this was different. She spoke about being filled with the Holy Spirit and speaking in a different language. As she laid her hands on me, I immediately began speaking in tongues as the Spirit gave me utterance. That very moment, the God of my mother became real. So real. Eternally real. I knew deep in my soul that our lives changed forever. Nothing would ever be the same. Although Maria did not have the same experience, she was all in and our journey of faith began. She invited us to a local church, and we began to learn the Word of the Living God. We began to build a true foundation.

When we entered Victory Christian Center in 2002, Maria and I were welcomed with so much love. Maria could not explain how she was feeling; she just knew she was home. We met the pastors and ministerial staff, who made every effort to pour into our lives. As new believers, we experienced excellence in ministry firsthand. We plugged into Bible groups and coffee ministry, and our children were getting a good foundation of the Word through the different activities in the children's ministry.

Everything was so good! We were on fire for the Lord. We were water baptized on 03-23-03 and we have never looked back. I ranked that day on the level of the birth of my children. The past was washed away and there was a resurrection of all things new. We were beginning to experience the one true God. The God of Abraham, Isaac and, Jacob. However, as our faith grew, the attacks began to come from those closest to us. Both families strongly rejected our newfound faith. "How could we do this to them?" Our parents were appalled at the thought that we would leave the Catholic Church for a cult. We clung onto Him even tighter and began to understand how important our church family had become. We attended regularly and paid our tithes. Friends that we met during this time are still our friends today. We had so much to learn but we were willing and obedient to walk the walk of faith. Our faith grew with every step we took. Despite the many unknowns, we were faithful in the little things and focused on the job at hand. Not looking back, we moved forward, keeping our hands on the plow.

Consistent faith brings the abundance!

For the last 20 years, Maria and I have been walking by faith. Faith on the mountaintops and faith in the valleys. We know that we have not arrived nor attained all that God has for us and we remain focused on the prize of the high calling. However, if there is one lesson that stands out over the years, it would be that only consistent faith will bring the abundant life. Only consistent obedience to the Word of God will bring the overflow. Yes, we praise God for those unexpected encounters with the King that can change your life in a moment, Maria is about to share one of those testimonies. It is the daily application of faith working by love that steadies your course and takes you to the next level. It is the difference between making Jesus your Savior and living with Jesus as Lord.

Everything in the Kingdom is accessed by faith. Without faith, it is impossible to please God. By faith, the worlds were framed. The currency of the Kingdom of God is faith in action. An intentional creator designed it that way so that anyone, and I mean anyone, can lay hold of His promises found in His word. An important question that all believers should be asking themselves is why am I not living in the abundant life that the blood of Jesus paid for? We struggle with finances, in relationships, in our workplaces, and at home. At times, the winds of our emotions can easily toss our ship back and forth. If I am leaving room for two opinions, maybe I am only exercising my faith when it fits with my lifestyle. I challenge you to give yourself a spiritual checkup and look under the hood to help keep your faith strong and active. This is rightly dividing the word of truth.

Active faith places a demand on the Word. As I feed on the Word, I am accountable for finding the promises in the scriptures that apply to my situation. Once I lay hold of it, I refuse to put my faith in anything else. My steadfast confession of that promise produces the substance of things hoped for.

The Voice Speaks to Maria!

On December 12, 2020, I went into the surgery center for a wellness colonoscopy. I was prepped and ready to get this done. I entered the exam room, very confident and carefree. The routine procedure did not take very long, and I was waking up from the anesthesia as the nurse was giving me post care instructions. Still somewhat sedated, I heard her say they could not complete the procedure due to a blockage in my colon. I was still foggy as I tried asking some clarifying questions. The nurse stated that she was not able to share any details other than I needed to call my doctor's office as soon as possible. The attendant quickly wheeled me to the car where Jaime was waiting for me. Jaime asked how everything went and the attendant handed him the post op instructions and the procedure images. I was stunned looking at the images and reading the initial report that showed a bowel obstruction of 40 cm. Rereading the report I was alarmed because being in the medical field, I had experienced seeing what my patients endured from colon obstructions. I tried to stay at peace, but I felt a heaviness in my spirit.

We shared the news with my son and his fiancé when we got home. As I shared the details, I began to cry and was fearful as I saw my life flash before my eyes. Thoughts began to surface about how I was not going to grow old with my soul mate. I will not be here to see my children walk down the aisle or be able to meet my grandbabies. I tried to keep my composure, but the thoughts just kept racing through my head. My son, his fiancé, and Jaime began to pray for my complete healing. I wanted so much to join my faith with theirs, but my medical background was in the forefront and all I could think of was the difficult road ahead and the treatment I was about to endure.

I called my daughter who is a registered nurse. On the phone, she reiterated all the possible procedures and treatments that my doctor would order. My head was spinning from the news, and I was in total unbelief at how my life had changed from the doctor's report. Still reeling, I phoned the GI (Gastrointestinal) doctor's office to see if I could get some answers. They immediately provided me a list of surgeons with whom I could consult. The office staff relayed a sense of urgency and said there was no need to come in to see the doctor but to follow up directly with the surgeons. I called my daughter again and asked for advice on selecting the best surgeon in town. Based on her recommendation, I called the surgeon's office, and they stated that a radiology procedure would be required prior to seeing the surgeon. Since I had been in the radiology field for 38 years and worked with the same group for over 15 years, I was able to schedule the procedure for December 24, my 59th birthday. I did all I could do in the natural, to get everything lined up for the surgeon.

The next day, I phoned my two brothers, and they were speechless. They did not know what to say of the news. I tried reassuring them that I was going to access the best care available and to keep me in prayer. They understood the seriousness of the doctor's report and were in agreement regarding the treatment plan.

Then on December 23rd, there was still so much going on in my mind. The thoughts kept echoing of an unfulfilled life. I kept myself busy with the daily tasks that needed to be completed but I was only staying busy to keep my mind from imagining the worse. That evening, I cried myself to sleep. I awakened at 2:12 am feeling restless. I got out of bed and went into the living room. In the stillness of the night, I prayed in the spirit and cried out to God for strength during this trial. It was at that moment I began feeling His presence and I heard the still small voice. I heard it as clearly as I am writing these words, "human error, benign." I knew that I knew it was the Holy Spirit. He said it, I believed it, and it was done! I felt His overwhelming presence as I had in the past, reassuring me, all is well. I went back to bed and fell sound asleep. I woke up refreshed and full of faith. I had such peace. A peace that only a word from the Master can produce. I felt assured and confident in Him that what He said was final and not the doctor's report. When I told our children that I had received a word from the Lord, they initially thought I was just saying it to comfort them. They did not sense that the Word of the Lord ignited the faith to defeat the fear of the present situation, as I knew that I knew it was going to be all right. My daughter begged me to continue with the radiology procedure I had scheduled for that morning. I assured her that I would keep the appointment so I could confirm God's Word to me.

Jaime and I drove to the appointment, where a colleague of mine performed the procedure. He quickly reported that there was an "error" in the doctor's report. My lower colon was more curved than the average patient, which appeared as an obstruction. There was no malignancy because there was no tumor, "benign" just as Holy Spirt stated. Human error and benign! We rejoiced as a family and gave all the glory to God! I enjoyed one of the best birthdays ever!

Faith begins where the will of God is known. Knowing the will of God for your situation will erase all your doubts and insecurities. When the voice speaks, fear is dispersed. As we listen to the inner witness, we need to trust and act on it by faith. Doctor's reports may or may not contain facts, but the Word of the Lord is truth. His Word will never return to Him void but it will always accomplish the thing for which it was sent. We serve a God who is faithful to His word. He is the same yesterday, today, and forever and therefore His will for us never changes. He is a good, good God, who has a plan for us, and it would behoove the believer to search out that plan. Our journey is a journey of faith. From faith to faith. From glory to glory. Let's touch and agree!

The story you just read is a testimony of a God who never relents and never surrenders in His efforts to know you. The God who created the universe with you and me in mind wants to have a personal relationship with His creation. A God who is no respecter of persons will perform marvelous works in your life if you allow Him access. Let's touch and agree.

Dear Heavenly Father. We give You all the praise, glory, and honor that You so rightfully deserve. I thank you, Father, for the person who is reading these words at this very moment. I pray, Lord, that You touch them in a deep and unmistakable way. That faith rooted and grounded in love ignites their spirit and reveals the plan and purpose that You have for their lives. I thank You, Father, that You continue to pursue them even in the middle of their messes. I decree and declare that nothing will ever deter the Father from pouring out His love upon you even when you are making haste in the opposite direction.

Today, Lord, we touch and agree to stop running. Instead, we make a firm decision to draw closer to You each day in faith, trusting only in the Word of God. We relish in the knowledge that it is just as true today as it was in the beginning, and on this rock, we are steadied in the storms of life. We are immovable, and we place Your Word above man's word.

Our prayer for you:

Father, we repent for the times when we ignored the still small voice. We make a conscious choice today to allow Holy Spirit to lead and guide us all the rest of our days, knowing that whatever direction it leads, it will bring glory and honor to You, God. And finally, *"I have been crucified with Christ; it is no longer I who live, but Christ lives in me; and the life which I now live in the flesh I live by faith in the Son of God, who loved me and gave Himself for me. I do not set aside the grace of God; for if righteousness comes through the law, then Christ died in vain"* (Galatians 2:20-21).

Day 25: WALKING BY FAITH

 Jeff E. Walker was born and raised in the State of Illinois. He attended Central Bible College of the Assemblies of God and is a graduate of Rhema Bible Training Center. He earned a Bachelor of Arts Degree from Western Illinois University, and a Bachelor of Science in Psychology and a Master of Arts in Professional Counseling Degree from Liberty University. He received his Master of Divinity and Doctor of Ministry degrees from Oral Roberts University, as well as a Doctor of Clinical Psychology Degree from Trinity College of Graduate Studies, which included an internship at the Betty Ford Center in Rancho Mirage, California. He is a licensed psychologist in the state of California.

Dr. Walker holds ecclesiastical credentials with the Rhema Ministerial Association International. He serves on the Board of Directors of Dwight Thompson Ministries and served on the Board of Trustees of Oral Roberts' Charismatic Bible Ministries organization for 21 years.

Dr. Walker has been a Reserve Deputy Sheriff and departmental chaplain for the Riverside County Sheriff's Department since 1990. He also served as a member of the Desert Regional Mental Health Advisory Board from 1994 to 1995. In 2008, he was invited by the Christian Association for Psychological Studies (CAPS) to be a presenter at their World Conference. The topic of his lecture, which was attended by both health professionals and pastors, was "Mental Health and the Local Church."

Having received a call to ministry at 18 years of age, Rev. Walker served two congregations in Associate Pastoral positions. He then felt led of the Lord to start a church in Palm Springs, California, in February of 1982. In 1985, the congregation embarked on its acquisition of eleven acres of land on Bob Hope Drive in Rancho Mirage, CA. The Victory campus is home to the church and the church offices, as well as Southern California Christian College (SCCC) which was established in 1985.

Rev. Walker, who has ministered extensively throughout the U.S. and abroad, resides in Rancho Mirage, CA.

You can email Rev. Walker at pastor@victorychristian.org

"You should go to Palm Springs and start a church!" Those words, which were spoken to me by a friend in December of 1981 while we ate homemade tacos, became God's fulcrum to free me from small thinking, little ideas, safe goals, and dwarfed dreams. Those 10 words would launch me onto a path that would determine the trajectory of my life, clarify my choices, and position me for kingdom fruitfulness. They have been my guiding light for 40 years now. But here's the thing about receiving such an assignment. Though thrilling, it brings out every fear, insecurity, and self-doubt imaginable. Remember how Moses responded to God's call on his life? Moses began immediately to explain to the Lord why he was not qualified to carry out the task which God had just laid upon him. I had a similar response to my call. Too young, have never been to Palm Springs, no one knows me there, don't have any money, and so forth.

Simultaneously, those words would anchor my mind and infuse my soul to such a powerful extent that I could face every challenge and impending danger with courage and faith. Those words birthed a dream in my spirit, and that dream has empowered 40 years of ministry. The reality of that dream has brought success, victory, breakthrough, and blessing to me, to my community, and to thousands of men and women around the globe.

It all began when my fellow Bible college graduate, Joe Bergeron, invited me to preach at his church in Burbank, California. I journeyed from my hometown of Mattoon, Illinois, winding my way through the cornfields and soybeans that grew in the land of my birth into unexplored parts of our country. Just before reaching my destination, while driving on Interstate 10, I passed through the Coachella Valley desert and saw the freeway sign for the Palm Springs exit. I had heard of Palm Springs, and I wondered as I drove past the exit, what was out there. Too weary to stop, I drove the final hundred miles to Burbank and connected with my friend, Joe.

One evening after service, Joe and I were having dinner. I asked him about Palm Springs. I told him that I had driven past it on my way to his city, that I had seen things on television about it, and asked him to tell me more about the desert oasis. That's when Joe swallowed his bite of homemade taco, looked across the table at me, and blurted out his humorous retort, "You should go to Palm Springs and start a church." We both laughed. I had never even been there and didn't know a soul who lived there. What a ridiculous thought! But, in the ensuing weeks, God profoundly solidified that idea in me.

Little did Joe Bergeron know that his words would so lodge in my heart that the result would be a harbinger of faith. The next question became, how could a single, 22-year-old kid, who was raised in an Illinois cornfield and only had a hundred bucks and a beat-up Toyota, start a church in a city he had never even visited...where he knew no one? How? By the power of faith, that's how.

I went back home, and just 10 weeks later I loaded all my worldly possessions in the back of my sad little car, stuck the hundred dollars in my pocket, and with the Midwestern crops in my rear-view mirror for good this time, off I went... faith-filled dream intact. Upon hearing the words, "You should go to Palm Springs and start a church," I was on my way to do just that. The road ahead was to be lined with miracles, and the journey was to be filled with both joy and difficulty. I was to learn how God has an exciting plan for any man or woman who will dare to allow themselves to dream.

Hebrews 11:1 tells us, *"Now faith is the substance of things hoped for, the evidence of things not seen."* In other words, faith gives tangibility, both seen and unseen, to the dream, the assignment that God places upon our lives. There are seven things regarding my kingdom mandate that have been a reality in my journey as a result of walking by faith. As I share them, my hope is that they will bolster your faith and confidence to fully pursue what God has placed in your heart. Here are the Seven Powers of Faith!

Power #1: Walking by faith will draw the right people to you.

You might think that walking by faith has enough power to work all on its own, just between you and God. A heart of faith has a lot of power, but not that kind of power. The fact is, while we all might wish we could do life on our own, that's not how we were created. We are not designed by God for a solo existence. We need other people to be happy and successful. If you think you are going to accomplish your assignment on your own, you are kidding yourself.

Part of the power of walking by faith is that it will attract the right people to bring your dream to pass. You are going to need those people. They are the ones who are going to assist you, encourage you, and support you. They are going to bless you, give to you, and counsel you through the ups and downs until the dream becomes a reality. Jesus had a purpose and a mission, and He was filled with faith. He was the Son of God, but He also had the right people working with Him. They were drawn alongside Him.

Power #2: Walking by faith will reveal those not called as your partners.

This is a tremendous truth to grasp. Your faith assignment will actually repel the kind of people that will hinder you from fulfilling it. If you have a clear assignment and you are going somewhere, you are excited about your future and your gaze is fixed on that goal, there may be some people who just don't want to be around you anymore. As you proceed to work out that assignment, those people will drop out of the picture. Even with Jesus, people were either attracted to Him or repelled by Him. So don't be surprised if, as you move forward, you are not always the most popular person on the block.

Power #3: Walking by faith gives you the strength to carry on in the hard times.

Speaking of Jesus, the Bible says in Hebrews 12:2, *"Who for the joy that was set before Him, endured the cross, despising the shame."* Jesus had an enduring joy, and that joy was His strength (read Nehemiah 8:10). The clarity of Jesus' assignment enabled Him to see that through His sacrifice, you and I would be reconciled and restored to a relationship with God. That enabled Him to live a sinless life and to suffer being misunderstood, persecuted, mocked, unjustly tried and convicted, scourged, spat upon, and crucified. He was able to endure all of that because He was solid about His assignment. He had the stuff to see things through to the end.

I launched my church in February of 1982. After almost a year of my best efforts, having started with only one, we had 14 in attendance. When I called my folks back in Illinois, I informed them that we were up to that number. My dad offered to send me money to come home. He was concerned about me, but I was totally oblivious to the fact that having only 14 people was not great. Yet, it was great for me. After all, God had multiplied the church many times over!

Power #4: Walking by faith provides hope for a better future.

"But the path of the just is like the shining sun, that shines ever brighter unto the perfect day" (Proverbs 4:18, NKJV). If you tend to think negatively and hopelessly about days to come, please back up and say, Lord, "I know You want to give me hope for a better future. You want to give me a vision of something better, of going higher with You, and walking with You in a greater dimension. You want to give me an exciting life that's filled with Your supernatural intervention, joy, wisdom, and power. I want to receive all of that now! Thank You for giving me a dream that stirs my soul and ignites my spirit."

Jeremiah. 29:11 (The Message Bible) says, *"I have it all planned out—plans to take care of you, not abandon you, plans to give you the future you hope for."* Anything birthed by the Holy Spirit in your heart will empower you to see things more clearly. It will destroy confusion and doubt and provide a sense of hope for a brighter and better future.

Power #5: Walking by faith will change the atmosphere and the culture.

Think about the life of Jesus. Although His mission seemed unlikely to the Pharisees and the Sadducees and the other skeptics of His day, it revolutionized the world. What Jesus did redeemed humanity, providing a way for us to return to the original position and state of being with God.

Think about the life of Dr. Martin Luther King, Jr. His God-given dream changed our nation, altering our culture and political atmosphere. Our lives can too! Our lives may not have the far-reaching impact of Jesus or Martin Luther King, Jr., but they can make a difference in people's lives, bringing change in the atmosphere and quality of life in our world.

When my youngest child was 11 years old, he was hit by a car while riding his bicycle. After being in a coma for over a month, having suffered a traumatic brain injury, broken legs, contusions, and abrasions, he began physical therapy. One day, I went to visit him during therapy. The curtain was pulled in his hospital room and neither of us could see the other. He wasn't aware I was there until he caught my fragrance. He said, "My dad is here, I can smell his cologne." My presence changed the atmosphere. You and I carry the fragrance of Jesus...a sweet-smelling savor. And, when we show up, the potential for changing the atmosphere is great. Your walk of faith has within it power to conquer what opposes you and dispel darkness with light!

Power #6: Walking by faith provides proper priority and parameters.

One of the things I appreciate about having a clear vision is that it makes so many decisions for me. Over time it just winnows out all the peripheral, unnecessary stuff and gives me a clear sense of direction. This also eliminates a whole lot of decision-making. I don't have to struggle with, "Well, should I do this? Or should I do that?" I know I am going somewhere, and I must invest all my energy and my time in moving my assignment forward. I cannot and will not be sidetracked if I can help it.

When Nehemiah was rebuilding the city of Jerusalem after it had been sacked and burned, two men by the names of Sanballat and Geshem tried to get him to stop work (read Nehemiah 6:1-3). They said, "Hey, Nehemiah, come down into the plain of Ono, and let's have lunch together." Nehemiah answered, "Sorry guys, but I can't come down. The work I'm doing is too important. I must stay focused on the rebuilding effort." The assignment God gave Nehemiah exposed all the distractions and nonsense of his world and his life, and your assignment has the power to provide proper priorities and parameters so you can live simply and successfully also.

Power #7: Walking by faith fosters insight and creative solutions.

One of my spiritual mentors, Oral Roberts, used to say that when he prayed in the spirit, he was believing for a Holy Spirit revelation in the form of "ideas, insights, and concepts." Our assignment and walk of faith create an atmosphere for these same supernatural blessings. Part of the inherent power of your dream from God is that it produces in you the creativity you need to accomplish it. As you press forward, insights and ideas will begin to flow into your heart, your mind, and your awareness. You will have the tools and the creative solutions for problems that arise.

A fine example is Joshua at the battle of Jericho, where God gave a word of wisdom to him. Joshua had a problem on his hands—a crowd of people with a history of saying things that got them into trouble. The stakes couldn't be higher, and he couldn't afford another plague from God because they grieved His Spirit with doubt and unbelief toward His promises.

As Joshua faced this problem, a creative solution bubbled up from his heart to tell the people to be silent until he gave the signal. But, in the meantime, "Shhhh." Shhhh? What kind of solution was that? "My feet hurt!" Shhhh. "I'm tired." Shhhh. "I don't know if...." Shhhh! At the right time, Joshua commanded, "Shout!" And, the wall came tumbling down, all because of a simple but effective idea that Joshua's faith produced in him. The power of faith is increased creativity to bring your dream about.

My prayer for you:

Heavenly Father, I pray for those who will read these pages. I ask that You give them a clear assignment, a distinct dream, and knowledge of their divine purpose, which can only be fulfilled by a response of faith in You. You are the Alpha and Omega of our journey. If You start us on a path, You will help us and cheer us on to the finish line. Holy Spirit, do

Your wonderful work of leading my friend into all truth, bring things to their remembrance, empower them to be bold witnesses, be their comforter and guide, and show them things to come for we need Your partnership to accomplish all kingdom work. Lord, I thank You for peace that passes understanding that will stand guard over the heart and mind of Your precious child. Ultimately, we pray Thy will be done in our every endeavor. Grant this reader good success and joy for their journey.

In the mighty name of Jesus, our Redeemer.

Day 26: FAITH IN THE FIRE

Rochelle Wright is the fur mom to three amazing and loving fur babies. She is a 16-year Special Education educator. She is passionate about collaborating, connecting, and empowering all educational stakeholders in the success of students' lives. Rochelle has served in various leadership roles in her educational journey and was recently honored by peers for both the "Teacher of the Year" nomination, as well as "Educator of the Month."

Rochelle currently serves as a Worship Team member at Life Empowerment Church. She also serves in her community as a Homeowner's Association Board Member, helping to build community and camaraderie among neighbors. Additionally, Rochelle loves to make beautiful happen one face at a time as a Beauty Executive and Self -Care Specialist in her small business. Her heart's posture is to see the beauty in all God's people and to empower others to show up as the best version of themselves daily!

By Faith...

Faith in the fire has been my most recent testimony to share with the world. In the most recent times, our world has faced a global pandemic that has shifted life in general as we see it, especially in the world of education. March 13, 2020, would shift the trajectory of my world forever, as it was the day we received the "Big Announcement" that schools would be closed due to a pandemic hitting the land. What was a pandemic? How would this impact educators, scholars, and their families? How would education look and be delivered, if it were not delivered in person; these were just a few of many questions that perplexed many educators' minds.

In addition to the "Big Announcement" (unbeknownst to myself), I also returned home from a work-related conference to my family, infected with the COVID-19 virus. My symptoms began to become apparent as each of the next seven days of my life would unveil new symptomatic discoveries, including loss of taste, loss of smell, headaches, fevers, shortness of breath, body aches, and pains, to name a few. Because this was the beginning stages of a global pandemic, there were limited resources, research, and access to testing for COVID-19. This is when fear began to creep in, due to a lack of knowledge and direction on how to conquer and navigate this viral disease as a family. I held onto and very frequently spoke out the scripture, 2 Timothy 1:7, *"For God has not given us a spirit of fear; but of power and of love and of a sound mind.*

Eventually, the Covid-19 virus would spread to my parents, with one being extremely symptomatic and one being asymptomatic. This began an extended quarantine journey for my parents and I. For the next eight weeks, quarantine would be necessary due to a lack of resources and available testing at the beginning stages of the pandemic. The struggle was real, the guilt of spreading this viral disease to my family was real, the journey was real, and so was the road to recovery. Through my family's faith, we were going to be healed of Covid-19 and by declaring in faith we were healed by God's stripes - no matter what the circumstances presented - we stood.

Our faith muscles were stretched, watching my symptomatic parent's health decline daily, while my health began to slowly improve. Because this parent is a non-believer, it made the journey to healing sensitive and yet troubling at times. This caused my asymptomatic parent, myself, and the family of believers to stand in the gap and intercede in prayer and faith on behalf of them. We watched on as his appetite decreased, his taste buds became inoperative, his breathing became labored, and his mental state became concerning. One thing that remained constant was his stubbornness, which would prove in the end to be a life-saving factor in his journey to eventually overcoming Covid-19. We believe to this day in faith, his refusal to go to the hospital upon his condition worsening actually saved his very life.

As he lay dormant in the bed, I felt helpless at times, but not without hope. The asymptomatic parent and I tag-teamed to tend to the ailing parent/spouse's health while also balancing being educators. It was time for a fast and to call upon the elders to pray. In addition, we allowed worship to be our weapon. A sound of praise would consume the atmosphere, whether he wanted to hear it or not as a non-believer. He was too weak to refuse care and intercession from loved ones. As the elders and family of believers gathered to pray for him, we began to see an unspeakable turnaround in his health within three days' time. He would have an encounter with God (like that of Paul) that began to shift his language of faith and soften his heart while beginning his personal journey with the Savior. God is still working on his heart, and I know by faith, my biological father will come to know the Heavenly Father for himself. He shares in current time, acknowledgment of God saving his life from Covid-19. HALLELUJAH!

As health symptoms improved within the household, we would soon receive news that our Covid-19 test results were in. After a 3-4 week wait, we finally had the opportunity to get tested. By this time, all three of the quarantined family members had very mild to little symptoms of the virus. We received a call from a medical research group with the news that my asymptomatic parent tested POSITIVE for Covid-19. While my results showed a NEGATIVE test result, this would reset our course of quarantine for the next 2-3 weeks. Ready or not, here we grow again in faith.

This journey of faith was different because we had to isolate and truly quarantine the asymptomatic parent to what we refer to as the "west wing" of their home. This allowed her to be alone with God and rebirth a childhood dream of hers that had been put to rest for over a decade. She had been a self-taught seamstress since the age of nine years old. In her time of personal quarantine, she began to draw closer to God while also drawing out her dream to fulfill a worldwide need for facial masks, due to the shortage of Personal Protective Equipment (PP) for medical heroes. On the other side of her closed quarantine door, she was creating a prayer war room and a space to let her gift be utilized once more.

A few weeks later, Mom would re-test for Covid-19 and her test results came back inconclusive. What did that mean? Did she need to remain quarantined and isolated? In her intimate quarantine time with God, my mom was directed by God to go on a fast and to commune with Him. She was obedient and was healed from this nasty virus, once and for all. Her extended time in this period allowed her to put aside distractions and tend to her needs first, while also communing with God. She enjoyed it so much she even went a little period longer in the atmosphere. The pandemic caused our family to prioritize the most significant things in life. It caused us to strengthen our faith and deepen our relationship with the Lord, bringing a healthier balance to our lives, and causing us to pivot for the better.

The biggest pivot in the pandemic would come in the personal relationship with God, the personal relationship with myself, and the professional relationship established within my world of education. This pivot unlocked and unleashed a faith from within me that I once knew in my journey as a believer. Because Covid-19 personally visited my household and impacted half of my family, we were forced to embrace the pivot and the new normal early on. In the coming 18 months of life, the word pivot became my first and second nature in navigating my spiritual relationship, life, career, and personal business ownership, finding a balance among them all.

God was the navigator who would anchor me throughout it all. Although it may seem unorthodox to be grateful for the global pandemic, I proudly praise God for every stage of growth I experienced in the midst of it. My spiritual and emotional growth were two areas of simultaneous growth and development. My journey began in March 2020. While faced with enduring the virus early on with my parents, finding balance to be their caretaker in quarantine while caring/nurturing and continuing to develop the brains/skills of my learning "handicapable" scholars became a God-led journey.

The world of education would impact how the entire world operated as a whole for the coming year and a half. Educators were faced with the challenge to completely pivot and transform the way they had traditionally delivered education to their students. We were all set on the journey to build a new plane while also learning how to fly it at the same time. Whew, now faith truly had to be the substance of things hoped for and the evidence of things unseen (read Hebrews 11:1). Education became a faith walk in real-time for educational stakeholders, including parents, teachers, administrators, and service providers.

To add to my faith muscle flex, I began this educational pivot while also living with Covid-19 and caring for two parents to whom I'd transmitted the virus. As educators, my colleagues and I literally shifted our entire delivery of how we presented educational concepts to children with a 2-week period to prepare the subject matter we had been trained extensively to introduce to scholars. And so, it began. The world of Zoom, CLEVER, and distance learning became the mission I allowed God to lead me through step-by-step.

As the first month of distance learning ended, God opened the door of opportunity and truly gifted me with a chance of a lifetime. I was invited to be one of 25 Kitchen Cabinet members selected out of over 700 Freedom Writer Teachers world-wide, to be a part of something bigger than myself. This invitation included the great task of creating and delivering learning curriculum that would cross states, countries, and even continent borders. The goal was to help the world pivot and embrace the new educational normal. Many lessons included social emotional learning and real-time discussions of racial injustices/social challenges globally.

My favorite lesson was a podcast led by *Grey's Anatomy* actor, Patrick Dempsey, who shared his experience as an individual with a learning disability (I affectionally refer to "learning handicapable"). As a student with dyslexia, Dempsey struggled to read. However, he overcame his limitations and learned to memorize lines, words, and phrases to improve comprehension and reading fluency. This gave us "Kitchen Cabinet" teachers hope that our students could do anything they put their minds and best effort towards. This was truly my safe and happy teaching place, in addition to my daily morning prayer call throughout the next 18 months of life. Having a strong, relational connection with God in addition to these two empowering platforms enabled me to navigate the upcoming journey from faith to the fire. It was a journey from a pit to His promises in the coming months.

As the beginning of the new 2020/2021 school year began, educators were slated to teach a full distance learning program for children. We now had a solid 2 ½ months of virtual teaching experience under our educational toolbelts. We had to be teachers of faith who firmly believed that we could be those superheroes that could do ALL things through Him who would give us strength to endure this extended venture.

This school year would be the best one of my career, yet the most challenging in a mental and emotional manner.

Early in the school year, I partnered with the most important teacher in a scholar's life, the child's parent/guardian. Each parent was empowered as their child's lifelong teacher with the assurance and support that "we" both would be on the educational journey alongside their child.

I packed all the supplies I purchased for my students and invited them and their families to come benefit from Ms. Wright's virtual learning school supply drive-thru at the school site. This drive-thru provided families with all the tools, resources, pneumonic devices, special education accommodation tools, a copy of our daily class affirmation poster, social/emotional tools, and essentially anything else that would help them feel like they had a piece of my classroom right in the comfort of their home. This assured students that their education mattered, as well as encouraged them to honor their home learning space just as they would in-person in my classroom.

My amazing scholars would show up as their best selves to my Virtual Zoom classroom daily. Following a daily social/emotional mindfulness lesson to begin each session, scholars were encouraged to tap in and take ownership of their learning. Parents and guardians were invited to my virtual classroom, as well, for extra support. Parent tutoring also enabled them to support their child's learning at home and oftentimes provide a simple prayer of encouragement. This school year would prove to be a euphoric year of teaching because for one whole school year, I felt like educational stakeholders were working collectively and cohesively together for the growth and development of the whole child.

As the year progressed, so did my scholars. Success showed up in many different facets within my student body. Many accomplishments included: achievement of Individualized Education Plan (IEP) goals, grade improvement, social skills improvement, and increase in student engagement and student confidence. It was apparent that the achievement gap that separated my scholars from their general education peers was coming much closer to a close.

All was going at a slow, yet steady pace in the learning environment for parents, scholars, and I. As the year progressed, I would be challenged to anchor myself in the Lord to help me navigate the deeper/choppier waters of this school year. If you were to visit my virtual classroom or speak with any parent/guardian, you would hear positive feedback about the special educational program created for their child's success.

Enter the district-appointed Equity Team to shake things up and subliminally shake up my faith muscles. After researching data from two prior school years, the results showed that students, particularly in my specific program, showed a significant decline. I essentially and abruptly became the face of the school's failure once more. It felt like a Joseph from "the pit to the promise" moment. My work ethic, integrity, and effectiveness as an educator were questioned by colleagues I had worked with and supported with all my being for the last 15 years of my career.

This assertion would draw me even closer to my Savior and into a place of humility, allowing Him to guide me through the deep shifting waves of this storm. The greatest hit in the pit was the moment a report was published with 19 bullet points spelling out my ineffectiveness as a 15-year veteran teacher and how I could improve by collaborating, teaching, and reporting what I do to my colleagues. As I received the email from my colleague with the "ouch" attachment, I immediately began to pray, seek His face, and humble myself to receive direction as to what my position would be in this assignment set before me.

The Lord directed me to stay right there in the high place with Him and remain unbothered. I began to consecrate and draw closer to Him because I refused to misstep in any direction that did not align with His will. My past trauma was telling me that I was triggered, and to run like the dickens. The toxicity in my work environment would grow like mold on a decomposing piece of food. There was someone to blame who wasn't defending themselves, therefore I became an easy target to dissect. In this dissecting moment, God was in turn performing emergency surgery on me, treating the wounds from my past childhood trauma. He revealed in my time of seeking and anchoring myself in Him that this circumstance was happening to allow me to see myself as He has always seen me.

It's in the refiner's fire that God's image can be seen through our purification process. When a metal such as gold is being refined, the purpose of the process is to rid the metal of all its impurities. The way one knows the metal is finally refined is by seeing their image reflected in the metal. Within the next three months, God allowed me to be purified, my character to become stronger, and my faith to be deepened in Him.

On one typical morning, while calling into my daily intercessory prayer line, I held on to a prophetic word that would bring about revelation, as it was a word of change and promise. The prophetess spoke the following word into the atmosphere: "There is someone on this line who God says He's coming to get you out of a place where somebody put you. You're in a spiritual place where somebody dropped you and is trying to keep you trapped, a place where they dropped the ball. Your supervisor did not do what they were supposed to do and now you must crawl out of that pit place. God says He's sending someone to get you out of there. There is going to be a divine release from a boss that is trying to hold you back." I held onto that word like the woman who held onto Jesus' garment.

Within one week's time, God would orchestrate a divine release and transfer me, providing me with the favor of three new job site offers. The Lord led me every step of the way through the interview process, even advising me of specific information I should list in three columns in preparation for a successful interview. With the three opportunities came the fight of choosing among three amazing and effective leaders who extended offers that one couldn't refuse. I wanted to ensure that I stayed in alignment with His promise. Although these three doors opened in record time, I remained obedient to God and accepted the position with the leader He prophesied was being sent to take me out of the pit. This journey showed me the goodness of God, His faithfulness, and how imperative it is to remain in His glory in our life. It was through this purification process that I also began to heal past soul wounds and see myself as He sees me. I AM ENOUGH because the God I serve is enough. My value does not lie in what others can't see within me, or how others treat me.

My prayer for you:

Gracious and Heavenly Father, I come to You on behalf of my brethren. I invite You to the very pit of our lives and release every challenge to You. Lord, draw us closer to You and help us not to lean unto our own understanding in the tough times. We cast all our cares on You, for You care deeply about everything that deeply hurts us. Help us to continuously be anchored in You on this journey as we seek Your kingdom. Guide us, Lord God, and direct our path, for the steps of a righteous man are ordered by You. We invite You to every twist, turn, and victory of our lives. We welcome You in every area of our lives, even those that can only be seen by You. We thank You for freedom from the yokes of bondage and ask that You loose liberty in our lives today! For we know that Your Word declares in John 8:36, *"Therefore if the Son makes you free, you shall be free indeed."*

We ask this is Your Son, Jesus' name, Amen.

Day 27: HOSPITAL ROOM FAITH

Ashley and Devin Duran started dating in 2017 and married in 2020. They are parents to a beautiful baby boy and declare their son is an answer to their prayers. They see him as a true blessing. The Durans have two German Shepherds and a Great Dane, who are also their babies. Safe to say they have a full house. The Durans are public servants who faithfully follow the Lord. They are persuaded, "In our darkest times, God has always shown us grace and peace."

I sit here in a hospital room, watching my newborn and husband sleep. I can't help but reflect on our journey as parents. God works in mysterious ways. I come from a broken home, and becoming a wife—let alone a mother—was something I never wanted. I'm also a sexual assault survivor, and affection doesn't always go well for me. Because of my trauma, I doubted my ability to be a loving mother and wife. It wasn't until I met my husband that my heart began to change. Devin is patient, kind, and so loving. Most importantly, he is a man of God. Devin's affirmations and leadership wholeheartedly changed my mindset. After we married, we decided we would try for a baby. I prayed for a healthy baby boy. I wanted a son who would have my husband's heart and my witty attitude. God spoke to me in a dream and said, "You are having a son." I knew I was carrying a boy long before my doctor was able to determine the gender.

Our son was prayed for, he was well desired, and he represented the strength we never knew we had. I had a difficult pregnancy. I had a doctor's visit three times a week. The constant blood draws and continually being on edge was emotionally and physically draining. We prayed for strength. We learned not to lean on-our own understanding but that of the Lord's.

Fast forward to December 1, 2021. Our sweet boy was born. All eight pounds of joy and purity. That little boy changed our lives. We named him Chancellor Anthem, and we declared that he would be a man of God. Chancellor means "noblemen, prince, or king;" Anthem in the Bible means "a hymn of praise or loyalty." Our son will be a leader who praises the Lord.

As excited as we were to be parents, we also experienced hardship. As we navigated into this new season, my husband and I began to grow distant. The sleepless nights, baby cries, and aches from being stuck under a sleeping newborn didn't help. To be honest, we had no idea what we were doing. I was losing my mind. During this time, I was also taking law school finals. Throughout the difficult weeks, I kept saying, "This too shall pass."

My husband and I really put in the work to rebuild our relationship. We reminded ourselves that marriage takes grit; we were a team. We needed to come first and continue placing God in the center of our relationship. We were getting lost in the chaos. Thankfully, this renewed strength would help carry us through our new trial.

Fast forward to February 5, 2022. I was driving 95 mph on the freeway. I was rushing my newborn son to the emergency room while yelling for help, feeling completely helpless and lost. It was raining and I felt God's tears. All I kept thinking was, "This too shall pass."

My son was poked and prodded with needles. He was screaming and crying in pain. The doctors couldn't give us an answer as to what was wrong. I was utterly exhausted; it was 2 a.m. I called my husband to ask him to be with our son so that I could sleep in the car. The hospital only allowed one parent in at a time. We are a team, so I was tagging him in.

A few hours later, we were notified that our son needed to be transported by ambulance to a specialized children's hospital. Seeing my newborn strapped into his car seat and then strapped onto a gurney was heartbreaking. There were a lot of unknowns. We didn't know how long we would need to be there. We didn't know who would take care of our dogs at home. We didn't know what was wrong. But we knew that God had a plan.

During our stay at the children's hospital, we saw our son undergo more painful tests. We saw our son suffering, but we couldn't do anything to help other than hold and comfort him. He was connected to machines, and it made it difficult to move him. Feedings were difficult; everything was difficult. My husband and I took shifts caring for Chancellor. He would sleep during the day, and I would sleep during the night. I would look at my son and pray that God wasn't done with him yet. I begged Him not to take him from me. It took a lot of prayer to keep our minds right.

On a few occasions, I completely lost control of my emotions. I looked into my husband's eyes and fell apart. I remember holding Chancellor as my husband embraced me. All three of us were suffering. Never in my life have I felt so useless, vulnerable, and terrified. My biggest fear was losing my son, and in return losing myself. In those moments, I prayed that God wouldn't separate us just yet. The verse, *"Be still and know that I am God"* (Psalm 46:10), was on repeat in my head. I needed to be still.

We had to keep faith that the same God who brought us this far would bring us through this. During our hospital stay, there was a man named Peter who was a "parent liaison" at the hospital. He told us where we could get free food at the hospital. He would come into our hospital room every morning and just talk to us about life. It was a good distraction. Looking back on it, I think God used Peter to remind us that He was watching over us. In the Bible, Peter means "rock or stone." It was God's way of reminding us that God was our rock.

We had more questions than answers. But we chose to walk by faith and not by sight. On day six, we finally got a medical diagnosis and developed a plan with the doctors. Our prayers were answered. I remember embracing my husband and telling him how proud I was of us. I was overjoyed at the thought of going home. God is good, especially during our darkest days.

As we reflected on our journey, it was a humbling experience. We felt God with us. Even when we began to question His plan for us, He was always there with us in that hospital room. He gave my husband and me the strength to carry on. He was with us at 2 a.m. when our son was screaming. He was there when we had to help hold our son down while the nurses drew blood. He was there counting every one of my tears.

Throughout my hardships, God has always provided. He has always remained faithful. Sometimes all we need is a little "hospital room faith." I know there are more trials and tribulations that we will endure...but if God is with us, who can be against us?

Our prayer for you:

Dear God,

We pray that whoever reads this knows that You are always with them. Even when earthly answers are unknown, and they have doubt and pain in their hearts, You are there. We ask that You cover them with love and grace. We ask that You give them strength to carry on through their trial. We pray that You remind them that You are their rock, a rock that is forever faithful and forgiving. God, remind them that "hospital room faith" is greater than any evil or uncertainty against them.

Amen.

Day 28: MATURING FAITH

 Arissa-Rose-Venegas is currently 22 years old and was born in Honolulu, Hawaii. Shortly after, she moved to California where she has lived most of her life. She comes from a blended family of twelve, nine of whom are her siblings.

Arissa moved to Arizona for college after graduating high school. She now attends Grand Canyon University and is majoring in Justice Studies with an emphasis in philosophy. She will be graduating soon and plans to pursue either family or criminal law. She is passionate about helping others in need. She enjoys the outdoors whether swimming, hiking, snowboarding, or running.

Something I have learned these past few months is the importance of prayer and the difference it makes. This alone has brought me closer to God while developing my personal relationship with Him. The last few months have been extremely challenging, both mentally and physically. At times I felt so overwhelmed with stress, anxiety, and loneliness that I felt as if I was drowning. But anytime those emotions and thoughts came up, I gave them to God. These trying times taught me how to put my faith in God and trust the plan that He has for me. Praying aloud to Him while putting my trust in Him was very difficult for me initially, but over time I noticed how easy it began to feel just talking to God.

Growing up, I experienced a lot of hurt and trauma, which made me struggle to connect with Him. As a kid, I didn't understand why God would allow these bad things to happen or why they continued to happen. I struggled when I was young and even as an adult with feelings of emptiness about not having a dad, but as I got to know God more and understand the love that He has for me, that feeling began to fade away.

I grew up in the church and have always believed in God, but it wasn't until this past year that I fully surrendered. I'm currently learning how to completely put my trust in Him, rather than trying to deal with everything on my own. I have watched God put certain people in my life who have taught me about the tremendous love that He has. These people have shown me grace, love, and compassion, which inspires me to continue to develop my relationship with Him while showing others the love that He has to offer.

My scripture for you:

Psalm 1 (New International Version):

¹ Blessed is the one

who does not walk in step with the wicked

or stand in the way that sinners take

or sit in the company of mockers,

² But whose delight is in the law of the LORD,

and who meditates on his law day and night.

³ That person is like a tree planted by streams of water,

which yields its fruit in season

and whose leaf does not wither—

whatever they do prospers.

⁴ Not so the wicked!

They are like chaff

that the wind blows away.

⁵ Therefore the wicked will not stand in the judgment,

nor sinners in the assembly of the righteous.

⁶ For the LORD watches over the way of the righteous,

but the way of the wicked leads to destruction.

Day 29: FINDING PURPOSE

Sophia Frech is 18 years old and newly married as of this past summer. She graduated high school at 17 and attended cosmetology school the following fall. She is now a newly licensed aesthetician and working on growing her experience. She has an amazing mom and dad and two sisters. They are her best friends and the most special people to her. She grew up in a Christian home and was always involved in church. Sophia's mom ran the youth program at one point. She, along with her siblings always helped her. Sophia attended summer camps all through middle school and high school. She began to grow in and learn her faith as an individual in her later years of high school and still believes she has so much more to learn and experience. Sophia knows that God is with her every step of the way.

For as long as I can remember, God was always in my life. From Sunday school to youth group to high school summer camp, I always called myself a Christian. It wasn't until a couple of years ago that I finally came to the realization and asked myself if I really had a relationship with God or if church activities were just something I always did. I started to wonder what I really believed in and if everything I had ever known was really it. I struggled to understand what I believe as an individual. I struggled to get to know myself. I worried whether I was living a fulfilling life. I doubted myself and started feeling like I was living with no purpose. Through these times of self-discovery, God has always provided and shown up. Since I was just a little girl, I have experienced the presence of God many times. I have seen my parents struggle to support their family financially, yet God has always shown up when we've needed Him and made provisions for my family. Not only has God provided for my family financially, but He has also brought forth healing for it. God has been with us through bouts of cancer with my nana twice now. He has healed her not just once but twice and I am so very thankful.

I have just nearly begun discovering my own faith and I have so much more room to learn. I know that I am not perfect, and I'm going to make mistakes. However, I also know that God will be with me through it all, through the ups and downs in all aspects of life. I can walk with my head high, knowing that I am not alone, even when life sometimes feels lonely. God is going to use us in so many other ways, more than we can imagine. He gives me a reason to have hope every day, even if I feel hopeless. If there is one thing I have taken away so far in my journey of discovery, it is that God has created us all to have a purpose, and without God, we are without purpose. *"The Lord will fulfill His purpose for me"* Psalm 138:8.

My scripture for you:

Psalm 138 (New International Version)

¹ I will praise you, Lord, with all my heart;
before the "gods" I will sing Your praise.
² I will bow down toward Your holy temple
and will praise Your name
for Your unfailing love and Your faithfulness,
for you have so exalted Your solemn decree
that it surpasses Your fame.
³ When I called, you answered me;
you greatly emboldened me.
⁴ May all the kings of the earth praise you, Lord,
when they hear what you have decreed.
⁵ May they sing of the ways of the Lord,

for the glory of the LORD is great.

⁶ Though the LORD is exalted, he looks kindly on the lowly;

though lofty, he sees them from afar.

⁷ Though I walk in the midst of trouble,

you preserve my life.

You stretch out Your hand against the anger of my foes;

with Your right hand you save me.

⁸ The LORD will vindicate me;

Your love, LORD, endures forever—

do not abandon the works of Your hands.

Finding Purpose

Day 30: PROMISED-LAND FAITH

Karissa Frech was born and raised in the Coachella Valley, where she lived with her parents Marisa and Greg, and her younger brother Hunter. She attended Grand Canyon University in Phoenix, Arizona, where she earned her Bachelor's in Biology with an emphasis in Pre-Physical Therapy. In August of 2022, she started her Doctor of Physical Therapy program at Western University of Health Sciences in Pomona, California. "Dr. Karissa" is a lover of Jesus, matcha, the beach, camping, and national parks.

As my mom, Marisa Frech, mentioned in her faith chapter, my name is Karissa. I recently was accepted to two Doctorate of Physical Therapy programs. I have wanted to be a physical therapist since I was a sophomore in high school when I was a patient myself. I was a competitive swimmer, so rehab quickly became a part of my routine.

In 2015, I started my freshman year at Grand Canyon University (GCU) with my idea of the perfect timeline. The way I saw it going, I thought I would graduate early in December of 2018 and start PT school in the summer or fall of 2019. I would be done with all my schooling in 2021. That plan was far from my reality. During my second semester at GCU, I was dealing with health issues that ultimately led to failing my first class. Up until this point, I had never really failed at anything I tried. I began to question if I was truly cut out for this educational path. At the start of that summer in 2016, I asked God for a very clear sign from Him if I was supposed to continue this path. The next day I was offered a Physical Therapy internship that I had applied for nine months before, an internship I had forgotten about by this point. During this time, I heard the Lord promise me I would get into Physical Therapy school but revealed that it would not be in my timing. The next six years were full of doubt, frustration, and lots of questioning. I continuously went back to the promise I knew the Lord made me in 2016 when I felt PT school was unattainable.

Fast forward to the 2020-2021 application cycle, I received one interview offer and was waitlisted at that school. It was a small taste of what was to come, and kept my faith in His promise. In the 2021-2022 application cycle I was offered seven interviews and accepted into two programs. It's been a six-year promise that has tested my faith but also strengthened my faith. I've learned to hold tight to the Word of God and trust His timing. I see it as the biggest miracle He has performed in my life thus far.

My scripture for you:

Jeremiah 29:10-14 (New International Version)

"This is what the LORD says: 'When seventy years are completed for Babylon, I will come to you and fulfill my good promise to bring you back to this place. 11 For I know the plans I have for you,' declares the LORD, 'plans to prosper you and not to harm you, plans to give you hope and a future. 12 Then you will call on me and come and pray to me, and I will listen to you. 13 You will seek me and find me when you seek me with all your heart. 14 I will be found by you,' declares the LORD, 'and will bring you back from captivity. I will gather you from all the nations and places where I have banished you,' declares the LORD, 'and will bring you back to the place from which I carried you into exile.'"

Day 31: CONFIRMING FAITH

Pastor Marcus Ruffin was born in the deep, yet warm southern parts of the United States — in Durham, NC. The second born, Pastor Marcus Orlando Ruffin is the sound epitome of hospitality and honor. His passion for life is to reach, build, equip, train, and maximize persons for life and eternity while silencing spiritual ignorance and compromised thinking patterns.

Pastor Marcus has two master's degrees: Christian Counseling and Marriage-Family Therapy, both from Oral Roberts University in Tulsa, OK. As the premier counselor of counselors/Licensed Marriage and Family Therapists, and in conjunction with the Holy Spirit, Pastor Marcus skillfully cuts through surface tension, landing upon the heart of sensitive issues while guiding the "willing and able" to their purpose possible. He innately discerns the fine line between spirituality and psychosis with "healing in His wings for all." Pastor Marcus' par none, effective, results-producing, prayer life takes great measures to ensure the unadulterated word of truth is effectively taught to the place where immediate and sustained application spontaneously erupts. The hearer awakens to reflect Jesus' words: *"Greater works shall you do than this, since you are called by My name!"*

His 17-year-young, by-faith twins, King-Marcus Oral, and Queen-Majesty Acacia are the legacy of his godly, intentional, deeply purposeful, anointed, covenant-partnership with the God-fearing, faith-walking, stately, and divinely postured—Bishop LaTerra Ruffin of 20 plus years. Together, they Pastor Life Empowerment Church and the world from Moreno Valley, California.

Confirming Faith

The Eunuch

I can recall telling my parents and others I would never get married and sensed a call to a eunuch lifestyle. At some point in my spiritual journey, there was a switch and I found myself looking for love! Now, I can't tell you that I suddenly became lonely or felt alone, but there was a heart's desire for marriage and family. Little did I know that I would find a bachelor's degree, a master's degree, as well as a marriage "degree," all at the same university! Due to a significant immoral life before Christ, I had "kissed dating goodbye." It wasn't until I recognized that I was "safe to date" that I opened the door to dating...Christian dating! What better place to explore than at a Christian University...Oral Roberts University (ORU).

The Mysterious Woman with a Bold, Red and Black Winter Coat

Now ORU had such an indelible mark upon my life before attending the university that it was only the Lord to make a match made in Heaven, on the earth, in a classroom! Yes, my first seminary/graduate school class, 8 am, is where the story unfolds. Being a young graduate student, 24 years old, I'm new on the scene and excited to enter a destiny opportunity. I understood my unique calling to "heal the soul." Now I'm fulfilling the second educational part to fulfilling this call. I'm ecstatic! Not to mention, I'm the first one in my family, both maternal and paternal sides of the family, to pursue a graduate degree.

Voila! Class begins, my first class. Scoping the land, it appeared that I might be the youngest in the classroom. As soon as class begins, I see this young lady come into the classroom with a bold, red and black winter coat. I'm sitting on the north side of the classroom. She takes a seat on the corner end of the table, the west side. There's something quite stunning and captivating about her and I can't help but notice that she has my attention for an unknown reason...at least for now.

From "The Mysterious Bold Red and Black Winter Coat Lady" to "Friend"

The class, "Counseling Diverse Populations," begins. The professor asked the students to introduce themselves. It was my belief that the older persons in the room were married, possibly with children. Therefore, I distinguished myself by stating, "I'm young, fresh from undergraduate, and single." Well, the mysterious bold, red, and black winter coat young lady eventually introduced herself and made the statement, "like that young man, I'm single also!" Now, I see her faith is at work! Faith is the substance of things hoped for...and I can see her faith!

I also hear her intelligent contributions to the classroom discussion, and I'm deeply impressed. Class ends. We go our separate ways. Later on that day, I'm headed to another class and there's the "mysterious bold, red and black winter coat young lady" ...now also "intelligent" woman, headed towards the water fountain. I thought this would be a good time to introduce myself. After all, my southern roots wouldn't have me be rude. I then briefly introduce myself and share my compliments regarding her intelligent classroom discussion. We made an amicable connection.

Time goes along and we develop a friendly relationship, later becoming good friends. We talked after class, shared an unexpected plane flight together, shared some meals, and made some good memories. She takes the time to introduce me to other graduate students and teaches me some of the ropes of graduate school.

One day, I noticed there was more to the connection that was seeping beneath the friendship and I'm already dating another person! The relationship between us has been integral and platonic, and throughout the friendship connections, there have been no questionable interactions from or towards the bold, red, and black coat. I can't deny that there's some romantic interest and attraction on my part, toward the bold, red, and black coat, but I'm already dating a young lady whom I've planned to marry.

Now my "bold, red and black winter coat" friend knows my girlfriend. They've met and shared some experiences in the once-famous Carlton Pearson's singing group, "Soul's A' Fire." I decided that I needed to make a separation. Without any verbal communication, I abruptly stopped hanging out with my new friend. After class, I leave. There were no hangouts, breakfast times, or any other types of hangouts. I'm still friendly and interactive in class, but I limit our time together. I thought I needed to protect my dating relationship over my newfound friendship with the lady in the bold, red, and black winter coat.

The Mysterious Wonder Woman Turns from "Friend" to "Big Sister"

After a time of absence, I returned and made her my "big spiritual sister!" There is an old saying, "Absence makes the heart grow fonder" and I began to miss my friend. We laugh about it today, but just recently I gave her a spiritual birthday card for her 40th and entitled it, "My Big Sister!" We resumed our friendship and I continued with my romantic pursuit of my girlfriend. Now one may ask how this changed the landscape of my heart, "I don't know, but it worked!" I think my context provided a safe place and heart boundaries!

I approached the lady in the bold, red, and black winter coat, now my friend, and asked, "LaTerra, can you be my big sister?" She tells me this level of friendship comes with unfettered heart access. I respond, "Trust is earned with time." We began to reconnect where we left off. The mysterious woman with the bold, red, and black winter coat, now aka, "Big

Sister," finished the semester and we both participated in Oral Roberts University graduation. I received my Bachelor's Degree in Psychology and my "Big Sister" received her Master of Divinity Degree. We all celebrated and had a group graduation, which was a wonderful end to my first semester in graduate school and her last semester in graduate school.

I enroll in summer school, and she enrolls in a chaplaincy program at a local hospital. She's working the third shift in the hospitality industry and I'm working 2nd shift in the mental health industry. We rarely talk, due to schedules, but we cross paths every so often. We're not talking on the phone and our usual after-class hangouts have ceased. We don't really connect by phone (this is the pre-cell phone era) and she's working the 3rd shift at the Marriott Hotel while I'm working the 2nd shift at a local group home facility. She's in her clinical pastoral program during the day and I'm in class and studying during the day.

Then, tragedy strikes! What my Big Sister doesn't know is that my two-yearlong romantic relationship is going south! I finally get the courage to end the relationship for unfaithfulness and in the painful devastation of it all, I remember my Big Sister is starting her evening shift and I'm ending my shift. I decided to pay my Big Sister a visit. She offered some consolation and recommended some reading for mending my heart. My big sister knew that I was emotionally hurting and offers her assistance. She checked on me at times as summer was coming to a quick end.

It was time for my Big Sister to head out west for her new ministry assignment. We decided to hang out for possibly a last hooray because I still had two years left for graduate school and she was taking a full-time ministry assignment in Palm Springs, California. We decided to have dinner and see the movie, "The Matrix!" Friends recommended this movie. They told me the movie has a lot of spiritual symbolism and relativism, and we were both excited to see it. She asked me if I was available to help her pack her items and we set a date to make it happen.

While we were packing the items and she was planning to drive to California that night, she asked me to drive her to the store for last-minute items. On the way to the store, we were laughing and sharing stories as usual, and then she said, "If we're not married by the time I'm thirty, we should just marry each other," and she started laughing. Well, those words pierced my heart, and I couldn't laugh; I was too nervous. My mysterious unknown classmate with a bold, red, and black winter coat turned Big Sister has now penetrated another layer! She noticed that I was not laughing and thought that maybe she had offended me. She apologized as if she had been inappropriately offensive. I told her, as I gripped the steering wheel with sweaty palms, "I would be honored to have you as my wife!" She told me, "Do you know that the U-Haul truck in front of us has all of my items packed and headed for California?" I told her that I couldn't lie and had to be honest. She would later give me three cards: one for her friend...one for her "little brother" ...and one for, "I don't know what's happening?"

The "Big Sister" Becomes a "Special Friend"

Now my Big Sister has reframed our connection to "Special Friend." We've decided to maintain a connection: a long-distance connection and a huge phone bill connection. Due to the pre-cell phone era, we only have a landline available for phone calls. Our schedules worked out where she's home at night and my day has ended. Unless I'm at work, we can talk often, but it was outrageously expensive. One month, we split a $500 phone bill, due to the long-distance, pay-per-minute system.

When the cell phone became available, we thought it was the best thing since God invented Noah's Ark, because we were drowning in phone bills. The cell phone, "Cingular" had a package deal, and one could have unlimited minutes after 8 pm my local time. We went from overwhelming phone bills to no phone bills or very little! We continued to chat and although my prior relationship had ended, I didn't want this potentially Godly romantic connection to be a rebound. A rebound is where you obtain another relationship in lieu of the old relationship, not because you are in love, but because you're lonely and just looking to replace the old love with a new love. It's just a temporary replacement and not a genuine heart-felt connection.

In October of 1999, I visited my Big Sister in Palm Springs, California. I shared my "rebound" concerns with my "Special Friend" and asked her to wait a year and not to take any romantic requests, dates, or any other potential requests. After I shared, I thought my Special Friend backslid into the "Big Sister" moment and told me that I needed to go back to my prayer closet because with that request, I hadn't heard from God! My Big Sister told me, "You don't know the kind of woman you're intriguing. To expect me to wait a year before entering a relationship with someone …. the devil is a liar!"

We continued enjoying my first trip to Palm Springs. Whenever she introduced me to her ministerial colleagues, she told them I was her "Special Friend!" She thought it was a creative way to say a lot without saying too much of anything. After all, I had told her to wait a year. I didn't want to have another heartbreak and especially ruin my friendship. I wanted to know from God if I was overlooking a dilemma and needed to hear from Him with clarity. We had decided to have another face-to-face visit in January 2000, and this would determine if "Special Friend" would last. I felt like I needed a miracle, a heavenly sign from the sky above.

Confirming Faith

The Miracle in the Skies

From October to January, I had recognized I needed to make a decision, and although it had been seven months between the last relationship and a new one, I was not really sure if it was time. I'm not certain my heart is ready to adventure down another romantic path. After all, I had kissed dating goodbye, and this is a new Christian adventure. I really sought the Lord, and as much as I believed I was ready, I needed more assurance to make this faith step forward. I asked the Lord for confirmation that only He could provide.

During this planning time for the January revisit, I learned that LaTerra's mother and sister would be visiting also. Now the pressure to not only be clear about my intentions but to also be interviewed (from my perspective, although no one ever said her mother would be interviewing me) added more pressure for me to have a confirmation from the Lord.

When I was attending Oral Roberts University (ORU), my father obtained employment with American Airlines. A part of his benefits entailed his family being able to fly for pennies on the dollar. I told my father that I wanted to go to Palm Springs in January 2000. The pennies on the dollar, catch-22 was that I had to fly standby. My father kept an eye on the flight options. He tried to secure a flight with the least amount of probability of being full. When flights were full, "standby passengers" did, just that...stand by! If you have ever flown standby, I am sure you might have heard the horror stories of canceled flights/airplane repair flights/holiday travel, etc. I prayed and asked God for a confirmation that the flights of LaTerra's mother and sister (from Philadelphia, Pennsylvania) and mine would arrive within 30 minutes of one another. Well, my father had secured my flight and I later learned that my "Big Sister's" mother had also secured her flight. Yes!!! You know it. The flights were arriving in California within 30 minutes of one another! Remember, my Big Sister doesn't know about my confirmation from the Lord. Well, I'm ecstatic because I believe the Lord has confirmed that my heart has a green light to go forward with a new-level relationship.

January 12, 2000, I arrived at the Tulsa International Airport and headed toward Palm Springs, California. I checked in for my flight with American Airlines (AA) and they saw that I was flying on standby. I then inquired if the flight was full. The AA agent told me that the flight had a lot of room, and I should be fine. I'm reminiscing on how the Lord has confirmed this miracle from the heavens above. Then, tragedy strikes! The AA flight before mine is canceled due to airplane mechanical problems! The persons from that flight are rolled over to my boarding flight and now I'm doing that thing again… "Standing by."

After a while I was looking at my flight take off into the heavenly skies, and now I'm going from standing by to saying, "bye-bye." I felt my heart lift as the plane lifted and I'm not sure what this means! I learned that there was another flight sometime later that appeared to have availability. Now, this would have been great on any other day, but my "miracle flight" had just left and taken my miracle with it. The horror of horrors was happening and I'm sitting there in bewilderment! Should I not leave…Should I just call and tell my "Big Sister" that I changed my mind? I waited for some time, never heard anything from the Lord, and my southern roots told me to be courteous and at least call and explain my flight's ordeal. I finally gathered myself and called and explained what had happened and told her the arrival time of the next flight!

Does Lighting Strike in the Same Place Twice?

I found the courage and made the phone call. I told LaTerra my flight had been canceled due to a mechanical error. She told me that she didn't know what was happening because her mother's flight had been canceled and changed too. There's no emoji that existed then or today to show the amazement on my face! Is there hope again? She told me that her mother's flight was canceled that morning, but she didn't say anything to me because she thought she would just pick me up at the airport, wait for her mother's arrival, and go from there.

LaTerra mentioned her mother's flight was coming in later that night but at the same airport. Well, you know what I asked next, right??? What time was her flight scheduled to arrive? When I tell you that she told me that the flight was now 15 minutes before my new arrival time, I felt like the Archangel Michael himself was going to come and translate me personally to Palm Springs at that moment! I was trying to contain my excitement because my "Big Sister" didn't know what the heavens had just confirmed to me...twice now! When I thought back on this moment, I recognized that for whatever reason my "Big Sister's" mother's flight was changed, and the Lord had to change my flight too. The double confirmation was heaven's way of telling me that there was a double blessing...double anointing...double confirmation...all of Heaven was behind me. I boarded my flight, as heavenly scheduled, and met my "Big Sister" and her mother and sister in Palm Springs, California.

"Special Friend" to "Courtship"

We both arrived at the Ontario airport and between the drive to Palm Springs and the next couple of days, we spent some time chatting and connecting. Remember, this was my first time meeting my "Big Sister's" mother, and she was checking me out with the "third eye!" We spent the next two days doing a variety of activities, enjoying home cooked meals as well as some local restaurants. It was a great time, especially with my double confirmation hovering over my head and around my heart.

On Friday, January 14, 2000, I thought this would be a great time to share my plan. One of the many things I told her was that the bracelet I gave her was my way of trying to get close to her ring finger! I elaborated on how the bracelet was a reminder of my love and commitment to her. I shared how the bracelet was a way to keep all those other guys at an arm's distance because I was on her wrist. I told her about the plan in moving forward and how I would graduate from ORU first before I make her my wife. I asked her into an exclusive dating relationship, and before she answered me, she said, "Wait, let me go and talk with my mother!"

Now my southern roots were all for parental approval. But the godly man in me thought, "After I just shared the double confirmation in the skies, you don't need anything else. Once you've heard from Heaven, "confer with no flesh," as the scriptures teach." She came back from her private conversation with her mother and told me, "Yes!" We've now officially started dating and I'm no longer just a "Special Friend." She's no longer a "Big Sister" but she's my woman and I'm her man. We have a "Heavenly Courtship."

A Heavenly Courtship

I flew back to ORU and finished my graduate studies. I told my woman, as the relationship progressed, that as much as we were a spiritual match in Heaven, we needed to become soulmates too. We started premarital counseling in January 2001. Every month forward, January to May 2001, we had two premarital counseling sessions with Dr. Arthur Tigney! We addressed a variety of details and had to work through our soul issues. As much as we had heavenly confirmation, it required "soul work" to have a marriage made in Heaven lived out on Earth. Now granted, I had never asked her to marry me while we had our premarital counseling, but the engagement would transpire on May 5, 2001, at the Grand Finale restaurant!

There we were, celebrating my graduation from ORU's dual master's degree program. Both our families, professors, and many mutual friends gathered on this joyous evening. Nearly two hundred plus were in attendance. Now, no one has been informed of the surprise at the end, except my two friends, Thomas and Tina Wyatt. They planned the graduation event. Each of the four graduates in our group was prepared to publicly share thankful words with their families. Due to my marriage proposal plans, we decided I should be last.

After I had thanked all the professors, my parents, and family members, I asked the mysterious lady who first struck my attention in the bold, red and black winter coat, who became my "Big Sister," transitioned to "Special Friend," and twice confirmed Heavenly Courtship, to come and join me on stage. After an appreciative introduction, I present my 1 Corinthians 13 revised Marriage Proposal:

"Though I speak with the tongues of Valentine and Cupid and have not you in marriage, I am become as a sounding poet and an arrow-less man. And though I have two masters in counseling and understand all mysteries and all knowledge, and though I have all the degrees in the world that I could influence the masses, and have not you in marriage, I am nothing!

And though I show you all my fortunes and potential to keep you from being poor, and though I have a prosperous career to be rich and famous, and have you not in marriage, it profits me nothing.

Our marriage will last long and be kind, full of love and not envy; a marriage that lifts Christ and not ourselves. I promise to behave myself seemingly, seeking not my own way and not being easily provoked when I may see a little bit of your evil ways.

We shall bear all things, believe all things, hope all things, and endure all things. Marriage with you could never be a failure. Whether there be prosperity it can fail; whether there be houses, they cease; whether there be diamonds, they shall vanish away.

When I was a bachelor, I spoke as a bachelor, I understood as a bachelor, I thought as a bachelor - but when I started courting you, I became a marital-minded man. I put away bachelor things.

For now, you see my commitment through a one-carat diamond with a VVSI-2 clarity (as I pulled out the diamond ring). I look at you, face to face. Now you know as I have known.

And now abideth friends, professors, family, and a proposal for marriage, and the greatest of these are professors, friends, and family encircling you and me in a marriage to be.

WILL YOU MARRY ME?"

At this point, I gave the mysterious lady, who first struck my attention in the bold, red and black winter coat, my "Big Sister," "Special Friend," and twice confirmed Heavenly Courtship fiancé and now soon coming bride, the microphone. As I placed the one-carat diamond ring with a VVSI-2 clarity on her finger, while the 18-carat gold bracelet hung from the same wrist, I heard these words, "Yes, today and tomorrow! Unconditionally yes! Forever YES!"

On April 20, 2002, in Rancho Mirage, California and June 8, 2002, in Philadelphia, Pennsylvania, we celebrated two weddings for the twice confirmed, Heavenly confirmed, Marriage made in Heaven on Earth, for the double blessing...double anointing...double confirmation!

At the time of this disclosure, we just celebrated our 20th covenant anniversary in our dream location, Paris!

Confirming Faith

My prayer for you:

Lord, you are well acquainted with the person reading this chapter. You know their hopes, desires, dreams, and steps. You also hear their prayers and are closely aware of their longings. I release a spirit of "wait upon the Lord for renewed strength, clarity, and confidence." I declare a mindset to know "no good thing will the Lord withhold from those who walk upright before Him." The partnership of these two owned and gripping revelations will safeguard every decision, thought, and opportunity. They will walk in step and in confidence with You.

You will surely bring it to fruition and confirm Your decision, in Jesus' name!

Amen.

AUTHOR'S CONTACT INFORMATION

Connect with me via email: FaithFaces2023@gmail.com

pastorlaterra@yahoo.com

Life Empowerment Church - LEC Website:

https://www.Let-God.org

Connect with me on Facebook:

https://www.facebook.com/profile.php?id=100092055824719

Connect with me on Instagram:

https://www.instagram.com/pastorlaterra

Phone: (919) 491-1553

Address:

P.O. Box 7958

Moreno Valley, California 92552

Made in the USA
Columbia, SC
06 August 2024

39579737R00176